West Wandering Wind

West Wandering Wind

W. R. GARWOOD
and
CARL W. BREIHAN

DOUBLEDAY & COMPANY, INC.
GARDEN CITY, NEW YORK
1986

With the exception of actual historical persons,
all of the characters in this book
are fictitious, and any resemblance
to actual persons, living or dead,
is purely coincidental.

Library of Congress Cataloging-in-Publication Data

Garwood, William R., 1917–
West wandering wind.

1. Bean, Roy, d. 1903—Fiction.   I. Breihan,
Carl W.   II. Title
PS3552.R366W4   1986   813'.54   85-24605
ISBN 0-385-23504-6

To Debby and Alex

West Wandering Wind

I

From the time I reached the old Spanish Trail to California, the wind had blown strong and always westward. And I followed that wind, or rather I and my little black mare and my pack mule drifted along with it, like ships upon an ocean; for the waves of the sea were patterned in the endless miles of ever shifting grasses that often came up to my stirrups.

So I rode west, seemingly free of the trouble that had uprooted and hustled me from Mexico and across three territories—like a windblown tumbleweed.

Camping in the partial shelter of a willow thicket on the fifth day since leaving the last of civilization, a run-down trading post at Vermillion Cliffs, I found myself doing some long and hard thinking about myself— Roy Bean, late of Mason County, Kentucky, and a devil of a lot later from that gunfight at Chihuahua . . . and the murderous event following.

Just a shade past twenty-three, as I hunkered by my lonely campfire on a windy June evening in 1849, I seemed to have lived several lifetimes already—and mighty busy ones! I'd flatboated from Kentucky to New Orleans at fifteen, spent a goodly hitch teamstering in the recent Mexican War, toting gunpowder and cannonballs for Zack Taylor, and finally becoming a sort of a counterjumper at my brother Sam's little trading post and groggery in the town of Chihuahua, until a few short weeks ago!

Early on that explosive morning, as I was dusting off the bar and thinking of the local girls, Sam had hurried into the place, all wrought up. "Gol-dummed knothead!" His eyes stuck out like he'd just been punched in the brisket. "You been out tomcattin' again with them Verdugo gals?" A couple of our early barflies stared up from their drinks.

"Might have walked out with one or the other." I wondered who'd been talking. Likely it was that green-eyed cat Conchita Peralta—and just because I'd dropped a hint or two that she might start looking toward becoming Mrs. Roy Bean—sometime. The trouble was I'd worked the same dodge around Chihuahua somewhat freely since joining Sam.

When I gave over freighting after the war and came to help my brother in his business I promptly got myself some visions of becoming a regular merchant prince. I was a go-getter, no matter what I went at—and I was mighty enthusiastic about the local belles, for one thing! One or the other could wind up as spouse to a whopping success, which would be me. The only joker in that deck was the fact that I just couldn't make up my mind which of the little señoritas to settle down with—and so kept trying to sample the merchandise, and getting away with it.

But now it seemed my sampling was catching up with me!

"Well, you're sure in one hell of a fix!" Sam shouted. "Esteban Domingo just galloped in, filled to th' brim with firewater and yellin' for your scalp!"

"Margarita's old beau? Thought he was in some Vera Cruz jail for slicing up a rival." A chill plunged down my backbone.

"He must have let himself out to come visitin'! And here he comes now!"

Sam was right. One of the meanest-looking Mexicans I'd ever set eyes on burst through the batwings, waving a mighty long knife!

"*Borrico!* Puckered horned toad! Two-faced coyote!" And those were the kindest of the volley of words shouted at me as he ran me around the saloon, scattering our early risers and bottles to hell and gone!

Wasting no time at peace talk, I leaped back of the bar and came up with Sam's big Walker Colt, hoping for a dry charge.

"Hold on! I don't know you, you crazy fool, let alone your infernal lady friends!" I cocked the heavy pistol with both hands, while the last customer plunged headlong into the street. Sam was already absent.

"*Sí*, I know you, though, you woman-chasing cockroach!" And with a drunken war whoop he flung himself at me, knife slashing a glittering streak.

Things happened fast. Came the ear-blasting roar of the Walker as its hammer slammed down and the weapon belched fiery lightning. That thunderous crash was still racketing through the building as the *late* Esteban Domingo thudded onto the sawdust with half of his ugly face missing.

For a tingling, humming moment I stood frozen flat-footed, staring at that sprawled body on the blood-spattered floor, then I dropped his big, silver-laced sombrero onto his face, or what was left of it, and staggered out onto the street. As I stood there gulping the air, a head or two poked around the nearby adobes. Other faces peeked from behind cottonwoods or stared out of the alley shadows. Feet began thudding, like rolling drums, as Mexicans ran up the street. Groups gathered, big straw sombreros tipped together as their owners whispered and rolled glittering black eyes in my direction.

Though Esteban Domingo had been a no-good drunken troublemaker, he came from an old Sonora family with plenty of pesos, which was the main reason he'd lasted as long as he had. He'd also served in the Mexican Lancers and was rated a jim-dandy Yankee sticker. Well, he'd sure enough stuck his last Yank!

Two of our regulars, Siquio Sánchez and García Tayopa, came pussy-footing in through the front door, brittle smiles lurking under their handlebar mustaches. More Mexicans broke away from the growing crowd and eased their way into our place to gawk and mutter.

Our *anglo* traders began to show up. Big Jim Wilson and cockeyed Frank Burris dashed over from Portales Street, with old Solomon Fancher, of the freighting company, waddling at their heels. My brother was with him and he tugged me off to one side.

"Wait a minute, that bunch in there'll steal us blind unless someone watches them!" I told him.

"Don't fret yourself over some bottles of pop-skull or a few yard goods —and give me that weapon!" Sam grabbed the Walker out of my fist and jammed it into his waistband. "Take a look at that!" He jerked a thumb at the growing crowd.

Though it was still early in the day, about the whole town of Chihuahua was up and out on the streets.

"Git yourself over to th' wagon yard and hitch up old Zack and Betty, and damned *muy pronto!*" Sam gave me a shove and Solomon Fancher grabbed me on the rebound and shoved me along through the milling Mexicans. He waved a hand at the wagon yard when we got there. "Thanks to you, Mr. Quick Shot, me and your brother and every gringo's got to pull freight fast—if we don't want our throats cut by these jumped-up chili con carnes. They're good customers but gol-damn hot enemies when their dander's roused. I oughta know. I was at Goliad!"

Fancher waddled around, yanking his beard and flinging orders. "When we heard Domingo was after your hide, we knew one or t'other would hit th' deck! And you, you unconsiderate limb, had to come out on top! Jest listen at that!"

The shrilling of women and the bellowed curses of the menfolk began to rise around town. I wondered if Margarita Verdugo was helping in that caterwauling, but I got busy hitching up our Dearborn wagon. Most of the American merchants used the big, heavy Conestoga freight wagons or lubberly Chihuahua high-wheeled carts with double-yoked oxen. I'd always felt that it gave us style to drive a span of horses, and now it looked as if we could use them to move in a hurry, for the uproar was swelling like the mutter of a coming storm.

"Hustle! Hustle! They're about ready to start th' hull darn war over agin!" Sam was back, wild-eyed and sweating, as he scrambled into the squeaking seat of our Dearborn. By now just about every *americano* was on the streets or gathering around the wagon yard with all of their weeping women and bawling kids.

Those glowering knots of Chihuahua citizens, milling about, waving hands and fists, had been neighbors, customers and apparent friends ever since Sam and I and the other gringos moved in after the signing of peace back in March of 1848. Since then we all had dug in and made the fur fly with our businesses—trading, grocery, dry goods and the rest. And now it seemed the honeymoon was over for good!

Not one man in all those staring crowds made a move to stop our leaving, even the local Jefes kept their distance as our makeshift wagon train began to rumble, cart and wagon, up Galagos, past the rows of stores and cantinas, but the racket over on the other streets was getting louder. There came the brittle clash of broken windows and the hollow thud of scattered shots.

Hearing those sounds we all whipped up our horses more briskly.

On the way, some of our party made several hurried stops to save trunks and other belongings. I got our small chest and some oddments from our comfortable adobe on Jalapa, leaving behind our Yaqui house servant, Texutla, to watch the place against our return.

It gave both Sam and me a wrench to pull up stakes and leave our dandy little place, with its walled patio garden and dozens of flowering plants. There in a corner, our huge chirimoya tree, festooned with a rainbow of orchids, lorded it over a regular little Garden of Eden, rioting with kumquat, lemon, grapefruit and golden oranges. Nothing like it in old Kentucky! And now we were being chased headlong out of that Eden.

As I dashed back from the house with the last piece of luggage, old Texutla, her broad brow creased more than ever with furrows, held up gnarled hands, wailing, "Return, O señores, return!"

I gave her a big hug and the keys to the place, joshing her about her tears as I jumped into the Dearborn beside Sam.

Tuxutla wiped at her eyes. *"Lágrimas de corazón son como una benedicción del cielo!"* (Tears of the heart can be like a benediction of heaven!) Then she smiled through those tears. Dear old soul, we'd not see her again.

Whips cracked, wheels creaked their rusty protest, and we trundled out into the sage and sand barrens, headed for anywhere but Chihuahua, women white-faced, men clamp-jawed and kids sniffling—all grieving for their own lost Edens.

For an hour or so we traveled on, most of the men on horseback, following their families in the heavy wagons, to the tune of forty-odd. And as we rode along the sandy track northward, we kept craning our necks back to gaze at the receding white cubes and oblongs of old Chihuahua; then at last the town sank away behind the rolling brown sand hills. But it was still marked by the drifting black plumes, smearing up into the bright blue sky dome, where some home or business place vanished in flames.

Gone out of sight were Margarita, and Conchita, and Emilita, and all the rest of those dark-eyed, red-lipped, soft-curved señoritas—as well as a year of hard work.

We expected to be followed, but it seemed the ranting citizens of Chihuahua had felt they'd come out ahead at that. Not only had they gotten rid of the gringo but they'd gotten their lazy brown paws on that bustling Yankee tribe's property as well!

I had figured to be ranked as a regular first-class pariah by all of our spontaneous exiles, but hardly a one, outside of old Fancher and Sam, gave me the slightest dirty look. Most seemed sort of proud of me. Those Mexicans back there might have booted us out, but I'd upheld the U.S.A. It was as though I'd won the war all over again—before our retreat.

So we stretched out our wagon train and dug into the hundred hot and sandy miles separating us from the town of Jesús María in northern Sonora, our nearest place of refuge.

II

Four days later our entire wagon train creaked up the sandy yellow slopes of the Padre Baca and unhitched on the outskirts of Jesús María in the surrounding saguaro thickets.

After old man Fancher, as wagon boss, had sent Jim Wilson and Ed Giddings into the town for news, we sat back, got the kinks out of our bones and viewed the countryside.

Here was another Eden in the midst of the empty wastelands. Orchards bloomed around the nearby mines and inside the town's crumbling biscuit-colored walls with masses of apples, quinces, figs, oranges, grapes, pomegranates and peaches. A goodly sized stream flowing out of the upper hills had been diverted through the fields in a series of irrigation ditches to bring forth these riches. And while we waited for our scouts to get back we filled our canteens and water barrels and tended to our stock.

I'd volunteered to ride into town with Jim and Ed, but Sam had jumped all over me. "We've got trouble enough without hotheads like you on them streets! Lord knows what you might do!"

Well, it didn't matter a smidgen who was on the usually peaceful streets of Jesús María. Within half an hour back came our scouts and, tagging them as fast as they could lash their wagons and carts, every blamed *americano* family in the place!

Somehow word had reached town, ahead of us, of our forced exit from Chihuahua, and all of Jesús María was bound to follow suit and drive away every gringo in sight. Before we'd finished hitching up again, at least ten families had joined us.

It was the same old story. Smoke of the Yankee buildings billowed up into the sky, like the pillar of fire the Israelites beheld—and like those old desert wanderers we took the hint and moved on, in our case toward the border and El Paso del Norte.

It was a right good thing we'd filled canteens and casks at Jesús María, for it was a long and hot trek to the great bends of the Rio Grande. But we stretched out, gritted our teeth and arrived at the Rio, across from El

Paso, on the third evening, going into camp in the blue dusk, while the yellow lights of the adobe town began to gleam in the nightfall.

Once ferried across the big river next morning on a pair of rickety flatboats that landed wagons and carts, one by one, at the foot of El Paso Street, there was a general meeting in the cottonwood-shaded plaza.

Most of our group, including Sam and old man Fancher, were for going on up to Santa Fe in the New Mexico Territory, while some were determined to head back to safer ground, such as Missouri, Illinois and other states.

It was while we debated and milled around, visiting with the El Paso folks, that word began to circulate of some sort of a gold strike out in California.

"That surely sounds like the right place to head for," I told Sam. "Besides, our brother Josh's been out there ever since he got out of the Army back in '46. He's alcalde at some spot in the road, San Diego, ain't it?"

"Yeah. And he's th' only Bean with enough wits about him to go tradin' where th' Mexicans ain't so full of chili powders!" Sam had always been saddled with a theory that Mexicans got their hot dispositions in direct proportion to the amount of chili they took on board during the year.

"Aimin' to go out to California?" One of the *americanos* of El Paso, who'd wandered up with the crowds, tackled me. "Think I'd like to git back out there. I used to sorta be in business around San Francisco. And if you cotton to company, I'll saddle and come along."

Bossy old Fancher, who'd tried to coax me along with the bunch for Santa Fe, cocked an ear at us. "I been all over this end of th' country huntin' and trappin' twenty years back, and I tell you right now, she's a long way from civilized." He yanked at his beard. "Like as not you'll run headlong into Apaches, or worse—Comanche wild men!"

The big black-bearded fellow, who'd introduced himself as Jeff Kirker, just grinned. "We'll carry along a little Blue Ruin. Best kind of insurance. Give'm a couple of jolts of whiskey and you can slick 'em even outa their squaws. We done it lots of times when I was ridin' with old man Carleton's California column."

"Them Californy Digger Injuns ain't one little patch on Comanches!" Fancher growled, and consigning us both to the devil he shook hands and turned away to boss some easier folks.

By settling accounts with Sam, I'd got enough of my money to pick up a nice little bay mare with four white feet at a nearby stable on Overland Street. Then Kirker and I pooled our cash and invested in a walleyed pack mule from the same place and enough supplies from Coon's Store to take us a good long piece.

Sam, who'd definitely made up his mind to go on north with Fancher and the rest of the wagon train, shook hands with Jeff and I when we mounted up the next morning. "Tell brother Josh to keep you in nights," Sam grinned. "If he don't, you just might be th' cause of losin' Californy back to th' Mexicans!"

When we rode down San Antonio, followed by the goodbyes of all the folks we were leaving, the early sun was just spilling its beams over the eastern foothills and turning the Rio Grande into one long winding path of pure gold.

We spent the next two days on a rough but passable trail that led along the east bank of the Rio toward the mission town of Albuquerque. The afternoon of the second day of our jaunt we were soaked to the very hide in one of the worst storms that I'd seen in all my time out in the western country, but we kept on and arrived at Albuquerque in the late afternoon of Thursday, June 30, 1849.

There were plenty of U.S. troops around the town, as Albuquerque was still an army base, but for some reason Jeff seemed to steer way clear of all bluecoats. "Brings back hard memories," was all he said as we sat over some downright warm beer in one of the local cantinas.

After supper of pretty passable frijoles and java at a seedy hash house on Alamogordo, we squatted on a bench in the plaza and watched the sunset smoldering like the tail end of a bonfire across the gloomy mountain the Americans were calling Mount Taylor, after old General Zack, but the locals still tagged Cebolleta.

"If we're gonna be pards," said Kirker all at once after clearing his throat half a dozen times, "we got to be straight with each other!" He rolled a cornhusk cigarro and peered hard at me in the red-gold light.

I rolled my own smoke, waiting for whatever he had in mind, and keeping an eye peeled for any spiffy-looking Albuquerque ladies that might be out taking the airs around the fence-lined plaza square.

We lit up with a couple of lucifers and smoked a bit. It seemed that warm beer had sort of gone to Jeff's head—and mine felt pretty buzzy as well.

"As I said, we oughter be straight with each other, if we're gonna be pards." Kirker fumbled at his shirt pocket.

"It's okay with me," I said, staring over at a nice young señorita, tagged by an old she-wolf of a *dueña*. The young lady looked back at me but kept on around the plaza.

"You're just a kid, young Roy, but I reckon you been around long enough to keep your mouth clamped if it's mean money into your pockets." Kirker glanced across his shoulder at a pair of U.S. dragoons, in their flat caps, all tipped on one side, sauntering along easy and careless after that señorita.

"This here trip could mean real money for a live wire like you if you wanter throw in with me," Jeff went on.

"Guess I'm your man," I said, puffing at my cornhusk and wondering just what in tunket he was getting at, so all-fired cautious like. I figured him for wanting to go into business, after he'd heard that my brother Josh was cock of the walk at San Diego.

He finally pulled his hand from his shirt pocket and held it out to me. "Take a good look at this!"

A United States ten-dollar eagle gold piece lay in his palm, shining in the late light with a fire of its own!

III

After Jeff Kirker had shown me that eagle gold piece, an odd sort of thing happened.

One of the pair of soldiers, tagging along after the pretty señorita, broke away and ambled toward us. Jeff got up from the bench in a hurry and stuffed the coin back in his pocket. "Come on!" was all he said.

The dragoon called something, but Kirker paid him no heed, and I stayed right on Jeff's heels until we'd gotten back to the run-down adobe tavern on Tijeras where we were to stay for the night, as my new pardner was all for hitting the hay early.

"That fellow wanted to pow-wow with you," I said as we piled into the creaking, double bed about eight o'clock.

"Just another drunk hoss soldier!" Kirker muttered as he blew out the tallow dip and rolled over onto his side of the crackling shuck mattress. "Git yourself *mucho* shut-eye! We got a power of hard ridin' comin'— gittin' through them blamed Sandia Mountains, and acrost a hell of a lot of desert and such before we hit California." He yawned hard and groaned like he was plumb worn out.

"Want to tell me about that eagle? Get straight with each other, like you said?" I waited, but Jeff was already snoring his damnedest—or seemed to be. I found myself wondering if I'd been halfway smart in tying up with a complete stranger.

About the time I was drifting off, it came to me what that dragoon had called out after Jeff. It was something like *"Red Rosita!"* But that didn't make much sense, and it wasn't long until Kirker's bucksaw snores had lulled me to sleep.

Before the sun was two hands high on the horizon next morning, we'd been on the trail a good hour or better. Kirker had rolled out at daybreak, poking me up to fetch our animals from the corral behind the tavern while he paid our bill.

I wasn't much on moving around so fast so early, but all he said was, "If you want to git to California in one piece you gotta travel early and fast." I took this to mean that we had to scoot along before the Indians were up and about.

I noticed, when we rode down the cottonwood-lined streets in the watery dawn light, that Jeff cast a number of hard looks in the direction of the local army headquarters at the Casa de Armijo, east of the plaza. It was plain that Kirker didn't want to run across any dragoons.

Later in the morning, after we'd picked our way through a boulder-clotted pass in the saw-toothed Sandias, we turned due west and headed across the high mesas on a line that would take us through the foothills of the Zuñi Mountains and on into Arizona.

On the second evening of our trip, as we camped near a water hole in the lee of a great orange-tinted bluff, Jeff broke out a bottle of his Blue Ruin from the pack mule's cargo. After several healthy belts, he leaned back against the rock and began to make a lot of talk. For a while he yarned about the war and the flocks of señoritas that had just swooned away at the sight of his manly carcass, though I noticed that none of them was named Rosita.

I could match him on tall stories. With no one around to call my hand, that scrap with Esteban Domingo had grown into a regular pitched battle with a whole gang of knife-fighting Mexicans. I really laid it on, for I guessed that Kirker was stretching the truth until it yelled for mercy himself!

But finally Jeff's yarns veered around to his shenanigans in California, and my ears pricked up.

"You say there was some trouble?" I put in to prime him a mite.

"Trouble's one way to put it." He downed another snort of the whiskey and grinned, sort of lopsided. "Y'see, I was in th' Army back then—sergeant of a six-man squad, ridin' guard on a hefty army payroll comin' up to Santa Rosa from San Francisco—and there was . . . some trouble!" He squinted at me through the amber bottle. His eye, magnified by the glass, looked hard and sort of wild, like the eye of a panther cat, before it springs with claws out. Then he tipped the bottle, drained the rest of that firewater, wiped his beard and gave a short, odd-sounding laugh.

"Roy, I like you, or you wouldn't have rid five miles with me!" His voice sent a prickle through my neck as it somehow changed. "Ever hear of Murieta?"

"Is this Murieta the jasper that caused this trouble?"

"In a manner of speaking." Kirker peered down the bottle as if he was looking for the right sort of words. Suddenly he got to his feet and heaved the empty as far as he could. The clash of shattered glass stirred up a couple of coyotes, and they began to yap their complaints about the racket.

"Like I said, kid," Kirker went on, "if I didn't take to you—and sort of need you for a certain job . . ." His voice dropped off again, as though something besides those coyotes could be out there in the dark. "You was curious about that trooper back at Albuquerque. If you thought he knew me, you'd be about right. Think his name's Sam Harper. He was at our Santa Rosa post when I got there, but he'd gone back to another fort before that—trouble. So he doesn't know *much!*"

"I heard him call out some name. Maybe Rosita? Know her?"

"Knew her, all right!" Kirker eased back down by the fire with a long sigh. "So did most every trooper with money enough for a proper introduction." He pulled his big bowie knife from his boot top and watched the reflection of the flames run along its edge.

I didn't like the looks of that knife. It reminded me of a dead Mexican with his face shot off—though I packed a bowie in my own boot.

"Don't worry." Jeff showed his teeth. "Like I said, you wouldn't lasted five miles with me if I didn't cotton to you!"

In a blinding move, he flipped the knife—and it shivered in the hard ground a scant inch from my big toe!

In that same instant he was staring into the muzzle of the Walker Colt, yanked from my waistband.

"Oh, hand back that sticker, Roy, and put up your weepon. That there knife only does its dirty work when I tell it to!"

Next morning we rode across the edge of the Painted Desert with its miles of red, blue, brown and splotches of purple, and it was like traveling over a great devil's paint box. While I gawked at the wildly strange landscape, I kept mulling over what Jeff had told me the night just past.

"Trouble" was certainly a good word for it! For Kirker was a deserter from the U.S. Army and wanted in California by the military authorities. But what the brass out there didn't know, or even suspect, according to Jeff, was the fact that he and a wild California bandit, Joaquín Murieta, had pulled off the robbery of an army payroll train. Murieta and his men had blown the whole six-man escort right out of their saddles, leaving only Jeff Kirker, the Judas goat, alive to tell it!

"We took that pack train of four mules and driv 'em into th' foothills west of Santa Rosa, hid fifty thousand dollars and more in gold eagles, then plugged th' mules twenty miles away. So I up and rid back into our post, all frazzled, and lettin' on that I was sole survivor of a dirty Mexican ambush—which I was," Kirker had said, grinning like some sort of a wildcat. "Everybody at th' post remarked that I was damned sure th' lucky seventh man!"

According to Jeff, he'd stolen the post commandant's favorite pacing horse, plus a brace of pack mules, and skinned out at midnight, two nights later.

He fetched up at the gold cache at daylight, uncovered the loot, loaded up his pack mules and headed blindly north into unknown territory as fast as he could push, keeping his eyes open for both bandits and Army.

"Found myself a place where not one damned white man had ever set foot. She's all hid there—and she's *bully!*" And that was all he'd told me about the hiding place of a king's ransom!

IV

As brother Josh used to say, you should never tempt the devil with loose talk!

Here we'd come all the way across the Arizona Territory to within a couple of miles of Zuñi Jack's trading post without having seen hide nor feather of a single redskin.

I mentioned this in passing and Jeff began, at once, to cuss out Indians in general and this Zuñi Jack in particular. I could see Kirker was toting a real skull ache from his bout with the bottle.

"You just wait until we git to his place, and see if he don't try to charge double for everything—damned highway robber!"

I didn't know this Zuñi Jack from a button but it struck me as pretty funny that an ex-highwayman like Jeff Kirker should be so all-fired self-righteous. But we needed some supplies and were running low on good water, and, according to Kirker, the Zuñi had a water hole famous for its sweetness.

"Indians are Indians," I grinned, "but it's funny we never saw any all this while. Old Fancher was positive we'd bump headlong into dozens!"

I was getting ready to chaff Kirker about highway robbers when a small, tawny puff of dust, hovering southward over the sloping mesas and cholla patches, began to swell and drift toward us.

"Indians only let you see 'em when they want you to," Kirker grunted, then stiffened in his saddle, looking south. "And a dollar to a bent peso we got some comin' this way right now! White men don't lambaste hosses like that—got more sense."

"What do we do, make a run for Zuñi Jack's or stay and powwow?" That cloud was getting mighty close as it swayed along all golden yellow under the blazing sun. Then we saw them! Five horsemen galloped toward us, rushing streaks of fluttering feathers and pounding hooves, darting across the mesa grasses like a swooping flock of gaudy birds. War crests and feathered lances glimmered over feathered shields of painted bull's hide. Naked except for a red clout flanked by two antelope tails, the leader rode up and lifted his long lance at us. A pair of his fellow riders held up their hands palms out, staring across at us with slitted, glittering eyes.

"Apache?"

"Comanche! And I don't know what they're doin' this far north," Kirker muttered out of the side of his mouth. "Don't go to makin' any quick moves, and let's see if one of 'em can parley." He raised his own hand, palm out and tried both sign language and Apache. The leader shook his red-feathered topknot like a wary hawk, then answered Jeff in Apache lingo.

Presently Kirker and the chief pushed their horses forward and shook hands. Then the Comanche offered his hand to me and I took it mighty easy like.

"This here's a war party on th' scout for Navajos or Zuñi. Seems some of th' Arizona Indians got too far south to suit these Comanche," Jeff translated the mixture of Apache and broken Spanish the chief used. "The Comanche got their own ideas of territory and this one says th' Indians up this way are jest too big for their clouts—and he and his bunch are out to cut some down to size!"

The Comanches kicked their spotted, paint-daubed ponies around us, growling like a pack of half-friendly dogs. The leader nodded his head and made motions with his wicked-looking lance.

"Wants to smoke th' pipe with us. They ain't on no warpath with th' white man right now," reported Jeff, "but keep your eyes wide and that cannon of yours ready, just in case."

We all dismounted, staked out our mounts, along with the pack mule, in the shade of a small stand of scrawny pines, and proceeded to smoke the pipe with those wild-eyed Indians. It went off pretty well until Jeff made the mistake of fetching out our other bottle.

Those Comanche grinned from ear to painted ear as that whiskey went around the circle. And each time the bottle circulated, the Indians grew more friendly, patting us on the back and nodding their plumes until it seemed we were squatting in the midst of a flock of crazy, glare-eyed hawks!

And just like any bunch of drunks, those Comanche got to bragging about how many coup they'd counted, and the number of scalps taken— including no small amount of Mexicans. They didn't mention whites, but I suppose they were just being polite. The chief, who was called Big Wolf, finally had to break down and show off his medicine bundle, tugging out a knotted linen rag from under his antelope-tail flap.

He untied the small parcel and shoved the contents across at us. It held, among other things, a dry, smoke-cured hand of a white woman! The hand was small and shapely, with a plain gold wedding band, and perfectly mummified. That pitiful packet also held one of the newfangled tintypes. The picture's oval frame dangled from a rawhide string around Big Wolf's neck.

"He says," Jeff interpreted, "he got that hand and pitcher th' spring of 1842. Says that dead hand is sure mighty big medicine, and there ain't been a bullet molded to puncture his hide since he's got that on him!"

I looked at the daguerreotype. A little girl peered out of the tinted picture. With wide blue eyes in a sweet, delicate face, framed by long blond curls, she looked to be no more than seven or eight.

"Where in Hades did that ugly murderer get a-hold of this?" I asked, while a chill rippled through me as far as my boots. That girl, young as she was then, would be sixteen or so by now—if she would have lived through the bloody butchery of a Comanche raid.

"Old heap Big Wolf here, when a young warrior, had a medicine man who told him that if he aimed to become a great killer and a taker of lots of coup, he'd need to get a-hold of th' left hand of a white woman who had a gal child—but he never got th' chance for such big medicine until he went with a war party nigh to th' California line," Kirker reported. "His bunch got th' bulge on an emigrant wagon train over there, and plumb killed off all th' folks and burnt th' wagons. While he was rummagin' through th' shambles he found a little white kid hidin' in a half-burnt wagon—th' one in that pitcher. Then he up and cut off th' kid's maw's hand and would have sliced her up and run a spear through that gal child, but some Mexican troopers showed up and th' Comanches all run for it. They know when to run and when to fight, like th' rest of us." He gave a short laugh and shrugged as if the story had got to him, hard as he was.

"So he got the hand and the picture from that dead woman—but what about the little girl?" I asked, but Big Wolf wanted to do some talking with me and clamped shut about that wagon train or its people. I had a feeling that he or some one in his band of butchers had killed the little girl before they left on the run, and looking at his broad, merciless face, I was sure of it.

When the Indians could see the bottle was finally dead, they got up and made for their ponies. Big Wolf and a skinny Comanche with one eye and black stripes across his ugly face stood muttering at each other, then the Big Wolf turned back to us.

"Like I said, he wants to know if you'll trade him for th' pitcher of that little gal child," said Jeff. "Musta watched you when you saw th' tintype. These devils don't miss much. He'd admire that Walker Colt in your belt, or th' big Tige rifle stuck on my hoss there."

So while the rest of the Comanches, back aboard their nervous, little ponies, waited and belched and grunted at each other, Big Wolf and I made trading powwow. I wasn't about to add to those Indians' firepower, for their three big flintlock horse pistols and a pair of U.S. percussion rifles made them deadly enough for any bunch of wild men.

At last the Comanche chief settled for my bowie knife and a cheap Mexican campaign medal and got on his horse after handing over the tintype; then the whole bunch galloped south without a backward look or a thank-you for the whiskey.

"Damned cheeky devils," Kirker growled as we rode up the great mesa he called Mars Hill in the direction of Zuñi Jack's place.

As we rode along, the purple-tinged San Francisco Peaks reached up over the skyline all the way around to the Coconino Plateau where we were headed. "Hopi call them mountains th' High Place of th' Snows. They say they're so high that when th' sun shines on one side, th' moon's shinin' on th' other," said Jeff, making talk, which seemed his way anywhere near a skinful.

I wasn't paying him much attention, for it was as clear as mud, as my brother Josh would say, exactly why Jeff Kirker'd latched on to me!

With the U.S. Army after him for desertion and that bandit, Joaquín Murieta, also on the scout for him, Kirker had to get some happy-go-lucky bonehead to scout along and see if the coast was clear enough to ride in and dig out that fifty thousand in gold. No dumned wonder he'd cottoned to young Mr. Roy Bean.

Passing through a scattered stand of ponderosa pine, we crested the hill and could make out the cabins and corrals of Zuñi Jack's trading post in a shallow valley just ahead.

Several small figures stood out by the corrals watching our approach. "There's Zuñi Jack," Jeff grunted, spurring into a brisk gallop. "Probably wonderin' if we're gonna fetch in his red brothers for a snootful of his bad grog." Jeff went on to tell me, as we racked downhill, that Zuñi Jack had been one of Kit Carson's scouts in the California campaigns and was said to be a pretty bad actor, tough as an old he-bear; in fact Jack had tangled with a mountain grizzly a few years back, with that bear coming out a close second best in a regular hand-to-paw Donnybrook!

Arriving at the corrals, we were hailed by a squatty-looking Indian in dirty buckskins who shuffled up, long musket cradled under his left arm.

Another Indian, this one as skinny as Jack was fat, and dressed as shabbily, stood behind him holding a rusty pistol.

"Hey now!" the first man shouted. "Thought you were part of that war party. They wuz here this very mornin' but we made th' red buggers clear off! Saw th' bunch of you up past th' pines but couldn't make out who wuz who, since I busted my spyglass." Zuñi Jack's English was passable enough, but sort of like he had a mouthful of hot mush.

"They was here before?" Kirker rubbed his black chin whiskers. "Well, they didn't git nuthin' from us, except a drink! And that reminds me, we need us some supplies." And Jeff followed the Zuñi into the trading post's dim interior, tagged along by myself and the other Indian, who'd turned our mounts into the corral.

"Other trouble around here?" Jeff asked the portly proprietor of the Blak Bare Tradin Stashun, which was the way the crudely daubed sign read across the adobe building's front.

"Naw! Hardly never see a soul, red nor white, since th' wagon trains are takin' th' old Mormon Battalion route southwest inter Californy."

"Why's that?" I horned in.

"U.S. dragoons keep that route open mostly, since that talk about th' gold strike," Zuñi Jack grunted, fiddling with the stub of an ear left by the bear. "You-all headin' that way? Y'can pick up an escort of soldier boys down ter th' Pima Tradin' Post as they ride through oncet a week or so on the scout fer hostiles—like them damned feather-sproutin' Comanche!"

I knew what Kirker would reply before he opened his mouth.

"Oh, we're goin' around th' old north route," Jeff answered shortly, then ordered another round of Mexican beer from Zuñi Jack's squaw, who hovered near the rickety bar, looking for all the world like a spitting image of her lord except for a red skirt and two whole ears.

By the time we'd taken on board half a dozen bottles of warm beer, Jeff Kirker had expanded into his usual talkative self, insisting we'd got the best of the Comanches in a little swap. He had me show the daguerreotype to Zuñi Jack and his help. "Lookit that! A genuine five-dollar tintype for an old bowie knife and a blamed jimcrack of a greaser medal!" Kirker crowed. "If that ain't tradin' them red devils outa their clouts, I don't know about it! And like I say, you can always git th' best of a dumb—" He suddenly shoved the bottle at his open mouth, and I knew he'd recalled what he'd said about Zuñi Jack's so-called shrewdness.

Jack took up the daguerreotype, looked long at it, then wagged his head. "Ugh hunh!" His voice sounded as if he'd a couple of mouthfuls of hot mush, so I figured him sort of roused up. "Ugh! I know that there pitcher, leastwise I know that little gal!" He tugged at his starboard, good ear. "Ugh! *Todo correcto!* And now I know why that blamed Comanche looked familiar when he rid in here this mornin' with his *compadres*. He's th' very one I took a shot at when I was scoutin' fer some Mexican Lancers out at San Pascual, where we caught them red-tailed rascals a-burnin' a wagon train!"

"Blamed rascal youself, ridin' with them blackhearted Mexicans." Kirker ordered another round of beer for all, winking at me.

"You saw this little girl?" I found it hard to believe but Jack had no reason to lie. "What happened to her?"

"Don't know for certain." Jack helped himself to our beer. "Do know she was th' only one of that whole train to keep her scalp. She might have been turned over to th' sisters at one of them convents, but which one's anybody's guess. Californy's got nigh as many as oranges."

I put the tintype back in my shirt pocket and went with a limber-legged Kirker to fill our water cask at Jack's spring out back of the corrals. Jeff had paid on the nail for our supplies—fatback, hardtack and another bottle of whiskey—and without any fuss. The warm beer had put him in a peaceful and forgiving mood.

When we rode off north, Zuñi Jack bowlegged down the trail a piece and called after us, "Watch them Comanche! They could still be hankerin' for your shootin' arns!"

We both waved at the Zuñi, then dug in and rode steadily for the next three hours, pulling up near sunset in a great stand of piñon pine atop one of the foothills of the San Francisco Peaks.

It wasn't long until I'd a fire going and sowbelly sizzling in the pan while the sun was burning out in a smother of blood-streaked cloud banks. For some reason I couldn't figure just then, the sight of all that scarlet and red flaming out there on the rim of the world gave me a case of pure goose bumps. A mournful wind was whistling its way through the pines, so I laid my feelings to that as much as to an odd-looking sunset.

Jeff had just come back from tending to the animals, which were staked out about fifty yards off on an open piece of mesa and had taken up his tin cup of coffee. "Well, kid, a couple of days and we cross San Juan River, swing west again for a hundred miles and we'll hit th' old Spanish Trail straight inter California!" He laughed deep and happy as he sipped at the hot java—and those were the last words he ever spoke, but four!

A musket cracked out and Jeff Kirker gave a grunt, folding over into the campfire, spilling skillet and coffee, and knocking ashes and brands galley west!

V

I was clawing for ground before that shot quit racketing through the trees.

Rolling over, I grabbed Kirker, hauling him from the fire, batting flames off his clothing.

"Where're you hit?"

He didn't answer; then he lifted his head to gasp, "That coin—Red Rosita!" His eyes rolled up; he stiffened and was dead!

There was nothing but brittle, hissing quiet; even that mournful breeze seemed to have died the same instant as Jeff Kirker. I stared bug-eyed at him, seeing blood spread on his chest. There was some on my hands and I hurried to wipe them on my shirt. It was the same color as that sunset. And in that bloody light there came the sudden screech of a war cry, and I knew Big Wolf was back to finish his trading!

Jeff's Tige rifle was still strapped to his bay on the mesa, and all I had to fight with was my Walker Colt. I rolled back, tugged the six-gun out and waited, not moving and scarce breathing, searching dark pines and scarlet mesa for movement.

Nothing stirred; then three Indians came leaping from somewhere and running toward the staked-out animals, a trio of devils darting through the blazing sunset.

I cocked the Walker, leveling down on the leading Indian—Big Wolf. The hammer clacked. No explosion! Damp powder in the chamber, or that dead hand was still big medicine.

I expected Comanches right on top of me by the time I'd cocked the weapon again, but they'd grabbed our two horses and were already astride, loping down the hill, while the third Indian dogtrotted behind, toting a sack of supplies.

I lowered the Walker and waited, then saw the whole bunch riding away hard as they could lash their mounts. As Jeff said, Comanches knew when to fight and when to let well enough alone. Besides, they had about all they'd come for—both riding horses and Kirker's rifle.

I leaned back against a tree, near Jeff's body, mighty glad I hadn't fired. I really wasn't any sort of an Indian fighter, and I knew it.

When the last crimson glints died in the ashy-blue west, I tugged Kirker back a piece, covering him with a section of canvas from the pack mule—the only live company left me.

I let the fire go on out, for if those Indians should come back, I didn't want any light showing.

Rolling up in my blanket, I waited it out until morning, shivering and shaking and filled with the kind of dreams I don't like to remember.

It was a long and lonesome night.

Gray dawn drifted through the trees before I fell into a hard sleep, worn with the turns and tumbles of the night. If Big Wolf had come back for my scalp, he'd have had it half off before I'd come to.

When I finally came back to the land of the living, the sun was high over the pines and some hellish commotion was ringing in my ears. I stumbled up, pawing for my pistol, only to realize my pack mule was out there on the mesa, braying its disgust and lonesomeness.

Moving the mule into the shade of the trees, near some gamma grass, I looked over what Big Wolf had left me. The water cask was still filled and there was just about enough supplies to get under way on north. I thought of going downtrail to Zuñi Jack's but the thought that those Comanches might be lurking below didn't set too well. It was a case of once burnt, never twice!

For a spell I lingered out in the hot sunshine for a chill stayed deep in my blood from thoughts of last night and what waited for me in the blue shadows of the piñons—Kirker's body!

I hadn't looked toward Jeff since scrambling to my feet at the tremendous racket of the pack mule's lament, but I finally turned and went back to our dead campfire. My poor saddle pardner lay beyond those cold ashes near a pile of upthrust boulders.

I walked over and tugged the piece of canvas off the stiffened corpse. Kirker still wore a surprised look, and for the life of me I couldn't keep from wondering if the six men of Jeff's squad had the same look when those bandits had knocked them from their horses. Kirker had been the lucky seventh man, but his luck had finally run out—with a bang!

Thinking of the robbery over in California, and all that bloody gold, fetched back Jeff's last words: *"That coin—Red Rosita!"*

Much as I hated to go through Kirker's clothing, I knelt and shoved his cold eyelids down over that vacant stare, then rummaged in his vest and discovered something. Kirker was wearing a money belt, stained and stiff with his dried blood, and it was chock-full of ten-dollar gold pieces. I slipped it off him and tossed it aside, then went on searching. In his vest pocket I found what looked to be the same coin he'd let me look at for a moment at Albuquerque. There were some odd scratches on one side, seemingly made with a knife point, but that was all. I stuck it into my pocket and looked over the ground. That pile of rocks and boulders would have to do, for I had no shovel or any means of digging out much of a hole.

I got to work on the pile of rocks, then took Jeff's bowie knife from his boot and dug hard as I could at the earth until I had a fair-sized hole hollowed out. It wasn't very fancy but it would keep Kirker from coyotes and other critters.

I tugged him over, wrapped him up as good as I could in the canvas, and covered him with stones and rocks until I had a good-sized cairn built. Taking the knife, I whittled out a crude marker from a fallen limb and carved his name and the date. He'd never mentioned relations, so I didn't know who to tell. Maybe this Rosita, whoever and wherever she might be? I'd wait and see.

It was odd but I'd worked up a mighty good appetite from all the lugging and digging. When I'd finished with the marker, I cooked myself the rest of the fatback, boiling a pot of coffee. Jeff wouldn't have minded, I thought, for his last happy moment was spent swigging down that hot java.

When I was finished, I picked up the money belt and counted all those brightly gleaming eagles—without doubt a share of that bandit loot.

When I was done stacking those gold pieces along the ground beside the fatback skillet, I'd exactly $720—more money than I'd ever seen since I was born. And it gave me such a warm feeling it completely burned away that deathly chill of the night just past!

It was certainly time to be moving on, and I packed as fast as I could, for I was still jumpy and seemed to hear the pounding of Indian ponies in every sound from the rap-rapping of the white-striped woodpeckers in the trees to the rattle of some wind-tossed branch.

Before I rode away from that pine grove, I went back to the mound of rocks that covered the seventh man—unlucky Jeff Kirker. Standing there in the green gloom of the pines, I bowed my head for a moment and said a silent prayer, for he was a right enough fellow, though he'd been a turn-coat highwayman with plenty of blood on his hands. But he'd been straight with me.

Riding the pack mule I'd christened Comanche, I traveled from water hole to water hole for the next week, skirting canyons and sticking it out through patches of pure desert hell. I lived mainly on what was left of the hardtack and what small game I could snare or knock over. At last I hit a branch of the old Spanish Trail, so marked on Jeff's map, north of the Kaibab Plateau in northern Arizona, and turned westward toward California proper.

Near the Horserock Valley, where I saw what seemed to be pure thousands of buffalo, drifting along like a sea of brown boulders, I struck another small trading post. This lonely station, run by a white man and his wife, was called Vermillion Cliffs from the towering rock formations of orange and green that loomed behind the buildings. It was a pretty rundown affair, but the man, one Whitmore, did have a fair string of horses.

"Ain't seed that kind of kale since me and Mert come out two years back." Whitmore rolled a quid in his lean cheek with emotion. "Don't git us much trade these days. Jest a few buffaler hunters and some traders, as most of th' movers are usin' th' south route inter Californy these days. More Army around to keep th' Injuns behavin'. Woulda thought you'd gone that way."

"Don't you go a-scarin' this boy!" Mrs. Whitmore leaned on her broom, tucked up her mousy hair, smiling at me as she smoothed her shabby calico Mother Hubbard.

"Guess I can get to where I'm going without too much commotion," I said, finishing loading Comanche, the mule, and adjusting a battered saddle on my new mount.

I steered clear of mentioning the run-in with the Comanches and Kirker's death, not wanting to spook the Whitmores, who still seemed to be tenderfeet. But that was the way things were going ever since we'd taken half of the entire Southwest away from Santa Anna and his Mexican *amigos*. The Easterners were flooding in upon this wild and brutal land, without a single idea of just what they were letting themselves in for.

Waving my Mexican sombrero, I rode away leaving my hosts to stand lonely and lost in front of their shabby cabin. The Whitmores and folks like them would need plenty of luck to survive, and so would I, when I came to think of it; but I was young and full of frijoles, and still believed the world was my private oyster, if I could just wrestle that shell open.

And I still had fifty thousand in gold waiting for me—if I could find it. That was enough to keep me on my way.

So it went day after day, moving on westward, in a lot better shape than I'd been before my stop at the Vermillion Cliffs. Now I was aboard a nice little riding horse, a black with two white-stockinged feet, with a decent U.S. Army carbine and ammunition.

Riding on toward California, I kept that blustering wind at my back that swept the vastness, and my thoughts, clean of troublesome worry. I was shed of Indians, it seemed, and that was one reason I sang to my defenseless animals as we drifted before that ceaseless wind, though I kept on the lookout for ambush sites.

Jeff's map guided us across grinding hot deserts, with their miles of cholla and joshua, and then through countless reaches of waving buffalo grass. There were, from time to time, great canyons to skirt, God-awful slashes in the deep earth that must have been made in the earliest days by the claws of some crazy animals hundreds of miles high!

Once in a while I, my horse and my pack mule enjoyed fording a clear-running creek, for the watercourses still wandered down from the distant mountains, though they were shallowing as the days wore along into deep summer.

My best time on the trail came at sundown, when the wind went to sleep, and the orange-scarlet of my fire bloomed out into the silvery twilight, putting to shame the faint green and amber of the dying sunset. Oh, I was mighty poetical like, all by myself, and I had to admit I'd have swapped a pile of eagles for the company of some pleasant young lady until daybreak—anytime!

But I was all by my lonesome, save for my animals staked out beyond the firelight. Both cropped at the buffalo grass and watched me shift and reshift my shining gold pieces, while the frosty blaze of a heaven jam-packed with stars rivaled and even outshone my glittering hoard.

VI

Night following night I camped along the lonely trail, nearly always serenaded by coyote choruses and roused out each dawn by the rusty braying of my pack mule Comanche.

Once up, I cooked my sparse rations, washed them down with a pot of ink-black coffee, tended to my animals and then struck on to the west, pushed forward by the unceasing wind, a wind that wandered in from out of nowhere with each sunrise and kept at its busy work until nightfall.

Following Kirker's rough but accurate map, I made my way to the rickety ferry at the Colorado crossing near the Riverside Mountains and was in California at last. Jeff had been a great help to me, though he lay in a hidden grave hundreds of miles to the east, for his location of definite water holes had kept me alive.

And now I traveled on the deeply lined tracks that remained after nearly three hundred years—the trail that Escalante's steel-suited troops and other old, hard-bitten conquistadores had also traveled.

Riding onward through the vast stretches of the empty land, with only the restless wind for company as it rustled the grass and tugged the gaudy yellow paper flowers of the mesas and whispered through the sword-blade leaves of the ocotillo, I found myself missing Jeff Kirker. So I fell into the habit of humming and singing along with the wind out of sheer lonesomeness and the need to hear any voice, if only my own.

I was singing along, pretty off-key, around noon in early July, putting my own words to an old-time hymn tune, when I got to thinking of food. It was a subject always close to my mind, what with spending nigh onto four weeks eating fatback, occasional jackrabbit and hardtack, boiled, fried and pounded into mush, and washed down with coffee so mean-strong it bit back!

What wouldn't I do for some buckwheat cakes, like those I used to get back in good old Mason County? I'd have done just about anything! And I sang:

> "The dark-brown cake is laid
> Upon a plate of spotless white;

And the eye of him who tastes it
Now flashes with delight!
Oh, cake that's buttered for me,
Why can I not partake?
Oh, my heart, my heart is breaking
For the love of buckwheat cake!"

I was tackling the second chorus with a lot of feeling and rubbing my middle with reminiscence when—

"*Alto!*" A small, portly Mexican, with enormous black mustaches and a gray sombrero, so big he looked just about like a toadstool astride a horse, rode up from a dry wash leveling a big Colt Dragoon dead at me!

"I hear your music, señor—if one might call it that." For a long moment the man kept his weapon trained straight at the middle of my belt buckle; then with a twisted smile lurking under his mustache, he lowered his weapon, and I did the same with my hands. "*Pardona!* By San Fernando's red nightshirt, I thought you might be from some bandit gang, for we are close to Murieta's country!" He flung a brown hand wide at the rolling acres of sagebrush and apache plume stretching off into purple distance toward the San Bernardino and Chuckwalla mountains to the southwest, then holstered his big pistol.

And when the little stranger tucked away his weapon in its long red holster, I caught sight of a badge of some sort pinned to his yellow suspenders.

I told him in a few words who I was, where I hailed from, more or less, and where I was headed.

"*Sí!*" He bobbed his mushroom of a sombrero, punched the badge on his galluses with a broad thumb, and introduced himself as Salvador Salazar, sheriff of Alameda County, which was about next door to San Francisco. He'd been, he said, out on a jaunt of two hundred miles and more scouting for some bandits who'd been raising hob along the coast highways and mining camps.

According to this fat little Mex sheriff, we were just a little less than one hundred miles northwest of the town of Los Angeles (The Angeles). But, said the sheriff, there were not many angels around those parts. "No angels, *amigo*, but plenty of *diablos*, let me tell you! And I've been chasing some for weeks. All the others of my company got saddle-sore and went back to their home ranchos." He grinned slyly at me. "But what can one expect from the Yankees! Now you have the look of one lucky *hombre*. For what you tell me, you've come many miles across plenty damn dangerous lands yourself. If you'd have traveled those sandy hells a month later, you'd surely have dried up along with the water holes and blown away!"

I admitted I figured I was a bit more than lucky to be where I was.

"See any hostiles? Apache, perhaps? I hear those accursed Comanche have been seen up north again."

"Had a run-in with one bunch back below Vermillion Cliffs in Arizona a couple of weeks back," I told him, but I didn't mention Jeff. One gander at that pie-plate badge and hearing Murieta mentioned was enough to put me on my guard.

From what this Salazar said, I'd got myself another trail pardner, for he was riding over to Los Angeles and thereabouts to check in with the local law before heading back up to his own bailiwick.

So now I found myself riding side by side and taking meals with Juan Ley (John Law), which was an odd turn of things seeing I'd darn near become right-hand man to an outlaw by the name of Kirker!

VII

After the blazing, empty deserts, huge stretches of lonely mesas and strings of brackish water holes, California was surely easy on the eyes with its rolling hills and bright green meadows, all ringed with groves of big, handsome trees—black oak, maple and sycamore. The long grasses began to be spangled with flowers of every sort, yellow daisies, wild red roses and dozens of other posies such as the big California poppies and golden coneflowers, all trying to outbloom the others.

Here was no wilderness of cactus, joshua and mesquite, with its sly bobcats and howling coyotes. This was a country teeming with wildlife of every sort from blacktail deer, antelope and even some elk to feisty chipmunk and loping rabbit. Birds filled the timber and whirled up into skies, from loudmouthed jays to pretty little wrens and dozens upon dozens of quail.

Yes, I was glad to be out of that wilderness and back into a land the good Lord Himself wouldn't have been ashamed to admit He had a hand in making.

It was also mighty pleasant to have Salazar along, after all the long, lonesome days on the trail, for the pudgy, little lawman was a lively saddle pardner, always ready with a story or a joke—unlike Jeff Kirker, who had to down half a bottle of liquor to get himself in any sort of a cheerful frame of mind. But then I guess six dead troopers weighed pretty heavy on him most of the time.

Salazar seemed to be of tougher stuff than Kirker. He didn't seem to let dead men bother him much—Mexicans or those shot in the war. And he didn't need any sort of bottled help to uncork his tongue. So we yarned through the days and evenings as we camped in lush meadows or rode along silvery-clear creeks and little streams, whittling down the miles to Los Angeles, our nearest port of call. And while we gossiped and talked, Salazar got most of my life and times out of me, though I kept Jeff Kirker from my story, only mentioning him as the fellow who'd got himself killed by Indians back in Arizona.

As I said, Salazar wasn't a bit shy in talking about himself. He'd come from a big hacienda near San Francisco, growing up there as a plain peasant kid. Tired of all the work and mighty little money (a peso a day), he ran off at sixteen, joining the Mexican Army and was at the Alamo fight. Later he fought Yanks all the way from Sonoma to Monterey, but he took it all in a day's work—like chasing down fellow Mexicans who'd gone on their own warpath after losing to the *americanos*.

"Some *hombres* can't seem to play the cards old Señor Luck deals," said Salazar. "I think I'm a reasonable fellow myself. I just take what the good saints provide each day, along with my dinner, and go about my affairs. I could bellyache and holler that we poor *californios* got kicked good and hard in the tail-bone. Me, I take vengeance from life itself; it's the best way!" He squeezed the air with both hands, rolled his eyes at the sky and then grinned.

"Speaking of cards," Salazar went on, "I think, maybe, you play some cards pretty close to the vest, young señor!" He twiddled at his mustachios. "*Sí*, you're a young *compañero* but you can keep some things to yourself, heh?"

I started to open my mouth, but he reached over to poke me in the ribs, and I knew he'd spotted that hefty money belt under my ragged hickory shirt. "Don't mistake me. Each of us has his secret or two," he said. "It's *solo bueno* to have your own, but be on your guard."

I wasn't sure what he was aiming at, but took it to be a friendly hint to watch my mouth and my money.

The night before we fetched up at Los Angeles, Salazar finally got around to mentioning his peculiar topknot, a thing I'd noticed the first time he'd doffed his big flopping sombrero.

I'd never spoke of his vanished scalp, feeling it wasn't up to me to remark on any of his beauty flaws.

"You've admired my tonsure," he said as he made a face but downed my boiler plate coffee. "That's quite all right, for by the arrows of San Sebastián I tell you right here and now there's not too many hombres around minus part of their head! And that little decoration came from those red hell-fiends when they pounced on a wagon train I was leading into Aguangua."

Right there I recollected what brother Josh, a better than average book reader, used to say: "Life's sometimes a damn sight odder than any storybook!" And I was grabbed good and strong with a hunch that this fat little Mexican was talking about the same raid where Big Wolf captured his medicine hand—and where that little girl had been scooped up at the last minute by the Mexican Lancers. Now this might sound a bit farfetched, but a person has got to remember that the old Southwest was pretty scant on population at the time I'm telling about, and some folks were just bound to cross trails.

Late the next afternoon we reined in at a fine little water hole a scant five miles from Los Angeles. When we were lounging in the shade of a great gnarled old black oak and letting the kinks unwind, I got out the daguerreotype and tossed it over to the sheriff without a word.

"*Ah, demonio!*" Salazar yanked away his headgear and beat a tattoo with a stubby knuckle on his scalped noggin. "*Sí!* that little one and I were the only ones—the only ones left alive after those *diablos* got through with their hellish work!" His black eyes bulged out of his dark face. "Those Comanche would have done us up *proplamente* but for the intervention of blessed San Miguel, who hurled the Lancers upon those *diablos rojos!*"

It puzzled me a mite just how he knew what particular saint was on duty, but only asked where that little girl had gone.

"Colonel Francisco Almada of the Lancers took her to the Convent of Santa María, north of San Diego. Myself, I was tended there by the sisters and saw her with those gentle handwomen of the Lord."

He handed back the tintype and we remounted and rode down a long plain, covered with clover. Within the hour we caught sight of the City of the Angels, where it sparkled in the afternoon sunlight beside a small river. A good dozen haciendas surrounded it, with their willow-fringed gardens, each filled with grape, quince, orange and pear along with some ancient fig trees. Old Fort Gillespie, with its American flag, loomed along the green hills beyond the town, while the cathedral sent up its twin towers into the mellow sunshine out of the cluster of white adobes and scattered two-story buildings.

As we rode down a dirt track that doubled as a road, Salazar, who'd been mighty quiet, squinted a curious eye at me. "But how did you—?"

I was ready for that and told him I'd come across the tintype of the girl at one-eared Zuñi Jack's trading post, halfway across Arizona.

"*Sí*, that would be the old he-bear himself who rode to our rescue with the Lancers—he and holy San Miguel."

I had to smile behind my hand to hear Zuñi Jack labeled saddle pardner to a saint, but then it could be so, for hadn't Jack brought along the Lancers in time to save a wistful-looking little girl—and Salazar himself?

Riding on toward that dreamy old Spanish town with its low, grassy hills, nearly little mountains surrounding it on three sides, we were in high spirits, and I cracked a joke or two while Salazar came back with a ring-tailed roarer about some Mexican ladies and a bullfighter that would never do for mixed company.

Arriving at Cahuenga Street, with its huge cottonwoods, we crossed what looked to be a wide alley filled with run-down saloons and billiard halls. Salazar pointed out the place as the Calle de los Negros, jerking a thumb at a bunch of roughs, both Mexican and white, who stood in front of the gaudy gambling dens, along with some fancy, but hard-looking ladies in bright dresses with shiny combs and feathery plumes on their sleek, dark heads.

"The cursed Three-Fingered Jack and that shifty villain of a Juan Soto came out of such a hole," Salazar growled, his usually cheerful phiz screwed up. "I haven't a doubt but this town's law officers have a time keeping such *diablos* as those back there in their places!"

"This Murieta—where'd he spring from?"

"Everywhere!" Salazar waved his hand in a wide circle. "Sometimes I think there must be a dozen Murietas, the way he pops up here and there." He was about to go on, but we'd arrived in front of Wagner's Saloon, and here the sheriff signaled me to dismount. This was, he told me, the newest place in town, with straight games run by a Yankee by the name of Dick Powers, who was one devil of a horseman as well as a sure-fire gambler. The bar was empty except for a scant-whiskered barkeep and several old Mexicans, drowsing over their siesta tequilas.

We had ourselves a couple of dust cutters at the long mahogany bar, and Salazar inquired for Powers, who he said had a saloon at San Diego as well as several other towns, only to learn the gambler was at Santa Barbara.

"This Powers came out to California with Stevenson's New York Volunteers. They were sure some scrappers! When he was going to be discharged at the end of the war, he made himself a stake by picking up a five-thousand-dollar bet that he could ride 160 miles in eight hours!"

"A thundering big ride," I said. "Who'd he bet with?"

"Some of the best riders in Southern California, vaqueros from the De la Guerra Rancho. They said it couldn't be done, and not by any Yankee!" Salazar grinned. *"Sí,* that fellow Powers's time was just six hours and a half! He used twenty-five mounts and galloped an extra mile to show them what was what!"

"Sounds like the sort of riding this Murieta must be doing," I said as I thought of fetching that phantom Red Rosita into the talk, but I dropped the idea when Salazar began to cloud up at the mention of Murieta.

We finished or drinks and went back to register for the night at the Bella Union over on Los Angeles Street, turning in our animals at a corral behind the hotel. When Salazar went off to check in with the local law, I headed for the nearest barbershop.

After a trim and a shave and an honest-to-God bath, in a tin tub in the shop's back room, I asked for the best clothing store and was directed to the Capital Clothing Emporium up on San Gabriel.

Standing there in front of the Emporium's full-length mirror a pretty hard jolt. Here I was, Roy Bean, normally broad-shouldered and broad-faced, hitting onto six feet of bone and muscle. And now I was staring at some sunken-eyed, wind-scorched, rail-thin beggar!

I'd lost twenty-odd pounds riding the winding trail out of Chihuahua. In my ragged yellow hickory shirt and cactus-tattered jeans, stuffed into dusty, scuffed boots, I was surely one sorry-looking sort of a scarecrow. No wonder Salazar had thought he'd run onto a regular hard case when we first met.

Another of brother Josh's secondhand sayings had something to do with new duds making some sort of a new man, so I decided to go the whole hog!

I bought the best tip-top garments and extras that place had to offer and put a first-class smile on the face of the turkey-necked young gent who waited on me.

When I sauntered out of the Capital Clothing Emporium, I might not have been a completely new man, but I was a darn sight better dressed one.

Scarecrow no longer, I was about as fine a dandy as could be found in the whole town. Turned out in black velvet trousers, midnight-blue silk shirt with flowing scarlet kerchief, shiny black hand-tooled boots, with the whole outfit topped off by a silver-spangled sombrero twice as stunning as the late Esteban Domingo's, I strode down the street and called on Salazar at the Los Angeles sheriff's office.

I made an impression, let me tell you, and even the hard-bitten old Sheriff Persifer got up on his bow legs for the introductions. He knew my brother, the alcalde of San Diego, and said as much, though I noticed he didn't toss any bouquets toward Joshua Quincy Bean—but, I thought, politicians were always leery of each other and this must be the case.

Bowing out like a copper-bottom grandee, I took Salazar in tow down to the finest cantina in town—the Blue Wing.

"You are a *mucho diverso hombre* from the one who rode into town with me two hours past." Salazar sat in the cantina lifting his amber glass of beer in salute. When he cocked his head admiringly, a sunbeam lanced through the shutters to touch the top of his missing scalp and give him a sort of halo, like one of his saddle-pardner saints. "*Sí,* you come to California looking like—how do you say?—a bummer, and here is *el caballero!*" He took a hefty pull of his beer, blinking at me with his bright black eyes. "If you had not a face, *sincero,* I'd think you carried *mucho dinero* from *somewhere.*"

So while we sat in the Blue Wing, tackling a prime good meal, all washed down with fancy Mexican wines, I let it be known all those eagles I'd been tossing around came from my family's venture at Chihuahua and were going to be used to start a new business at San Diego.

"Ah, San Diego." Salazar stuffed his face with tortilla, worked his jaws awhile and then came up for air. "Sheriff Persifer reports some trouble down there. Just like here in town and elsewhere. He says your brother, Señor Joshua Bean, *el alcalde,* had to throw some of the gold seekers into his *calabozo* when they tried to take over his town on the way to and from the mining camps—and also that there has been robbers on the loose about that country!"

It appeared things were lively at San Diego and that suited me, for I'd been dreading having to go back behind some counter and bow and scrape for pesos and dollars. I'd lost my appetite for being a merchant prince and made up my mind to apply for some job with the law force.

According to Salazar, the riffraff and toughs had been sweeping through the territory for the past year and times were getting wilder each month.

"It's getting to be a regular plague, let me tell you," Salazar grunted, stuffing away more tortillas. "And now, by San Miguel's pinfeathers, they're arriving from every blessed corner of the world! Just as I left San Francisco there were over one hundred abandoned ships in that harbor! *Sí,* sailors just row ashore and begin to hoof it for the mines. That bay up there looks like *la foresta* from the dozens on dozens of masts sticking up into the sky—captains and crews all out to grab off a fortune from those double-damned mines all springing out of the earth like mushrooms ever since they first found those infernal nuggets at Sutter's Mill!" He got himself so wrought up that I was afraid he'd choke on the food, but after he wheezed a minute, and washed down that wheeze with a generous gulp of wine, he went back at his plate with a will.

When I thought of all that gold out there just waiting for me, and without the need to sweat and strain to get it, my eyes narrowed and I smiled to myself. But Salazar, who seemed to have the knack of reading my thoughts, shook his head.

"Gold can be a blessing, *joven hombre*, but I think gold will prove a curse! *Sí*, a curse for many a man in California."

I didn't try to argue the matter, for I knew for a fact that my eagles—the entire lot of them—had brought death to seven men. And that was curse enough, I thought.

VIII

When I rode down Los Angeles' Main Street and out San Fernando the next morning, following a comfortable night's rest at the first-class Bella Union, Salazar rode at my side, astride his pudgy buckskin.

In talking to the local sheriff, he'd learned that some of the very rascals he was trailing were thought to be in my brother's *calabozo* at San Diego, or were a week back. *"Quién sabe?"* Salazar shrugged when we mounted up and headed out of the old town. "Those infernal jails are all made to be broken out of. A blind peon with a spoon could cut his way out of our accursed adobe. But they don't get away with that sort of thing at our Alameda jailhouse. That place is all stone and iron, let me tell you!"

About five miles out of Los Angeles we met a small crowd of folks coming toward us, mainly Mexican along with some Yanks, and all heading north to the Sacramento mines. Some rode bony mules and some forked worn-out nags that didn't seem able to make it to town let alone any farther. They certainly were one ragtag bunch, and I wondered if any of those hard-faced rapscallions, who stared at my fine horse and fancy duds with mighty calculating looks, had been guests of Josh's hoosegow.

All we learned in passing was they'd come across the southern Gila route and damned it for a red-hot griddle. All said they'd be blasted if they went back that way, not if they rotted in their tracks. They went on their way up the road yelling and cussing their heads off like a pack of wild men.

Salazar wheeled in his saddle to stare gloomily at the dusty mob. "They're getting worse each month—just scum rising out of every hellhole on earth and swarming like two-legged locusts toward the gold! That bunch will mean more trouble for the Los Angeles officers, and for me—if they get up as far as Alameda before they're tossed into jail."

I rode along, watching the sky above me, all filled with slowly drifting clouds pushed along by an easy wind like huge clots of cream swimming in an enormous bowl of blue. Several high pairs of dark wings cut across the sky in front of us, some sort of huge birds that swam through the same sunny air. Salazar pointed them out as California condors, the largest bird of flight, with an average wingspan of ten feet or better. "And now the infernal miners are shooting those birds right and left just for their wing-feather quills in which to tote their cursed gold dust!"

"There must be hundreds of those birds in such a big county," I said, thinking that I'd need more than some wing feathers to pack that fifty thousand in gold eagles—when I got them.

"Ah, señor, there'll come a time when greedy man will have taken and destroyed every creature—and, someday, perhaps even himself!"

The stunning big birds soon sailed away on the cool winds that blew first from the east, and then meandered back from the direction of the nearby coast. And for the first time I felt the spicy tang of an ocean on my face and could taste it in my mouth.

"Do you hear that?" Salazar cocked his great mushroom sombrero and shrugged a shoulder at me as he pulled up his horse.

"I thought I heard the wind in those trees there," I said, tugging on my reins and looking out across the rolling countryside, but saw nothing out of the ordinary.

"Turn down here." Salazar guided his buckskin onto a small lane that forked westerly over a low hill. *Then there it was!* As far as my eyes could see there was only sparkling, restless space, all filled with the reflection of the drifting clouds. It was like nothing I'd ever imagined—and yet, some-how, I fancied I could see the same grassy waves I'd drifted through on the wind-driven journey that fetched me to this.

"That, my young friend, is *el Pacifico!*" Salazar reined in beside me. "Great Balboa, they say, first beheld it in far-off Panama. And now you see it for yourself, young Bean! Wonderful, is it not? And out there, thousands of miles off, another land—China perhaps!"

I couldn't answer. As often as I'd thought of this Pacific, and rolled the name on my tongue, riding the hot, sandy miles toward California, I never had the slightest idea it would be as it was.

While we stared off into the shimmering horizon, white feathers of surf rolled and unrolled along the empty strip of yellow sands below us with a velvety whispering that blended with humming of the winds.

"Now come along, young *compadre.*" Salazar turned his buckskin's head. "We have close to thirty miles before we can take our supper at San Juan Capistrano. Then we'll be a good halfway to San Diego."

The tavern at the little pueblo of San Juan Capistrano seemed to be about the same as all of those along the King's Highway. A one-story, fortlike adobe, painted a dull yellow, with a sloping orange-tiled roof, it stood back from the wide white road among a grove of live oak and cottonwood, staring at us with its big green loopholed shutters, like a watchful kind of an animal.

We arrived at gray dusk as the Angelus bells were ringing from the one remaining tower of the decrepit old Franciscan mission where it stood, lonely and neglected.

A burly, dark-skinned Negro, in ragged pants and red undershirt, slipped up and took our animals around to the rear of the General Santa Anna Taverna, eyeing my silver-studded sombrero with downright admiration.

The large and smoky barroom was well filled for supper, with a patrol of five troopers from Fort Stockton, at San Diego, along with some local Mexican merchants and rancheros, plus a dozen gold hunters, or what they were beginning to call themselves, Forty-Niners. On the whole these miners were a decent sort and not tenderfeet, for they'd been at the mines for a year. This bunch had been down to the Mexican diggings below the border, but the pay dirt had been scarce and so they had come back north and were now heading for the American River.

One of them, a long, limber New Englander who named himself as Yankee Jim Carson, had been in the thick of it from the summer of '48, when he'd been a bank teller at San Francisco. He wasn't a bit backward about telling some of the lunatic events that swept across California from the time a Mormon merchant, Elder Sam Brannan, had sauntered into San Francisco's Portsmouth Plaza May 11, 1848, and hauling a bottle of gold dust from under his coattails begun to holler: "Gold! Gold! *Gold* from the American River!"

"Old Sam knew all about that strike at Sutter's Mill but had kept it under his stovepipe hat until he'd got himself at least four stores built and stocked up along the Sacramento," said Carson. "When the folks heard him bellerin'—the real gold rush started right that very day—and San Francisco began to turn itself inside out. Over a quarter of th' whole dumned population of menfolks lit right out for th' American River by next day. More than fifty new buildings goin' up around town were left where they stood, while carpenters, hod carriers and th' rest headed for th' diggin's. Just about everybody, includin' myself, came down with a ragin' case of gold fever!"

"And it wasn't just you civilians what ketched that there fever," a trooper grinned as he helped himself to another stack of tortillas. "Lootenant Ord's hull garrison deserted and went north—and I'd a been one of 'em but I was in th' guardhouse at th' time!"

Another of the miners lit a clay pipe, puffed out a cloud of smoke, fingered his chin whiskers and chuckled. "A pard o'mine named Jake Leese made himself over seventy-five thousand dollars in three months on th' Yuba with jest a pick and shovel! Another bugger with th' moniker of Sleepy Bill Daylor dug out fifteen thousand in one week, and when I was at Parks Bar th' average yield per man was over a hundred dollars a day."

"Yessir," chimed in Yankee Carson, "th' boys at Wood Creek cashed more than three hundred dollars each in chunks every evenin'. Guess I should have stayed put instead of leggin' it down to Frytown and them blamed Mex diggin's."

"And that was away back in the middle of last year," snorted the miner with the chin whiskers. "Lord above, just look what's happenin' this year of 1849!"

"*Si!* Death and destruction across the land, and it has only just begun. It is the beginning of the whirlwind!" Salazar butted into the conversation.

The company turned to look at the sheriff and took in his saucer-sized badge and the conversation dwindled away for a moment, until I signaled the bartender and ordered a round of drinks for everyone. That cheered up the bunch and a corporal began to tell of how he'd been riding up the coast from Santa Barbara and had been pitched from his mount when the sorry brute shied at a wind-tossed bush, leaving him dismounted miles from anywhere at sundown.

"That was bad enough," he said, "for I walked along most of the night until I found an empty adobe hut about dawn. I didn't look around in the dark—just up and rolled over in a corner of the front room and went sound asleep. But when I woke up, I surely wished I'd still been on my feet, and still walking; I'll say so!"

He'd roused up to find himself surrounded by dead bodies, all stiff and stark. They seemed to be what was left of an emigrant family that'd taken up squatter's rights to the adobe and must have had some money or property when they arrived. The dead man, about fifty, had his skull split completely open; a woman, probably his wife, had her head cut nearly in two; while their two children had evidently been struck down by blows from the same ax.

"Horrible!" said Salazar. And I felt his black eyes on my middle, where my money belt bulged. "That is the damnable scourge of gold. It calls up the demons in man!"

"Downright unpleasant to say th' leastwise," said Yankee Carson, who proceeded to liven up the gathering with a song.

I can't recall all the foolishness, and only some of the choruses, but they went something like:

> *"Oh, what a miner, what a miner was I!*
> *All swolled up with the scurvy,*
> *So I thought I would die.*
> *I went to town, got on a drunk,*
> *And in the morning to my surprise*
> *I found I'd got me a pair*
> *Of roaring big black eyes.*
> *And I was strapped—had not one cent—*
> *Not even my pick and shovel,*
> *My hair was snarled, my britches torn,*
> *And I looked the very Devil.*
> *Then I took myself a little farm*
> *And got me a señorita;*
> *Gray-eyed, humpbacked and black as tar,*
> *Her name was Marguerita.*
> *My pigs all died, hens flew away,*
> *Joaquín he stoled my mules;*
> *My ranch burn 'down,' my blankets 'up,'*
> *Likewise my farming tools!"*

There was more but I can't fetch it back. Another song one of the miners tackled, began:

> *"Oh! Susanna,*
> *Go to hell for all of me;*
> *We're all a livin' dead*
> *In Californ-ee!"*

They were still hard at it when Salazar elbowed me up and piloted me down the hallway to our room, as I was somewhat befuddled from the rounds of drinks.

"You hear!" Salazar spouted like a boiling teakettle, tugging off his boots. "Now that infernal villain of a Joaquín has got himself stuck right in the middle of a barroom *balada!*" He flung his boot against the wall. "Next, by San Gabriel's tinpot trumpet, he'll be a hero in some Yankee penny dreadful!"

IX

In spite of my heavy head, we were up and on the road by the first light while the stars were just fading out in the golden-red tint of a new day. It was a good hour or more before the Fort Stockton troopers caught up with us. For a spell there wasn't much said on either side as the soldiers were as much under the weather as I was and Salazar was glooming to himself—probably about the song of Joaquín Murieta. But after we'd halted at a small cantina called El Ruiseñor (the Nightingale), where everyone, Salazar included, had a couple of passable shots of peach brandy, the tales and songs broke out again—and lasted the rest of the way down the coast to within a mile or so of San Diego.

One sawed-off trooper, nicknamed the Flea, kept after the corporal of the unit, named Bates, singing the same off-key ditty so many times we all threatened to yank him from his horse and let him foot it the rest of the way to town. But that didn't bother the Flea one bit as he warbled over and over:

> *"Oh, what was your name in the States?*
> *Was it Thompson, or Johnson or Bates?*
> *Did you murder your wife*
> *Then run for your life?*
> *Say, what was your name in the States?"*

Corporal Bates, trying to squelch the Flea and change the subject, admitted many of the gold hunters, or what he called the Argonauts, had actually switched handles for one reason or another, but went on to say most were just cutting ties with an old life, and no known event, outside of the late war, had ever brought so many different men to one place. There were fishermen from Nova Scotia, loggers from the forests of Maine, farmers from New York's Genesee Valley, doctors from the prairies of Iowa, Maryland lawyers and college men from Yale and Harvard.

"Yes," said the Flea. "They's pigtail chinks, South Sea cannibals, Florida crackers, and all them high-tone Southern gents with their herds of slaves!"

"And whole bloomin' companies of New Orleans gamblers along with droves of calico queens and their lowlife macks," added a red-faced trooper.

"And whole squadrons of bandits!" said Bates. "And just about every dashed one a blamed Mexican." He shot a quick look over at Salazar where he rode beside me, hand on pistol butt, searching each roadside thicket and grove with his keen black eyes.

"*Sí,* but you are right, Corporal. It is the great shame of our land that so many of my countrymen feel they have to take to the highways to obtain honor for their losses!" Salazar nodded his mushroom sombrero so hard it flopped like a flag in the breeze.

"They takes to th' road for a whole lot more than any of their plaguey honor, I'd say," grinned the Flea.

"With such a crew loose as Three-Fingered García and old Juan Pico, it's a wonder anyone gets to his proper destination with a whole windpipe," said Bates.

"Don't you forget that slippery Joaquín Murieta! They say he's th' boy with horses and can be in one end of California one night and in th' other th' next," put in the red-faced private. "That's one feller to match our old pal from th' New York Volunteers and th' Crossed Muskets Saloon, Diamond Dick Powers!"

We were just then skirting a sizable woods, and as we passed the southern end of the timber the Flea let out a yelp. "Look at that!"

We hauled up on our horses to stare at a grisly sight. Two dead men dangled from a limb of a huge old oak. They slowly turned in the sea breezes, doing a silent sort of fandango all by themselves. Both were Mexicans. One was togged out in a mighty fancy outfit, silver-trimmed pantaloons and a fine yellow shirt. The other was just a ragged sort of a peon in dingy white trousers and a faded red shirt. They were a pretty ill-matched pair but surely equal in one respect: both were good and dead.

We all turned to stare at Salazar where he sat motionless for a moment. Then he swung down from his mare and stumped over to the hanging tree, and spat out: "Vigilantes!" He yanked a piece of paper from the shirt of the more prosperous-looking corpse and after studying it came back and handed it to me.

HIGHWAYMEN TAKE NOTICE!

This will serve notice to such vagabond outlaws as "The Avenger," "The Blade" and "José California" that the citizenry of this land will no longer tolerate further criminal acts! All perpetrators of robbery,

rape and brutal violence will be dealt with in the most summary fash-
ion—as these two villains graphically depict!

Signed:
Men of the Night!!

"Knew things was gettin' bad, but I didn't think they was ready to call in old Judge Lynch down here." A gangling trooper spat on the off side of his horse with a wry face.

"Men of th' Night? And who might they be?" The Flea wondered.

"Men of the devil!" Salazar gritted. "Corporal, cut down those poor devils. We'll take them along to the alcalde. Villains, or not, they deserve a plot of their own ground."

Bates snapped out the order and the two corpses were soon stowed, facedown, over the cruppers of the troopers' horses.

We rode the rest of the way down to the San Diego River without much to say.

Arriving at the muddy river a little past noon, we were ferried across the water by the old Mexican flatboatman, four at a time. He looked long at the troopers' stiff cargo but said nothing.

Riding on into San Diego, we crossed Taylor and went on down Washington through a sleepy little hamlet of red-and-green-tiled adobes, parting from Bates and his men after they'd deposited the two corpses on the wide veranda of the Casa de Lopez on Twiggs Street, headquarters of the alcalde.

In scant moments the pepper-tree-shaded plaza began filling with quiet groups of citizens. I noticed one pair of pretty young señoritas in mantillas and flowing gowns of watered silk at the side of the gathering crowd, fans fluttering.

"And just what in the name of the old ring-tailed coon is this all about?"

I didn't need to ask who that was! The voice booming out of the casa in that Kentucky twang could only be my brother Josh's!

That mob of folks parted like the Red Sea before Moses as Joshua Quincy Bean strode forth in all his glory.

If I thought I'd cut a fair swath with my silver-studded sombrero and velveteen pantaloons, I was left far in the dust by that outfit of the alcalde of San Diego.

In gold-encrusted jacket, brilliant green sash around a pair of flame-red trousers, all gussied up with the embroidered outline of birds and flowers and wearing a gold ring in his right ear, Josh stood, one hand on his hip and the other twiddling with a narrow goatee, glaring first at the dead *bandidos* and then back at the crowd.

Then he saw me!

"Suffering hoop snakes, Roy!" He brushed the gawkers aside and grabbed me by the hand. "Welcome to California, you young coyote!" Then he marched me into the casa, leaving one of his flunkies, a big, scarfaced Mexican to get rid of the bodies and take Salazar up to the *calabozo* to look over the current catch of hard cases.

Once inside, Josh sat me down at a long, beautifully carved table and bawled out for wine. It wasn't long until a skinny little Indian with long hair and dressed in a snow-white coat and pantaloons trotted in with a dusty bottle and a pair of sparkling glasses, with all the style of a regular butler.

"Well, Roy." Josh leaned back in his big arm chair and grinned. "I never thought to see another Bean out here. Though I've got to say I had some word of your escapades at Chihuahua." He lit up a long, twisted cigarro from one of the candles on the table and shook a finger at me. "I've got to caution you, you young devil, that I keep a tight hand on affairs at San Diego, and if you upset the traces, well—!" He stopped grinning and blew out a cloud of blue smoke around my head.

I began to explain how we'd been forced to vamoose from Mexico, but he cut me off, shoving the gilded cigar box over to me.

"No matter, there won't be much of that sort of thing here. For one thing, our ladies are pretty well chaperoned." He reached out and poured us each a healthy belt of the golden wine, then laughed. "Oh, don't you look so sober-sided, Roy! You'll get to meet a pair of lively fillies at dinner tonight. Yes, I travel in the best society here; there's no hog meat and grits for us Beans! San Diego may not be too much in the way of towns, but, by Jasper, I run it—right along with my American Flag Saloon, and make 'em both pay!" And Josh grinned with tight jaws.

He went on to ask about brother Sam and my trip over to California, keeping the wine coming while the afternoon gradually became all golden and mellow like that wine.

I yarned away until the sunlight outside the half-closed shutters of the big, low-beamed room had moved its golden bars across the painted floor, then faded with the hours. The candles in their tall silver sticks grew brighter, burned down and were replaced by the little Indian. Off in the distance the bells of some mission were chiming and somewhere within the big casa an old clock creaked out the time of six o'clock. But for the rest, and where the afternoon had wandered off to, I wasn't one bit certain.

The only thing I was sure of was that Salazar had come back sometime during the afternoon to say goodbye. He'd decided the batch of small fry in the jailhouse weren't worth toting back to his bailiwick. He didn't happen to have warrants for either one of them—a pair of brothers who'd run off with a string of mules from the American River mines. "If I took them back, those ruffian miners might try to take the law into their own hands," he said as he shook hands with Josh and I. "By Santa Clara's night rail, there's already enough of this vigilante business—here and elsewhere." As he clapped on his oversized sombrero, he dropped his voice a peg. "Watch your gold, young Señor Roy! Gold will be the death of many a man along these coasts, and for years to come!"

When he was gone, Josh poured us each another glass and cocked his head, peering through the yellow wine at me. It gave me an odd feeling as I recollected poor Jeff Kirker pulling the same stunt with a whiskey bottle!

"Gold, Roy?" Josh drank off his glass and poured himself another.

"Just some money left from the store at Chihuahua."

He changed the subject and called the Indian back with another bottle.

An hour later, after I'd had a good tub bath in my room down the hall from the alcalde's reception room, and the little Klamath Indian, Abraham, who doubled as butler, cook and bookkeeper, had shaved me and dusted up my clothes, Josh came in. By then I was just about sober again.

"Come along, Roy, I'm late for dinner at the Bandinis'."

On the three-block stroll across the plaza, past Josh's American Flag Saloon, and down the side streets and lanes, my brother talked about his problems as judge, jury, constable, mayor and tax collector—all rolled into one official called alcalde.

Josh, who'd served as an officer in General Kearny's U.S. Infantry, while I was getting by as a teamster for Zack Taylor, had always been a great schemer and reader of books, the law included, though he'd never practiced at it. So when the new government needed a military man for alcalde of San Diego, he was already in town running his saloon. He up and asked for and got the appointment from the military governor of the territory, his old boss, General Stephen Watts Kearny.

But it hadn't been any sort of a picnic for Josh, and he made that clear. "Things have been going downhill with a swoop ever since this gold strike business," he admitted as he took my arm to guide me up to a large, wrought-iron gate set in a high wall at the end of a lane.

"Here's Casa Bandini. I surely thank my stars that I've got such old

California families on my side, even though I do sell rum for a living. Some of the Spanish tribes still resent the Yankees, and between them, the miner riffraff and the growing horde of bandit gangs, it makes us a rough row to hoe!"

We walked through the gate, held open by a bowing Mexican servingman, went down a flower-lined walkway and up the steps of the big timber-and-adobe mansion.

Señor Bandini, a well-set-up old California gentleman with white goatee wearing a beautifully embroidered black suit, greeted us at the open doorway. Señora Bandini, a plump little lady with a pretty face and dressed in a sweeping white gown, mantilla to match and large ruby earrings, stood smiling beside the señor.

After the introductions, the Bandinis led us down a long hallway, filled with suits of Spanish armor and decorated with one oil painting after another of proud-looking señoritas in their mantillas and lace, and downright mean-eyed señors in old-time outfits.

The hallway opened onto a tree-bowered patio, lit with dozens of Chinese paper lanterns of every color from green to scarlet—all hanging among the branches of the orange trees. Scores of lighted candles stood in silver candelabras along the linen-covered table, which was filled with dishes and set for a party of six.

I was about to mention the empty places to Josh when a couple of fine-looking girls came hurrying up through the small orchard toward the patio, chattering like a pair of schoolgirls. I recognized them as the same young ladies who'd been in the crowd when Salazar and I arrived with the troopers and the dead bandits.

After more introductions, Estrellita, the black-haired girl, sat by me, and Lucia, the blonde, sat by Josh, and we began the meal. After soup, one dish followed another, served by a staff of white-clad Indian servants —boiled mutton, beef, roast fowl, boiled pears, four kinds of beans, potatoes and corn as well as a good dozen side dishes. When we'd worked our way through all of that, along came the fruit—mammees, cherimoyas, and all sorts of oranges, peaches, plums and even sliced melon, served with one sort of wine after another. To top it all off we had dozens of little sugar cookies of every size and shape and washed down with some of the blackest and strongest coffee I ever tried to pour down my throat. I'd been to more than one fiesta at the homes of our so-called friends at Chihuahua, but I never had a feast like that. And along with the coffee and cakes came the fun-filled small talk with the young señoritas, while the older folks plodded along after.

The girls insisted on hearing of my crossing from Mexico and when I'd told parts of it they declared it rivaled anything they'd borrowed out of the alcalde's private library.

"Your tales are far better than Señor Gulliver's voyages," said dark-eyed Estrellita.

"And I thought, right away, of Don Quixote and his fat, little Sancho Panza when you all rode into the plaza today," said the blue-eyed Lucia. "Though you were a much handsomer Don Quixote than the fellow in Señor Joshua's book," she added in a hurry.

I hadn't mentioned the Comanches beyond the bare facts of our fight, but now, with Josh and the elder Bandinis deep in a discussion of civil affairs, and filled to the brim as I was with fine food and wine, I decided to make the tale of my wanderings even better by heaving in the story of my hair-raising trading session with Big Wolf.

The hour was getting late. A lopsided moon wandered in and out of the drifting mountains of clouds. The candles had gone out of most of the Chinese lanterns and a gusting wind, coming up from the nearby bay, swayed them along the branches of the orange trees like a strange crop of restless little paper moons. The tall candles on the table winked and fluttered their flames, casting shadows that stretched and shrank back into themselves again. It seemed the proper time for the telling of tales!

While the local gossip went on down at the end of the table right along with a lot of fan-waving by the señora, the lively Bandini sisters huddled across the table from me, excitedly poking at each other as I spun out my tale of wild Indians and Big Wolf's terrible medicine hand.

"And did you hold that thing in your very own hand?" Lucia asked, dark eyes glowing in the shifting candle light.

"It's just like a story by that wicked Señor Poe," said her sister. "You know the one where the poor hero finds a lady all sliced into little pieces!"

"Silly, you are thinking of Bluebird's wives." Lucia poked at Estrellita with her little red fan. "And then what happened, Señor Bean?"

"This!" And I took the daguerreotype from my pocket and held it out in the flickering candle flames. You'd have thought I suddenly shot off my old Walker Colt!

"*Dulcima!*" Both girls were on their feet. Estrellita, the nearest, darted to me around the table and had me by the arm. "Come, señor! Come and look at something in our parlor."

Before her parents or Josh could scarcely look up; with Estrellita tugging me along by the arm and Lucia poking me forward with her fan, I found myself in a big chamber off the patio.

It was a stylish room, furnished in some sort of crimson damask, with fine inlaid tables, mirrors and handsome furniture, with a dozen or more small paintings along the walls.

"Look!" and both girls pointed to an oil painting on the wall directly over an expensive pianoforte.

It was *the girl in the tintype!* She was older, perhaps nearly the same age of the Bandini sisters, who I'd guessed at between eighteen and twenty. The portrait was that of a young woman, dressed in a white low-necked gown, with a set of pearls around her graceful throat and with her golden-tinted hair done up prim and proper in the Spanish style. She needed nothing more than a comb and mantilla to look just like one of the señoritas of old Spain. Yet she was certainly American.

I was plain thunderstruck. Here was the girl of the daguerreotype. This was the daughter of the poor lady of the medicine hand. How near was she to me at that very minute?

"She is now away at a finishing school near San Francisco," said Estrellita, positively reading my mind. "And she is our dear friend, and when home, lives with her aunt, Señorita Rosita Almada of the Rancho las Fuentes, not ten miles to the west of us here!"

"And she will be home for the summer within the month," her sister chimed in.

"And you shall get to meet her and tell how you found her picture," said Lucia.

And all I could say was "Yes."

X

For the next few days, after I arrived, I looked over the little pueblo of San Diego and the country around. There were scarcely a dozen shops in the whole town, plus a pair of saloons, or cantinas, the American Eagle, owned by Josh, and the other, the absent Dick Powers's Crossed Muskets.

There were plenty of towns in California that must have offered better pickings for the new Yankee alcaldes, but there was no doubt in my mind that Joshua Quincy Bean would make out at San Diego—one way or another.

Looking over my brother's adobe palace at the Casa de Lopez, his string of fine horses, his servants, his fancy clothes and fancier vittles, not to mention his tip-top wine cellar, I had to admit that San Diego might be a small puddle but Josh was surely the big frog!

There seemed no need for another store in town, and as I didn't feel like starting out to be another merchant prince, I presently sounded out Josh about joining his staff or working in his saloon.

"I've been studying that," he answered, pushing up his specs and putting down a big account book he'd been thumbing through at the dinner table. "I know you've got plenty of sand, Roy, and you've been through the mill, seen the elephant and all that, since you were a young 'un the same as the rest of us Beans. I know you've got the nerve to stand up to bad men and Indians, and while we're a bit light on Comanches, we've got a mighty good supply of the former. With the gold strikes, after the war this whole country just exploded. It was nice and easy, all around, but now hell is plumb out for noon!"

"Well, I'm ready to pull my weight," I said. "I'd just as soon earn my keep by helping out your law force, for it seems you could need help."

"Right as rain, but as county treasurer, along with everything else, I need more help in our tax collections. Sánchez, my constable, has been trying to get around to all the ranchos and farms, but he's the best man I've got at the cantina, and he can't be in two places at once, so there's a couple dozen places he hasn't been able to collect as yet."

"That the only reason?"

"I'll admit there are a couple of reasons. Sánchez had some run-ins with some of the rancho owners, and also the little farmers. They just don't cotton to a fellow Californian prying pesos out of their hides. So they resent him, and his methods. Peons and ranchers both have come to grouse at his actions. *Tacaneria—infamia,* they call it—and they may be right, but taxes are taxes."

"What's the other reason, beside Sánchez's meanness?"

"That damnable will-o'-the-wisp rascal of a Murieta!" Josh clapped the ledger down with a crash, tipping over a glass or two. "He's been seen around here several times in the past few months, and though he's yet to pull off any big robbery, I'm sure that some of his gang—and he's got dozens of the blackguards on call—have been mixed up in holdups on the highway and at some of the ranchos owned by Americans. Sánchez has a damned healthy fear of falling into Murieta's hands, and says he's been trailed, and even shot at. So if you're game, you can take over the tax job until it's cleaned up."

"Seems those night riders could handle him the way they stretched the necks of that pair we brought in."

"They've got to catch him first," said Josh with an odd look, then he turned to his strongbox and hauled out the tax book.

I noticed right off those taxes seemed steep and mentioned it.

"I don't set the figures. They come down from the territorial governor's office at San Francisco," Josh answered sort of snappishly. "But I'm not looking for your advice. All you've got to do is collect the rest of those accounts before the first of the month. That'll give you nigh onto two weeks."

"I see Señorita Almada at Rancho las Fuentes is down for a hundred pesos."

"That's the largest amount, all right. She'll pay, but you'll have to catch her home. Lopez never could find her. And there's more just like her."

"When do you want me to start, and how do I get the lay of the land?"

"I'll send Abraham along with you tomorrow. He knows every square mile of this country. His tribe was here before the Spanish arrived." Josh scowled at the ceiling. "And you'd better have an escort from Fort Stockton. I'll take care of that."

I thanked him for his time and went out to keep a riding date with the Bandini girls. We'd been ranging the countryside around San Diego nearly every day since we'd met at their place. And contrary to the way most Spanish ran their families, with *dueñas* and chaperones, the two Bandini sisters did just about as they blamed well pleased. They were as independent a pair of señoritas as I'd ever run up against. In fact, both had sewn the first American flag that flew in the plaza all of three years past, when it wasn't too popular to take any sort of interest in an American flag.

Several young officers from the fort came regularly to call at the Casa Bandini but the frisky señoritas weren't about to give up their freedom, and so they made jolly companions for me on rides that took us down around the bay and as far off as the old mission of San Diego de Alcalá in Mission Valley.

But now I had to tell Lucia and Estrellita that I was going to be busy for a few weeks, collecting taxes for the alcalde.

We'd reined in at Point Loma to watch the big gray whales drifting along the sparkling ocean like huge floating boulders, while the waves kept rolling slowly in toward the beach, all vasty green and bursting with a roar that surprised me every time as they flung clouds of white foam at us, only to hiss and grumble back into the next incoming line of waves.

"Señor Roy!" Lucia wrinkled her pretty nose. "That naughty Señor Joshua should not have you do such things! That ugly Lopez has so upset folks with his highhanded ways that I'm sure you'll have some trouble."

"*Sí*, it really isn't fair to ask you to do such things," her sister chimed in. "Most of the people at the ranchos and the little farms just don't have that sort of money this time of year."

"Well, I'll have to use my head," I told them as we turned our mounts to ride back toward town. "And if they can't pay, then I'll just guess they'll have to owe for it."

"They won't owe one damn thing!" the alcalde shouted when Abraham and I swung up into our saddles in front of the Casa de Lopez next morning. "Not one gol-damned peso do any of them get out of paying! They've got plenty of money hidden away and you collect! The governor of California wants you to collect, and the whole blamed Congress of the United States wants the same thing! *Comprende?*"

"I understand, but I don't think I'm going to like this job after all," I said. And I was right in spades!

Away I rode toward the fort to meet my troopers, mad clean down to my boot soles. Here this stuffed peacock of a brother of mine expected me to hustle up his infernal tax money however I could get it—and yet he'd already told me that the big, burly Sánchez with his ugly face and two pistols had fallen flat on the same job.

I was so disgusted with Joshua Quincy Bean that I had half a mind to head back toward San Francisco and forget the whole affair. But two things wouldn't let me. I had to see that girl of the tintype, Dulcima, and I also had a strange hunch that her guardian, the hard-to-find Señorita Rosita Almada, could just be the Red Rosita of Jeff Kirker's story, though the Lord knew the woods were full of Rositas! So I had to stick it out for the time being and see for myself.

When we halted in front of the adobe-and-log walls of Fort Stockton, who should be sitting their horses waiting for us but Corporal Bates and the Flea!

"Bates and me have been down to the American Flag five nights runnin', but divil a sight of you," yelped the Flea.

"So we figgered it was time to hold us a reunion," Bates finished.

"Though we're all set to cut and run for it if those hot-blooded Mexicans rise up and go for you with them machetes!" added the Flea.

"The first on our list is Señor Xavier Hechavarría of the Ranch of the Little Wood, Rancho Montecito," said Abraham in his perfect English, brown finger marking the page in our long calfskin-bound book.

The Rancho Montecito sat, all by its lonesome, on a wooded hill about two miles west of town in the foothills and seemed pretty much abandoned. Several adobe sheds and barns looked empty and the only ranch hands to be seen were a couple of old men lying on their backs in the shade of a big cottonwood, smoking cornhusk cigarettes. These ignored our little party as if we were twenty miles away.

While Abraham and the troopers sat on their horses and waited by the corral, I dismounted and went around to the front of the old ranch building with my tax book. After I'd pounded on the door for a while and only managed to rouse up some cur dogs that set up a tremendous racket inside, I heard the tapping of a stick. There were two or three good whacks, some yelps and then a little peace. The door creaked open and a bent old man who reminded me of a tired hawk asked me to enter.

I saw that he was stone-blind and down on his luck, for his gilt-edged jacket and even his pantaloons, were patched, particularly at the knees. The old fellow introduced himself in the finest of Castilian Spanish as Colonel Don Xavier Hechavarría, and politely asked how he could best serve me.

When I told him who I was and why I was there, he nodded sadly and then answered in English. "Señor, it has become the jest of the whole world that we Spanish always say *mañana*, yet that is what I must answer. As you have seen I have only two old ancients out there, no doubt sleeping, when they should be working in the gardens, if nothing more, for we have neither cow nor pig left on the place. But they are old soldiers like myself, who have fought long and hard for Mexico; and now . . ." He paused and I saw a tear slip from his blind eyes to zigzag down a wrinkled face and into a white goatee.

"There is merely the little matter of just fifty pesos, for your half-year taxes, Don Xavier. That, and I'll be on my way," I said, looking around the empty room with its rickety table and several battered chairs. The only decoration upon the cracked walls was that of a painting of a handsome young officer in the uniform of the Mexican Army. I made him out to be a lieutenant of the Tululancingo Cuirassiers, one devil of a fighting outfit. I mentioned the portrait to make conversation.

"My only son, killed on the field of honor at Buena Vista. Our family is *funesto*. There is no one to help me run the rancho. We have nothing." The old man sank into one of the flimsy chairs with his cane and leaned his head upon his clasped fists. "We have nothing for the tax. This I have told to that abominable blusterer of a *renegado* Sánchez when he was here last."

I pulled up my shirt and fished out one hundred dollars in gold from the money belt and put it on the table, while the pack of lop-eared curs sat around laughing at me with lolling tongues. "The tax will be taken care of, Don Xavier—by a friend. And if you're asked about it, say it was taken care of—and that is all!" I fixed the money belt, tucked my shirttail back in and went out the door.

When we rode off, I handed the tax book back to Abraham. "Mark down fifty pesos, collected."

Even the Flea was quiet for a while as we traveled on toward our next stop. But he finally broke loose. "Even the Good Book doesn't have many kind words for tax collectors, but I got to hand it to you, Bean! I didn't hear not one cussword—nor any racket but some dogs getting lambasted. You're surely smooth, if not particularly human." But he grinned when he said it—and it was a good thing he did, for I was ready to tangle with anyone!

By the time we got around back to town at sunset, I'd called on a total of six places, three ranchos and three small farms, and hadn't got my hands on one damned peso, though I'd credited them with $175 "paid." And I'd left $120 in ten-dollar eagles with the owners, on the sly, threatening them with bodily harm if they ever spilt to anyone where that money had come from. It was bandit gold I left behind me, but I knew where to get a whole lot more—or would when I got to talk to Rosita—if she were the right Red Rosita. Then there was the coin of Kirker's, with its odd markings—a map of some sort, I was bound. That would take some ciphering, but I figured I could do that, also. This Rosita, if she happened to be the right one, and my marked eagle could be twin keys to that gold.

About the only thing Josh had to say when we sat down to supper, served up by a poker-faced Abraham, was he found it sort of odd such folks could pay up in U.S. gold pieces. He went on to say it might be bandit gold (though he'd no idea it came from me), and he'd get around to that item in due time. But what really mattered was the fact that I was getting his taxes in—and it proved I was a *real Bean* for getting a job done!

"It's not the easiest job in the world," I told him, not looking at Abraham.

" 'No man was glorious who was not pretty laborious,' " said Josh, swiping another saying from old Ben Franklin.

Myself, I didn't say anything.

XI

The very next morning we started out again, but without our troopers, for both Bates and the Flea had been assigned to scouting duty by the post commandant, and I didn't feel the need of anyone else riding nursemaid.

So we traveled on a southwest tack toward Spring Valley, with its hundreds of red-limbed manzanitas. Though summer was getting along, Indian paintbrush, California poppies and acres of whitethorn still flamed across the foothills, and along the meandering creek beds the cottonwood, sycamore and willow all turned and danced their leaves in the breezes wandering over the land.

California was truly a fine country, and I would have felt mighty fine myself except for my tinhorn job. I cursed to myself when we rode down to a small farm with its scraggly grove of walnut trees and parched cornfields, telling myself that I'd get those taxes come hell or high water—and damned if I was going to part with any more of Kirker's ill-gained gold. I was already down to little more than $370 in ten-dollar eagles!

When we rode away from the farm of one-legged Silvestre Sandoval north of Spring Valley, I considered myself lucky to get off with only the loss of sixty dollars—forty to help feed his four motherless brats and twenty dollars to credit to his taxes.

With well over a dozen calls to yet make and the stolen gold dwindling like a chunk of ice on a red-hot stove, I decided to try to get to see the Señorita Almada at Rancho las Fuentes on the other side of the El Cajón Valley, though it was a ride of nigh thirty miles.

The route took Abraham and me up out of the grasslands and onto a stretch of desert with its monotonous brown stretches broken every so often by greasewood, mesquite, yucca and here and there a towering saguaro. But presently we were threading among the brush-covered Laguna Mountains that brought us out into a small valley. Abraham, never much of a talker, volunteered that this place was El Valle de las Viejas (the Valley of the Old Women), named by the old-time Spaniards when the tribesmen living there ran for the hills and left their women and children flat.

Another hour found us on a good wagon road that led straight as a die over rolling hills while the purple smears of the Lagunas swept up along our left. We began to pass small farms, with flocks of sheep grazing on grassy slopes as well as quite a few wild hogs. Abraham pointed out a small valley on our right as La Cañada de los Coches (Gulch of the Hogs). Another mile or so and we rode past the humpbacked bulk of Mount Selix and turned north at Allison's Springs.

"There, señor!" Abraham pulled in his horse and pointed ahead at a broad mesa dotted with groves of oak and chinquapin. And beyond, flanked by a pair of great pine woods, stood Rancho las Fuentes.

A long yellow wall, covered with roses, ran across the front of the rancho, as thick and sturdy as a fortification. To the south of the ranch buildings, reaching nearly to the woods, orange groves, almond orchards and scattered figs were in early fruit. At the north another orchard of pear, peach, apricot, apple and a stretch of vineyard ran to the thick pine forest.

The ranch house itself stood squarely behind those walls and up to its arched gate we rode, dismounted and pulled at a bell rope. A silvery chime sounded from somewhere inside the shady courtyard. Almost at once a wizened little man in a striped serape and white duck suiting shuffled crablike toward the gate, swung it aside and bowed me in, while Abraham stayed out with the horses, watering them at a long stone trough behind the hitch rail.

I followed the old servant through a shrub-filled garden and around a large, carved fountain that shot up lacy fans of spray. Off to both sides of the painted flagstone walk smaller carved fountains filled the afternoon with soft musical sounds. Rancho las Fuentes was mighty well named.

A sunny sort of peace seemed to hover around the gardens and house, yet as I tagged the old serving man up the rancho's broad steps I got a look at a huge, gray mountain of cloud looming up past the pine woods, and a distant rumble of thunder threaded through the whisper of the fountains.

Coming up onto the shady half light of the broad veranda, I wasn't sure of who or what might be waiting for me; then a low, pleasantly husky voice sent a sudden shock through me. "Señor?"

I squinted through the gloom and then saw a young woman seated in a hammock in the midst of the golden shadows.

"Señorita—Almada?"

"*Sí, Señor Bean.*" That low, rich voice sent another tingle through me, and I knew as sure as I was standing there that here was Red Rosita! I'd have bet every dollar of that hoard of eagles!

"You know me, Señorita Almada?" Now I could see the whole

curvesome outline of the lady. A low-cut green gown revealed about as much as it hid from view, while a pair of rounded ankles peeped out of her flaring dress to end in a pair of stiletto-heeled scarlet slippers.

It was a sight that kept me clamp-jawed.

"You may have been told, Señor Bean, that it is rather impolite to stare at a person on such short acquaintance." She flared a sudden crimson fan, waving it in a sweep to indicate a pair of comfortable chairs near her hammock. "To answer your question, yes, I do know who you are, and why you appear here in the midst of a long afternoon and without a proper invitation."

I plunked down into the leather chair and looked at her, without seeming to stare. For a minute I forgot plumb about taxes. I forgot that wistful-faced little girl of the daguerreotype—forgot everything except that here reclined the most wickedly lovely female I'd ever laid my eyes on. She was what the writer of *Belle Martin the Heiress*, a book I'd been reading nights from Josh's library, would have called "a woman fit to inspire a man to desperate deeds and yet lure him to the very brink of disaster by her charms!"

Rosita Almada was all of those and a lot more: fiery, flaming red hair, flashing emerald-green eyes, perfect nose and when she smiled at me . . .

"Señorita," I rasped when I got back some of my power of speech, "I guess you do know why I'm here and—"

"And—I'm ready for you!" She suddenly reached under a pillow beside her, and I stiffened, waiting for the crack of a pistol or the flash of light on a dirk.

"Close your mouth, Señor Bean! You look so much more handsome with it closed." Her voice rippled with a sort of laughter, and I thought those fountains out there had the same musical sound.

Taking a second look, I saw she held out a small leather bag to me in her smoothly tapered hand.

"The taxes. One hundred pesos, I believe." Her voice quivered with that same sort of hidden laughter. "I know you must have heard that I am quite unapproachable. I'm sure the worthy alcalde, your brother, has informed you that I stand firm against all of the Yank's tax bullies. And I might have done so today but for one thing." She paused, watching me fumble with the moneybag, then stuff it into my britches pocket.

I guessed she was waiting for me to say something. "One thing, señorita?"

"*Sí*, I have a most hard heart, señor—a flinty heart, I might say, but I have heard certain tales that may have softened it, somewhat."

"Tales?" But I knew what she was driving at, all right.

"Yes. You have given away considerably more than you have collected. Old Colonel Hechavarría couldn't rest until he'd got the news to me—news that there was at least one Yankee in sympathy with our poor disinherited people."

I didn't know how to answer beyond saying I hoped such word wouldn't get around to any of the others on my tax list, as I still hoped to pry some actual cash out of them.

"I won't trouble my mind about them, señor, you'll take things as they come. I can see you are that sort of a man." She swung herself up from the hammock and stood looking at me, a sweetly languid woman who could have been anywhere from twenty to thirty or more; I didn't care a tinker's damn which!

I hurriedly got up and stood turning my silver-mounted sombrero around in my hands, and wondering if now could be the right time to fetch out Kirker's marked eagle, or if it was the proper time to mention that tintype of her young ward. Then I got the feeling that Rosita knew about Kirker's gold eagles! But why hadn't she said anything about my scattering them around the countryside to her stove-in fellow Mexicans?

Just about then a muffled bell rang out at somewhere in depths of the great ranch house. Rosita gave a slight start and her knuckles whitened on the hand holding the red fan. I saw, then, that she must have been waiting for that sound—for who made that sound! And right on top of that came the rumble of thunder—closer than when I'd arrived at Rancho las Fuentes.

A storm was on the way, and we had ourselves a long ride back to San Diego. I only hoped that Abraham knew of some quicker route.

"You must come again under happier circumstances, señor." Rosita held out her hand and I saluted those perfumed little fingertips in the best manner of a real don. "My ward, the little Dulcima, will be home from San Francisco within a week, and you must return for our celebration. I understand you are friends of the Bandini girls, and that will make for a jolly time. Say you will come!"

I answered that I'd be most happy to attend, then bowed myself out and hustled down the veranda steps, while the señorita vanished into the house. The thunder seemed closer and the trees in garden and orchard were swaying and dipping their boughs to the sudden wind gusts.

The same old majordomo appeared from around the breeze-tossed spray of the center fountain and let me out of the great metal gate.

"Señor! It will storm in a minute!" Abraham was ready with the horses, and we swung aboard. "Should we wait or ride for home?"

I took a hurried look at the low, wolfish clouds and then back at the rancho. I didn't trust myself to be cooped up inside that place with such a woman. The good Lord only knew what I might do.

"Let's ride!"

"Bueno! I know of a different road that can take us back to town by a shortcut."

We put the steel to the horses and flew down the dusty road away from the rancho, turning off into a thick pine woods to the southeast.

On we galloped while the rumbling crack of thunder behind us swelled up like a battle. A battlefield in the sky. Mexico City all over again, I thought as we swung out of the woods and onto a mesa, heading for the crossroads Abraham was after.

At that moment, three horsemen came spurring hell-for-leather from behind a clump of oak to the south. A musket boomed out, then another! Bullets chirped overhead, like the song of some deadly little birds.

"Bandidos!" Abraham poked a finger at the trio of riders heading their horses toward us.

"Get going," I yelled, lashing my own horse for all I was worth, Abraham following suit, and we dashed on toward the crossroads. Another gun banged and then Abraham shouted, "Señor, behold!"

A rider mounted on a great gray stallion had loped out of the pine woods behind and was pounding across the mesa to cut between the pursuers and ourselves, flinging up his arm in some sort of a signal.

Glancing over my shoulder, and losing my sombrero, I was flabbergasted to see the robbers pull up and wait for the man on the big gray. Then the first raindrops struck the road with the force of bullets, and the storm broke!

"Keep going!" I shouted above the crashing storm roar, while Abraham mouthed something at me that I couldn't catch.

We finally halted in another woods, ten miles away from the attempted robbery, and huddled under some trees, but the full force of the storm had already gone brawling on out to the coast and the wide Pacific.

"Now, what were you shouting about?" I asked my companion as I sat in a wet saddle, mourning for my lost silver-mounted sombrero and still wondering about Rosita, and that damned handy stranger.

"I said, señor, *that was Murieta!* Joaquín Murieta upon his steel-dust stallion who halted those villains at the crossroads!"

"Murieta?" I stared at him and over my shoulder. "Keep riding!"

XII

"Murieta? You certain?" Josh waved a copy of the *Alta California*, just down from San Francisco on the stage. "Look here. It says Joaquín Murieta and his blackguards have been raiding mining camps up along the Sacramento not three days before this paper came out, and it's just two days old!"

"Could have been mistaken, I guess, but I know some *bandidos* tried mighty hard to puncture our hides at the Las Fuentes pine woods." I was crawfishing somewhat for I didn't feel like tipping our Indian's hand. He'd been mighty positive that the rider on the big gray was Joaquín Murieta! I didn't want Josh sweating him over the fact that he knew Murieta on sight. I suspected Abraham was wise that I had handled all of the tax collections on my own hook, and he'd not peached on me.

Josh, busy totting up the tax figures, ignored my last comment. "So our high-and-mighty señorita of the Fountain Rancho paid in good old Mexican pesos. She's one lady too keen to handle any *bandido* gold!" His lip curled in a way to raise my dander. Somehow I didn't care for the way he was talking about Rosita Almada. But before I said anything, I thought to myself that it was no business of mine what he or anyone had to say about such a woman. And such a woman!

"You might as well wipe that silly grin off your face, Roy! It's plain to see that stuck-up Mexican has her claws out for you. She's been playing the high-toned señorita since she came back here around a year past to take up her father's rancho. The old man, he was a Mexican officer who died just about that time. Heard there was a son somewhere, said to have been killed in the war. So without anyone at home the place had been going to rack and ruin until she showed up. That Rancho las Fuentes used to take in hundreds of acres from an old Spanish land grant, just about half of the whole valley."

"Place still looks pretty good," I said.

"Don't know where she got enough money to bring that rancho back out of it," said Josh, squirting a stream of blue smoke at one of the candles on our table and fingering his goatee. "There's something sort of odd about that young señorita."

"Meaning what?" I was curious myself just what the folks around San Diego had to say about Rosita.

"Oh, I don't know. Never had the time or inclination to pry into her affairs nor listen to much gossip. All I know is that she showed up on the stage one day with a young girl who she said was her father's ward. But that girl is pure *anglo*. You've seen her picture over at the Bandinis'. They and the Almadas always seemed to be pretty tight. These Spanish stick together, as you know, I guess."

"I've noticed," I said, glancing at Abraham from the corner of an eye. But he was as blank as an adobe wall while he poured us more wine.

"Well, let's see," Josh thumbed through the tax book, "looks like you've got less than a half dozen stops to make and you'll have her all shipshape. But I think you better have some protection again."

"I'm all for that!" I took the book back and hoped I had enough of Kirker's eagles left to finish the job.

I wound up my collections in the next two days, with the Flea along for company, as well as Abraham to guide me to the remaining farms and ranchos. It went off without a hitch, though I was left with only a little more than one hundred dollars in my shrinking money belt. Word must have gotten around like wildfire that a brass-bound sucker was making the rounds, though not a whisper had reached the alcalde—so far.

There'd not been the slightest trouble while we rode on our way, though the hair on my neck bristled up more than once when we got near to a woods or some other possible ambush site. I'd said nothing to the Flea of our recent run-in with bandits, as he seemed to be sort of trigger-happy, and I didn't want him whaling away at some wind-tossed branch or cloud-swept shadow.

But in the late afternoon of the second day, when we'd just one more stop to make, I caught several glimpses of a distant horseman who seemed to be dogging our trail. Finally even the Flea spotted that far-off speck drifting across the skyline near Spring Valley.

"Wouldn't be Murieta?" I asked Abraham as we jogged down a slope and through a scattering of chaparral. I hadn't said a word to the little Indian about the rider on the great gray since our mad dash through the storm, for I had a hunch that Abraham would explain in his own good time. But now it had just slipped out.

"I'm not sure," Abraham said, watching the tiny mote as it vanished behind a ridge of blue-tinted hills. "It might be—"

"You acquainted with that there gent?" The Flea, nearly swallowing his cud of golden twist, had spurred his bay mare beside us, his six-gun out and in his fist.

"Put up that weapon, unless you can pick off that fellow from half a mile away," I told the Flea. "And he's out of sight now anyway."

"Murieta?"

"Whosomever," I said, while Abraham said nothing at all.

Then I made my last collection (contribution) to the alcalde's tax fund and we three rode back into San Diego while the wild lilac covering the hills turned from smoky blue to crimson in the flaming Pacific sunset.

With my job of collecting done, I spent most of the next week pretty profitably, hanging around my brother's cantina and the other saloon, bucking the tiger and playing close-to-the-vest poker.

Sánchez, Josh's scar-faced constable, worked part time at the American Flag as bouncer and sometimes dealer. One day found us in a game of stud with some of the locals. After a hand or two, he braced me. "And how do you like our California by now, Señor Roy?"

I'd never taken much to the big devil. "Pretty well, but I don't take very kindly to having your friends doing their damnedest to drygulch me —especially the one on the big steel-dust stallion!"

He began to cloud up like a thunderstorm but then his jaw dropped, and even the scar on his chin turned a sort of yellow white.

"You saw *that one?"* It was as if I'd said that I'd bumped into the Old Nick himself outside the door!

"So I guess." I hadn't told anyone but Josh about the affair and I knew that Abraham had stayed mum. So it seemed to come to Sánchez as a real jolt.

"Ah, that *diablo!"* Sánchez got himself up and called one of the regular dealers over while he stalked to the bar and began to work on his private bottle.

As Josh had said, Emilio Sánchez had one big respect for Murieta!

The game went on until suppertime, with a few polite questions from the players concerning my run-in with Murieta, which I turned off as pretty much of a joke.

But Sánchez never bent his ear toward us and never left his spot at the bar until his bottle was bone-dry.

When I got out of the game, fifty pesos to the good, Sánchez lurched past me toward the door, muttering something about *hombres* and *noche*. *Men of the night?* Then I recalled that placard on the hanged man!

"I don't know just what was about," said Josh when I quizzed him at our evening meal. "Looks to me like Sánchez had himself too much liquor. Said he was working away at a bottle all afternoon, didn't you?"

"Yes, but I was thinking that it had something to do with those poor devils we fetched in when I first came to town—the ones you had Sánchez plant over in Boot Hill."

"Well"—Josh helped himself to another plate of grub—"you may be right. That message on them was signed Men of the Night, wasn't it?" He looked sideways at me, and then nodded at Abraham for another round of wine, while he began to talk about some actress named Lottie Crabtree.

Somehow I had a feeling that my brother would just as soon not talk about night riders and stretched necks at the supper table, so I dropped it —for the time being.

When I rode over to the Casa Bandini on Calhoun Street for our regular Tuesday-morning jaunt, I found both Bandini sisters already up and waiting for me on their mounts.

"Señor Roy, my and don't you look the *brillante* one in your *bonito* new white sombrero," said Estrellita, laughing as her sister shied a riding crop at her to be still.

"Señor Roy, pardon that little minx; she knows you still mourn for that *esplendido* sombrero you lost when that *estupido* horse bolted with you in that storm!" Lucia spurred her black mare over to me and put a hand on mine. "You must never mind that tease! I think your new topper is most becoming." She glanced at her sister and her eyes sparkled with mischief. "Besides I have something to make you forget any number of old sombreros."

Estrellita gave a cry and shook her finger at Lucia. "You very bad thing, you! You know we agreed to both tell Señor Roy when we rode together— and—"

"Never you mind, you tease!" Lucia bent toward me, whispering, "Our dear Dulcima arrives on the coach from the north this very Tuesday afternoon, before the supper hour."

"*Sí,* and we are asked to come over to Rancho las Fuentes this Saturday eve for a grand *baile,*" her sister rattled on, trying to get in her share of the news. "Her aunt has sent an invitation to us and others in town and about the country."

"She tells us in her note, Señor Roy, that you have had a personal invitation from her when you were at the rancho last week—which you never told us, you sly rogue," Lucia chattered away, breaking in on her lively sister. "Señorita Almada also sends another word to you—that she expects to see you again—"

"At the *baile*," Estrellita began.

"Or before, if Señor Roy comes with us to the stage station, for the señorita expects to come over in her conveyance to pick up Dulcima."

"You know we plan to ask them to stay at our Casa overnight. It will be late for them to travel back to the rancho, even if there is nearly a full moon tonight!" Estrellita got in her final shot before putting the spur to her white horse. "And Señor Roy might be asked to come for supper!"

We left town in a flurry of dust and laughter, loping down to Point Loma and a picnic lunch.

That afternoon I was standing in the small crowd at the little brown adobe station under the cottonwoods on Crabillo, along with Señor and Señorita Bandini and their girls.

"It is getting on for five o'clock"—Lucia, who hadn't changed her riding habit, was bouncing on the toes of her little, red riding boots—"and Señorita Almada isn't here yet—and the stage should be arriving anytime now."

Estrellita, fine and furbelowed in a wide white silk dress, kept her yellow fan flickering like some sort of butterfly. Suddenly she snapped it shut and waved it over the heads of the crowd, knocking several sombreros galley west. "Wrong, dear sister; here she is now!"

A red-topped surrey, driven by the old Mexican from the rancho, drew up alongside the hitching rail, and there sat Rosita Almada in the back, a small, dark sombrero in her hand, and with her flame-colored hair blowing about her shoulders.

She saw the Bandinis and waved to them, but before she could alight, the two-mule mail hack from Los Angeles came pounding around the corner, with a pinto stallion loping along behind. It wheeled up to the station in a cloud of dust and a volley of shouts from the bearded driver.

The first person in the hack that I spotted was Salazar, his big sombrero flapping as he peered from the rig's side curtains.

All was uproar as the driver leaped down waving his arms, and we learned that there'd been an attempt to stop the stage—and not five miles outside of town.

"Young Bean, well met!" Salazar shouted at me over the hubbub. "Watch this scoundrel while I get my horse secured!" He tossed his Walker Colt underhand to me.

I managed to catch the heavy weapon and keep it pointed at a ugly-looking Mexican with one eye, who stood glaring at the crowd as if he'd like to eat them all.

"That there hombre is one of th' jaspers which tried jumpin' us at Washerwoman's Gulch!" And the hack driver shook a big red fist under that hard-case's flat nose. "If'n it hadn't a been for Sheriff Salazar and Dick Powers there, bein' on board, we'd a been gone goslin's fur damn sure!" He pointed to a dapper-looking stranger in a dark frock coat and a gray topper who was getting out the far side of the hack. The dude was helping a prim young lady step down beside himself and fussing with her baggage.

I was so busy staring at her I was suddenly jolted back to the three-ring circus when Salazar grabbed his weapon out of my hand and jammed it into the robber's midsection.

"Hey there, *borrego!* So you thought you'd take yourself a stroll, did you, Juan Pico? Well and good if you took a stroll while this gentleman stared at the ladies, eh?"

I could feel my ears getting bright red as the young woman coming around the hack with the dude looked me full in the face. It was the girl of the tintype, blue eyes clear as the summer sky and that same fine-featured face, suddenly alight with a soft rosy tint. Then she dropped her gaze and was surrounded by the lively Bandini sisters and their parents.

"Guess I forgot what I was doing for a minute," I told the sheriff.

"*Sí,* young Roy!" Salazar grinned. "I know what you are thinking. And I know, also, who that young señorita is! I must say we had a fine talk on the way down. By San Luis's double halo, it ain't every day that two survivors of those devils of Comanches can ride along in one coach, let me tell you!"

"Señor Bean! Señor Roy Bean, come here, if you would, please." There was Estrellita and Lucia, arms around the girl they called Dulcima, and both waving me over to Rosita's surrey.

"Go along, young Bean." Salazar nudged me with an elbow. "I'll see you later on. I got to get this one to your brother's *calabozo!*" Away he went, shoving the hulking road agent along, followed by half of the crowd, while the rest stood stock-still, listening to the hack driver jaw away just how the sheriff and Powers had stood off a trio of *bandidos* and dropped one of them by puncturing the robber's horse dead center.

I skirted the bustling knot of gawkers and found myself the target of those unforgettable blue eyes. The Bandini girls had been telling the girl of my daguerreotype.

"Most interesting, I'm sure. But Señor Bean will have an opportunity to talk of such things when he comes to our *baile* on Saturday," came the vibrant voice of Rosita from her surrey. "But now we must start out for the rancho—if we are to get there before midnight."

She reached out and helped the new arrival into a seat beside her, while the old Mexican finished stowing the baggage onto the front seat of the rig.

There came a flurry of protests from the Bandinis but to no avail. "Señorita Almada," Señora Bandini sputtered, "how can you even consider riding back to Las Fuentes now—and with such ruffians roving our countryside?"

Rosita rummaged down into a straw handbag and pulled out a Colt Baby Dragoon pistol, while the old Mexican on the front seat flourished a pair of man-sized six-shooters.

Then I saw that slow, tantalizing smile, I remembered, quiver at the corners of Rosita's red mouth, while her brilliant green gaze swept over me; then she murmured an order to the driver, wheels creaked, and the carriage rolled away through the yellow afternoon sunlight.

The man called Dick Powers stood with gray topper in hand, staring with a furrowed brow after the dwindling rig. Suddenly he gave a short, odd laugh. "Heaven help the highwayman who tries to meddle with *that lady!*"

XIII

The night of the *baile* at Fountain Rancho was just about as fine as I can remember in all my time in California. A moon, at the full, gleamed down from a cloudless sky jam-packed with millions of glittering stars, as I rode up to the gate of the big old house where it sat flooded in the silvery light and flanked by shadowy orchards and lowering black pine woods.

I'd ridden over from town in the late afternoon, taken myself a room at the Casa de Oro (House of Gold) tavern just two miles from the rancho on the crossroads and was ready for a lively evening. I'll admit that I had a couple of second thoughts about those rascals who'd given me that merry chase a week back, and I wasn't about to ride all the way back to San Diego in the small hours of the night—even if the feisty Señorita Almada had no qualms about jaunting through the dark.

From the look of the wagons, buggies and saddle horses strung out along the hitching rails, I was far from being the first arrival. Over the whispering of the breeze-tossed fountains behind the walls came the twang and tinkle of guitars and the murmur and laughter of voices.

Dismounting, I tied up my horse and tugged at the bell pull once, twice and then a good dozen times before I roused out the old manservant. From the whiff I got when he swung open the gate to bow me in, I figured he'd been celebrating with the *botella* pretty lively himself.

Just before the gate clanged shut another rider, decked out in a dark riding outfit, serape and sombrero, came loping up. The stranger piled from his horse, flung the reins to the Mexican, then swaggered into the patio beside me.

"Say there, isn't this our good alcalde's relative?" The man was none other than the dude gambler Powers—my brother's rival in the local saloon business.

I allowed as much and was about to make some talk about the fine night when we were surrounded by a noisy crowd of guests. I recognized more than one that I'd visited on my tax rounds and saw they knew me, but I was mighty glad they only bowed and smiled and went on with their visiting. They hadn't forgotten my threats about talking out of turn!

A sudden hand tugged at mine and Estrellita Bandini was laughing at me and at her side, the girl in the daguerreotype—and both as pretty as two just-minted gold pieces.

"Roy! Come and dance with us," Lucia Bandini swept up out of the dark crowd, swirling her new silver ball gown for my benefit. The music rang out in a gay little tune, and as the partners moved out on the patio floor, I found myself dancing with Señorita Dulcima!

All I could think of as we circled and swayed around the floor, while the fiddle, flute and guitar swelled into the silvery moonlight, was that here was the very girl I'd thought about many times through long nights on the trail, and how downright strange it was that I now held her in my arms.

While we danced, she sang the words along with the rest of the folk, in a gay little voice, all sweet and lively:

> *"Aforrado de mi vida!*
> *Come estas, como te va?*
> *Como has pasado la noche,*
> *No has tenido novedad?*

> *"Y vente con migo*
> *Y yo te dare*
> *Zapatos de raso*
> *Color de café."*

When the little orchestra finally ran down, the guests broke into applause and chatter while I looked around for my partner.

Lucia suddenly popped up and poked me in the ribs with her fan. "If you're looking for Señorita Dulcima, she's over there by the far fountain."

I followed her directions and saw the tintype girl standing near the orange trees in the tawny glow of a string of Chinese lanterns. She and the gambler Powers seemed to be mighty busy talking.

"Señor Bean?" I recognized Rosita's unforgettable voice and turned to find her standing just behind me, one hand on her hip and the other holding a closed fan that she tapped against her perfect chin. "I'm happy you could attend our little affair and that you were gallant enough to attend to my young ward." She smiled that slow smile that never failed to send a jolt of fire right through me. Turning, she nodded to Lucia, who immediately bobbed her head and walked away.

"From Dulcima's appearance when she danced by, it is easy to see that she finds her fellow *americano* a person of *fascinación*," she went on.

"But I'm not the only interesting Yank here, it seems." I made a slight

motion toward Powers and the girl Dulcima, where they stood chatting in
the wavering lantern glow.

A look passed across Rosita's face, so swift as to be almost invisible.
"Yes, but I have no way of supposing how such a person got in here. I gave
old Carlos definite instructions that you or your brother were to be the
only anglos allowed—or invited."

"He arrived about the same time I did, and your sentry seemed to have
thought it was Josh with me."

"He is as familiar with the alcalde as the rest of us." Bringing up her
painted fan, she fluttered it like a watchful cat switching its tail as she
stared at Powers, then she turned back to me. "I've heard that you ob-
tained a daguerreotype of Dulcima out in Arizona someplace and were a
bit—how shall I put it?—somewhat taken with her."

I admitted that I'd come across the photograph in a pretty strange
manner, and, as she seemed to want to talk, went into the details of just
how I found that tintype. I hoped it would put her off somewhat.

"How unusual." She smiled up at me in the lantern light. "You might
allow me to inspect that picture sometime, as it may be a relic of some
relative who perished in that wagon train tragedy. The poor girl has had a
most sorrowful beginning, hasn't she?"

All the time Rosita was speaking, her brilliant gaze was scanning my
clothing, my face, and particularly my eyes.

"*Sí*, my niece has the effect of often fascinating the sterner sex—as I've
said." She nodded in the direction of Powers and Dulcima.

I mumbled something about the beauty of the night and the fine crowd
at her affair, but the mistress of Las Fuentes seemed determined to keep
me on the griddle for the time being.

"You must now be aware that Dulcima has some talent in the manner
of singing." Rosita's eyes remained fixed on the strolling pair. "Unfortu-
nately she also possesses quite a streak of waywardness—and that has
sometimes led to her association with such undesirables as flashy, shallow
theater folk and some of the gambling fraternity. I've had to insist that
she leave all such people alone—and I believe she has done so as far as I
can tell."

When I said something about Dulcima not bumping into that sort
when she was away at her finishing school, I was wishing that Rosita
would trail off onto another subject.

"*Sí*, it would be much better for all concerned if she were actually back
at school," Rosita went on, touching her lovely chin with her closed fan.
"But in the meanwhile, during her vacation, she needs other diversions to

turn her away from possible mischief during the time she is at home, particularly as the Bandini girls have invited her to town." She paused again as she watched the gambler and her young ward where they strolled under the orange trees.

"You want me to keep that gent out of the picture as much as possible?" I wondered if Rosita had any idea of my reputation back down in Mexico—and hoped she didn't. Besides, I seemed to have a different feeling toward the little lady, who'd been so charming and lively during our dance—sort of protective, you might say.

"*Sí*, I want you, as you say, to keep an eye on Dulcima while she is in town." Rosita suddenly took my hand and a real jolt of electric fire shot through me. "Now come over to the veranda, if you will; I have a friend who would like to greet you."

She led me around the little orchestra at the end of the house and up the steps where old Colonel Hechavarría sat in a chair near the open door. The ancient Mexican houseman stood by the blind officer, a glass and bottle in his hand. When he saw us approaching, he hustled to pour out some wine for the colonel.

"Esteban, would you go in and bring out that present for Señor Bean," Rosita told the old fellow, who made himself scarce.

"Sit you down, Señor. Sit you down." The blind man waved a thin hand and I plunked down into a nearby chair as soon as Rosita had seated herself in her hammock.

I made some polite talk about seeing him again, asked after his health, and all the while was aware of the brilliant green eyes of Rosita on me. She said nothing at all, but seemed to be waiting for something.

"Señor, as you see me, I am come up in the world a bit, all thanks to your generosity." And the old gent spread out his arms, displaying a new jacket, and patted his middle, where a fancy gold sash held up his red-slashed trousers. "*Sí*, it is good to again seem like a gentleman, if only to dress like one."

"Clothes make the man, I've heard." I fingered my own gold-filigreed jacket but stopped when I saw Rosita's amused glance sweep over my outfit.

"But I must tell you, Señor," the old man went on, "that a certain *hombre* has been asking questions of my man Pacheco when he has been in San Diego for supplies!"

"Questions?" I asked as Rosita leaned forward in her hammock, fan waving slowly in the orange lantern light.

"*Sí!* I sent Pacheco into town, as I said, and he stopped by one of the cantinas—'The Crossed Muskets,' I believe. There the proprietor, Señor Powers, had word that my man had brought some gold to San Diego, and he got our poor Pacheco somewhat tipsy as he endeavored to discover where that particular coin had come from."

"What did he find out?" So this Powers was some slicker than brother Josh, nosing out that gold I dropped around the countryside. But perhaps the gambler was just fishing for whatever he could find. Certainly he couldn't connect a few golden eagles with Jeff Kirker's hidden hoard.

"He told Señor Powers that it was coin from a good friend, but that we had possessed it for some years," old Hechavarría answered, long fingers tapping on the side of his empty glass.

"Hush!" Rosita held up her hand. "Don Xavier, say no more for now. I think I know why this gringo has been asking such questions—but I'll explain later."

The little orchestra had struck up another tune and the patio was again filled with the shadows and silhouettes of the dancers. I saw both Bandini girls sweep by in the arms of some young *californios,* and then the gambler and the tintype girl swirled past in the laughing crowd.

"Señor Roy," Rosita called over the sound of the music, and I turned to see her standing by the doorway, a sombrero in her hand and a strange young man at her side.

"Señor, I believe that is your property." The stranger spoke English with a pleasant accent.

I took back my long lost sombrero. *"Gracias!"*

"It is nothing. I came upon it last week during that storm—and Rosita tells me it belonged to you." He bowed and turned back into the interior of the house without another word. Whoever he was, he had the run of Rancho las Fuentes.

I stood looking from Don Xavier to Rosita. Both seemed about to say something when the stranger returned to the porch. "Your pardon, Señor Bean, but I've just arrived from a most tedious journey and my manners are not of the best." He put a hand to his heavily inlaid red jacket and made a graceful bow. "Permit me. I am Francisco Almada, as my dear sister could have told you."

My eyes must have opened wide, for he laughed and, throwing up a hand, clapped me on the shoulder. And when he did so, his jacket parted and I glimpsed two six-shooters thrust into his green sash.

I told him that I was mighty happy to make his acquaintance, and thanked him again for the return of my lost lid, but I didn't mention how taken aback I was to meet Rosita's so-called brother!

We bowed to each other again and this time Francisco vanished into the house and stayed gone.

"Sit back down." And Rosita patted the hammock and held out a hand. My head was humming like a nest of bees—and then, all at once, I had that old Bean hunch.

As I sank back down beside Señorita Almada, I knew that I'd just met none other than Joaquín Murieta *himself!*

What Rosita said next just helped to nail down my suspicions. "Roy, why did your brother not come out this evening with you?"

I knew that she was somehow aware that Josh, Lopez and several of his deputies had stayed in San Diego to guard the jail. "We've got pretty straight word that Murieta and some of his gang are in the area, and that could mean that he may try to break those rascals out of the *calabozo*, including his right-hand man, Juan Pico," my brother had told me that afternoon as I left town to ride to Rancho las Fuentes. Josh hadn't seemed too ruffled about me riding all that way out into the country, with the possibility of a gang of cutthroats on the loose. Well, if he wasn't too worried then neither was I, though I wasn't about to ride back to town after midnight.

Rosita was still waiting for my reply and I felt her fan tap my knee. "Business in town, I guess," was all I could reply, while the blood began to pound as I felt the soft curve of her thigh against mine.

"And you had no business but that of seeing my little ward." She rapped me gently on the ear with that fan. "You needn't hold on to that sombrero so tightly; I shall see you don't lose it again."

Somehow the words slipped out before I could clamp my jaw. "Joaquín does as his sweetheart tells him?"

Then I expected to feel that little dagger at my ribs again, but after a gasp she turned and her eyes blazed into mine.

"You heard, my *brother!*"

"Well, I'd been told that he—Murieta—was your—"

"*Lover?*" I could feel her body stiffen. Then she laughed softly.

I knew I could be skating on about as thin ice as a man could and not plunge right in over his head. "No offense, señorita, but that was what a friend of mine told me." I could have added a few other things, but had sense enough to keep my jaw shut.

"This *friend* wouldn't be named Kirker?"

Now it was my turn to stiffen up. "It might have been."

"That is what I have feared. You've been tossing around Jeff Kirker's stolen gold." She grasped my arm with fingers soft yet strong as steel. "Roy Bean, you could be in the deepest of trouble!"

"Does your brother know about the gold?" I looked hurriedly at the door, but it stayed empty—and old Don Xavier seemed to have dozed off in spite of the musical hullabaloo in garden and patio.

"It's not just Joaquín. In fact, he's—" She paused and looked around. "I have much to tell you, but it must wait until later."

The music had stopped again and we could hear the guests clapping and calling for Rosita.

"I promised I would sing a song for them, and it's growing late, and many, except the Bandinis, have a long ride home. So I'd best play the more proper hostess." She arose and I got up also, holding my two sombreros. "Meet me at your golden tavern after the *baile* is over—at midnight."

XIV

It grew late. The moon, covered with misty clouds, eased down over the pine woods and night birds were calling. A chill breeze had drifted in from the Pacific and the guests were starting to look for cloaks and traveling gear when Rosita came out of the ranch house and down the broad steps into the patio.

A murmur of pleasure swept through the garden when the company saw their hostess. She'd put up her flame-tinted hair in a bright-green scarf and her curvesome but slender figure was clothed in a short, ankle-length cloth-of-gold gown, edged in a beaded fringe. As she moved toward the little orchestra, she jingled with necklaces and bracelets like a young gypsy princess. Her bright scarlet slippers clicked and clacked on the painted stones of the patio, while an anklet of coins tinkled and rang on one slim ankle.

With a signal to the musicians under the pepper tree, she spun around on her slippers, keeping time with a pair of castanets. While fiddle, guitar, drum and flute swept on in a flurry of music, her dance became that of a tattered, golden leaf caught up in an ocean tempest, as glittering skirt and sea-green scarf flared out into a misty blur under the silvery glow of the dying moon and the flickering lantern light.

On and on she danced, twirling, spinning and weaving breath-stopping patterns in motion until I knew I'd never seen anything so wildly beautiful. When she stopped, with one last whirl of arms and legs and twang of guitar, the whole garden broke out into delighted applause, while I stood staring, too charmed to make a move.

Lucia Bandini, slipped up beside me on the steps, munching away on a honey cake, whispering, "Isn't she wonderful? They say she was on the stage with Lola Montez and the toast of San Francisco before she returned to this rancho."

"There wasn't anyone else to run the place when her father died?" I wondered what she knew of Francisco Almada—or *Joaquín Murieta!*

"They say there is a brother, but a perfect scapegrace; a ne'er-do-well who rarely comes to the rancho. I've never seen him, nor have many."

We were soon joined by Estrellita and with the Almada ward, Señorita Dulcima. The gambler was nowhere in sight, though I was sure he'd not gone. Both young ladies were chattering and full of plans for the night's sleeping arrangements. Dulcima smiled at me when I asked how she liked her. "She is wonderful at whatever she does." Then she fell silent and looked off into the distance toward the orange trees.

"See, they ask for another song," Lucia said, pointing at the milling guests around Rosita. Suddenly the music clashed into a Spanish patriotic serenade, and her thrilling voice rang out:

> *"La augusta Cristina,*
> *De España embeleso,*
> *El mas tierno beso*
> *Imprime a Ysabel:*
> *Y 'Reina,' le dice,*
> *'No ia sobre esclavos;*
> *Sobre iberos bravos,*
> *Sobre un pueblo fiel.'*
> *"Triunfamos, amigos,*
> *Triunfamos enfin,*
> *Y libre respir*
> *La Patria del Cid."*

Standing balanced like a golden angel on the edge of the west fountain, Rosita, with arms flung to the night sky, sang the entire seven rousing verses, joined by the entire crowd for the fiery choruses.

On and on she sang to the explosive end:

> *"And thou, messenger*
> *Of peace and joy,*
> *Hear the pure voice*
> *Of our loyalty;*
> *Hear the accents*
> *Which we raise to heaven;*
> *Hear what we cry,*
> *Country! Liberty!"*

And the audience chimed in, roaring their answer to the military hymn:

> *"Triunfamos, amigos,*
> *Triunfamos enfin,*
> *Y libre respir*
> *La Patria del Cid!*

[Let us triumph, my friends,
Let us triumph at length
And let the country of the Cid
Breathe freely again!]"

When the song finished there came shouts of *"Viva la España!" "Viva el México!" "Viva la señorita Rosita!"* and the uproar was tremendous.

At last some young caballero, two sheets to the breeze, shouted out, *"Viva todo el mundo!* [Long live everybody]," which bit of foolishness was followed by a gale of laughter.

When the applause and excited conversation eased off, the guests began to leave the rancho with many goodbyes, while the guitar and flute played and the rest of the little orchestra sang them on their way with a clever little drinking song:

"Ah! que bonitos
Son los enanos,
Los chiquititos
Y mexicanos.

"Sale la linda,
Sale la fea,
Sale el enano,
Con su zalea."

Rosita, who stood by the gate, bidding farewell to the folks, took the old Don Hechavarría by the hand as he came up, guided by his servant. She lowered her voice but I was near enough to hear her mention Francisco by name. It was plain that the old gent was one of the few who knew that her brother was nearby, though he couldn't see him.

The Bandini girls hurried up to bid me *buenas noches.* "We'll be back in town in a few days and Dulcima comes with us—so you must promise, Señor Roy, to be as attentive to our dear friend as you are to us!"

They playfully shoved Dulcima forward while she struck at them with her fan but smiled shyly at me.

I allowed that I'd come calling at the Casa Bandini as usual and, feeling like a regular don myself, took the fingertips of each young lady and saluted them in the best fashion. When I seized Dulcima's tapered fingers, she pulled them back for an instant and then surrendered them to me. I brushed them with my mustache, and as I did two people watched my shenanigans, besides the Bandini sisters and some of the departing guests.

Rosita's green eyes were on me for a long moment, while Dick Powers, hand shoved in his sash, stood in the shadow of the wall staring at us.

With one last bow to the ladies, I followed the jovial, chattering crowd through the gate, hard on the heels of Powers, who'd managed to leave while I bade Rosita a good evening.

Untying my horse from the rail, I thought I saw a light in the upper story of the big old house and wondered if Joaquín Murieta stood there watching us leave, but it could have been just moonlight upon a window-pane.

"Well, Bean, I see we're heading the same way." Mounted upon his big black stallion, Powers waited for me in the road while the traps and wagons pulled around us on the way to their ranches and farms.

"Only as far as Casa de Oro," I said as I spurred up my horse.

Powers kept on beside me. "Golden House? That's a prime name all right." We rode in silence for a piece, then: "Plan on staying in the vicinity for a spell?"

"Just for the night. It's a long piece back to town in the dark."

"Not for a gent with any sand!" He opened his coat and displayed the handle of a six-shooter in his belt.

I let that pass and didn't feel that I had to show him my weapon. It was plain to see that Powers was trying to rile me for some reason, and I wasn't about to rise to his bait. "My nag can stand a rest. I pushed her pretty hard coming over. And I may do some swapping at the Misión San Carlos. They say the fathers have some prime saddle stock over there."

"Swap your crow bait like you swapped sombreros tonight, eh?" He gave a short laugh and spurred up, leaving me by myself in the dimming moonlight.

Dick Powers didn't appear to care much for my company, and that was one hundred percent with me.

All the way to the tavern at the crossroads, my mind was in a perfect muddle. When I tried to think about Rosita's warning, I got to pondering what she'd said of her brother, the man called Joaquín Murieta. And when I began to cipher just how Joaquín Murieta could be related to the mistress of Rancho las Fuentes, I got to thinking of the tintype girl and her odd connection with that strange family . . . and so it went, never landing on one subject long enough to decide what I was going to do about gold, girl, Murieta—or Rosita herself!

Several of the guests had taken the same road, and as I loped past they wished me the best of the coming day. More than one had felt the benefit of Kirker's gold eagles, and others had heard of my soft-headed approach to tax collecting. But to give all due credit, none that I knew of, had breathed a word to anyone in San Diego—though Dick Powers had begun to sniff around for whatever he could find.

Once in a while I passed small groves of trees looming up dark and dismal-looking in the tarnished half light of the fading moon, but never did I have more than a passing doubt as to who might lurk nearby, for I was about certain that no one thereabouts made any moves unless Francisco Almada, otherwise Joaquín Murieta told them to—and if I was to believe Rosita Almada, and my own sixth sense, he was in or near Rancho las Fuentes.

There was no sign of Dick Powers on the road. He was probably long on the way back to town, for as a horseman with few equals, only Murieta had the reputation for moving faster and farther in a given time. And as my thoughts drifted back to Powers, I found myself wondering why he'd come out to the Almada place all uninvited. The answer seemed to be Dulcima herself.

When I pulled up at the tavern there was a battered tin lantern hanging over the entrance, but no light within. I pounded away on the big oaken door and finally turned out the tavern keeper, who came waddling with a candle, digging at his pouchy eyes with a dirty fist. As soon as he got himself around and recognized me as the gringo who'd come by earlier and paid hard cash for a presumably soft bed, he helped me stable the horse out back in a shed and then led me through the bar to a room that looked out upon the road and the empty mesa beyond.

Wishing me *buenas noches* in a wheezy voice, he shuffled away to bolt the front door and left me with the guttering stump of the candle and a rickety cord-and-shuck-mattressed bed.

I tugged off my boots, squinted at my watch and wondered if Rosita would actually follow me down to this shabby crossroads hostelry—and in just about half an hour at that!

Lying back on the creaking bed, fully dressed save for my shirt, I tried again to puzzle out the odd parade of events that had seen me practically run out of Mexico to fall in with a red-handed robber, learn (or nearly learn) the secret to a golden bonanza, discover not only the little girl in the tintype but that her very guardian was none else than Jeff Kirker's Red Rosita! And to put the cap sheaf on the whole affair, find that Rosita's brother was actually the noted bandit leader Murieta!

How I wished that Salazar had been close at hand to help me solve such a mixed-up puzzle—and what to do about my discoveries. But the little Mexican sheriff had left the bandit Juan Pico in Josh's *calabozo* until he returned from an expedition down into Southern California, below the border.

And if I told Salazar that Joaquín Murieta was as close by as Rancho las Fuentes in the person of Rosita's brother, would he laugh or take off his flopping sombrero and rub his vanished scalp?

And did I want to tell Salazar anything at all? I didn't know.

The whole matter seemed to be as wild as one of Salazar's hated penny dreadfuls, yet it was as true as the fact that I had a hole in the stocking of my right foot.

Staring at that toe, wriggling it and keeping an eye on the dwindling candle, I kept hoping that Rosita was on the way and began to get all hot under the collar, even with my shirt off.

Then came the rapid beat of hooves—hooves pounding down the road from the direction of Rancho las Fuentes, and I got off the bed and pushed open the shutter to peer out.

Shading my eyes, I could only make out the hazy forms of rider and mount in the dimming starlight, but knew my candle had been seen.

The figure dismounted and I heard bit and bridle jingle. Then the shadowy person drifted toward my window. I stepped back and waited, beginning to burn, again, with anticipation.

The shutter eased full open. An arm poked in through the window. Something glinted in the candlelight—a long-barreled pistol.

As I froze against the wall, my six-shooter buried under my pillow, the stranger flung a booted leg over the sill, swung up—and I was looking at Joaquín Murieta!

XV

Francisco Almada stood quietly in the vague candlelight, pistol held on a line with my belt buckle, then giving a short laugh, he thrust the weapon back into his waist sash.

"Easy, señor. You might as well invite me to stay, for I'm certain to be the only guest, invited or not, that you'll see tonight."

"You took me a mite unawares like, señor—ah?" I waved him to a seat on a corner of the bed and sank back down upon my creaking mattress, waiting for his next move.

"It would seem you are somewhat in doubt as to my correct identity," Almada smiled with a flash of even white teeth. "Please be assured that my true self is that of Don Francisco Almada—brother of the beautiful and sometimes dangerous Rosita!"

"But you are also *Murieta!*" I was wondering how to get at my own firearm, but it was under my pillow—and I was sitting on top of both.

"Guilty as charged, Señor Bean." Almada removed his gold-encrusted sombrero and inclined his sleek head slightly. "But have no misapprehensions as to my visit. It is necessary, for I wish you to carry a most urgent message to your brother, the alcalde. You'll be seeing him shortly?"

I allowed as how I'd be setting eyes on Josh about as soon as I got back to San Diego in the morning. Then, as Murieta seemed to be thinking, I looked him over. I'd seen quite a few playactors in my brief span, for I'd always had a hankering after the theater, and this dashing young fellow was about as handsome as any leading man I'd ever laid eyes upon. In a later time when folks began to make a sort of royalty out of those on the boards, he'd have been called a matinee idol. Now as he sat back on his corner of the bed, relaxed but ready to spring on the instant, like some dangerous, graceful cat, I found myself thinking that had I been some young lady I'd have come close to swooning, seeing those piercing black eyes flash under their long lashes and his handsomely regular features darken and brighten with each turn of our talk.

There was only one minor flaw in Joaquín Murieta's overall appearance. He was shy a piece of his right earlobe, and as he spoke from time to time his hand would travel up to fiddle at his damaged ear. But that hand never strayed far from his pistol sash.

"If you are able to get in a word or so with your brother, as you say, tell him, if he values his life in the very least, to beware of what he might do to the men of Murieta!" And young Almada's hand again dropped to the butt of a six-shooter while his eyes locked with mine.

"I'd guess that Josh knows how to handle his jailhouse without much jawing from me."

"His *calabozo* is one thing; *night riders* are another!"

"Night riders?"

"Sí! Perhaps you were unaware that your fine relation has been hand-in-glove with those foul night birds—those devils who carry off poor, helpless prisoners into the darkness—even those guilty of as little as the theft of a sheep or a cow—and—!"

"And?"

"Ah, you *are* aware of what happens to them, and I have information the stranglers plan to murder the trio now held in the alcalde's *calabozo."* He tapped me on the knee with a long finger. "If that should happen, as sure as my name is—never mind which name—your brother stands to be a dead man!"

"You would kill my brother?"

There came a silence that seemed so deep and long that the guttering of my guttering candle crackled like a little bonfire, and the night wind, ever prowling outside, moaned like some lost, whimpering animal.

"No! I'll not kill your foolish brother, *but Joaquín Murieta will*—if the alcalde and his brutes lynch those prisoners!"

"But you just said—?" I rubbed my eyes and stared hard at this debonair young caballero, who sat so calmly in the wavering, lemon-tinted candle glow, face a handsome mask, without the least expression.

"Señor Bean, do you think I am the butcher who slew a dozen men to seize myself a fortune in bloody gold—the gold that villainous renegade Kirker ran away with?"

"But you—you're Murieta!"

"I am, *but there is another Murieta*—at least the one who rides and slays under that name." He suddenly bent forward, his shadow doubling out to stretch black and menacing across the wall behind him. "Keep your hand away from that weapon under your pillow, and I shall tell you of the two Joaquín Murietas."

So while the flickering candle slowly died away into a pool of pale wax, I sat and listened to the calm, even voice of the man called Joaquín Murieta, as he spun his tale in that small hour of the night.

"You've met the parent of my alter ego, Carlos Hechavarría, the poor old Don Xavier. Most certainly the cruelest part of this whole tragic farce remains the fact that Carlos is determined to never make himself known to his ancient father, nor return to his home until the *americanos* are driven from the country—impossible as that event seems to be.

"My sister and I have both pleaded with him many times, but he remains steadfast to his vow to stay 'dead to all but honor,' as he expresses it.

"You should know that both Carlos and I, being from the same valley, were officers in the Cuirassiers, in fact the same company. And both of us were wounded at Buena Vista. I took several bullets. The only one showing damaged a small portion of my manly beauty; thus you behold my abbreviated ear. But Carlos himself was left for dead upon that terrible field. I went forth to hunt him out on the night following the battle, but he had taken a head wound and wandered away into the wilderness, where, amazingly enough, he dwelt amongst a small Indian tribe for nearly a year. This was all unknown to our Army or to his family, which was told of his apparent end.

"When I returned to California, I was certainly *sin blanca,* or, as you Yanks would say, 'busted!' Things were in a complete shambles. My father had died while I was gone, and the American government, in an effort to raise funds to help pay for their oppressive war, had levied a great amount of taxes upon our rancho! There was little hope of any gainful employment here and so I rode north to the recent gold strikes in an effort to earn money enough to pay off my parents' debts and save the family place from complete disaster. Though I'd been an officer, the only job available to a greaser, another of the *americanos'* charming epithets, was that of mule driver at the diggings.

"Everything went along quite decently for a time, then one of the officials, in charge of our particular mine, desired my job for a lately arrived relation. There was nothing he could find to fault in my work and so he accused me of stealing from the miners themselves, and I had to flee away to the mountains for my very life.

"Hiding out and roaming around in the wilds like some unwanted animal, I fell in with all sorts of landless men—vagabonds, thieves, murderers and rebels like myself, who'd refused to knuckle under to the Conqueror. I gathered the best of these fugitives and molded them into a small, well-mounted company of guerrilla cavalry, with our horses coming from the best *americano* ranches. Then we began to extract a portion of our vengeance, as well as gold, from the invaders!

"And now I observe your furrowed brow as you begin to wonder just how this person, this Joaquín Murieta, came to be, and how he split, eventually, in two.

"It so happened that about six months after I'd founded my little band, and we had begun to make many of the Yankees regret ever having come out to California, Carlos Hechavarría himself rode into my camp. He had heard of us, and being determined to levy his own brand of vengeance upon the *americanos*, sought me out and disclosed himself as an alive—but strangely changed—man, indeed!

"When we were mere youths at home, dodging school and labor on our respective ranchos, riding the hills and valleys, like our fathers before us, and, finally, courting the neighboring señoritas, Carlos was the very merriest of companions. Always ready for an all-night frolic or a gossip and a bout at the bottle—that was Carlos. Even when caught up in the stern events of a war, fought to retain our country's honor and independence, Carlos Hechavarría had been the dashing, careless caballero—in fact a very devil of a fellow!

"So you can well imagine that I greeted his return from the dead with joy. And when I found him wrapped in never-ending gloom, I endeavored to jog him from his intractable moods by reminding him of our secret names, names that we had used years before. This foolish fancy had seen us, each in those lighthearted times, writing notes and cryptic messages back and forth. Every minor confidence we felt like exchanging, be it an appraisal of a new schoolfellow or just some petty devilment, was hidden in the bole of an old, twisted oak on the border of our two ranchos.

"In signing my messages I used the name of Joaquín, from the given name of a black-sheep ancestor who'd voyaged to Mexico with the great Cortés, and promptly deserted to live among the Aztecs—certainly a man with a mind of his own.

"Carlos called himself Murieta, taking the name of a hero from the old Spanish folk tales, *Murieta of the Twisted Sword,* one of the valiant followers of El Cid, who fought long and bravely against the invading Moor—almost a case, on Carlos's part, of prevision of coming events.

"It so happened that my reminding Carlos of our youthful games took an unusual turn. He at once proposed that as the only two experienced officers in the band, we divide the available forces and raid the Yankees in earnest, seizing all the gold and specie we could until there was enough wealth on hand to purchase a sizable amount of arms from our foreign sources. Then, with additional recruits, we would wage unmerciful guerrilla war upon all *americanos!*

"His plan, good in part, called for the two bodies of riders to be commanded each by a captain bearing the same name. In this case he proposed that the combined Joaquín Murieta be used as one alias for the both of us. Thus we would bring confusion to our warfare. It became so successful that several ruffianly road agents took up the name for themselves, and caused the so-called authorities many a puzzled day and night as they rode hither and yon, chasing Joaquín here and Joaquín there.

"All this jogged along in fine style for the next several months, until I fell in with that accursed *renegado* American sergeant—Kirker!

"This happened in a gambling saloon and theater in San Francisco, owned by the actress Lola Montez and managed, at the time, by a young señorita of your acquaintance—my sister, Rosita Almada.

"Many of the *americano* troops from the camps around San Francisco and thereabouts frequented the place, with Kirker among them. The sergeant was a great gambler and had already run up an enormous debt by the time Rosita learned some highly interesting facts about him.

"It so happened that my sister, who always keeps her pretty ears open, overheard Kirker boasting of a fortune in gold bullion that his squad would be guarding in transport in less than a week's time, actually on July twenty-first. It turned out to be federal money needed to pay half of the entire force of federal troops in northern California.

"She hurried out to me at my secret headquarters at Portolo Valley with this most intriguing news. I immediately dispatched a messenger to Carlos, where he camped near one of the main trails to the mines while waiting for a fat ore shipment.

"He arrived the next day, and after a meeting at our main camp, I rode into San Francisco at dusk and, luckily, found Kirker still cooling his heels at Montez's Melodion Casino on Market Street.

"Kirker was already half in his cups when I arrived that evening and down on his luck, as usual, but I managed to make his acquaintance, under another name, and advance him five hundred pesos as a friendly loan. The sergeant was as unlucky as reported, and though he 'bucked the tiger' with a right good will, managed to drop the entire amount of money by eleven o'clock.

"Rosita had little trouble in coaxing the rascal upstairs to one of Lola's private dining chambers, where I joined them, in the guise of Rosita's sweetheart, to that villain's chagrin, I'm sure. But, with a goodly amount of passable wine and a bit of harmless flirting by Rosita, we had him openly discussing the upcoming gold shipment by midnight. And it wasn't much longer before we had him agreeing to a plan that would allow myself and a few 'friends' to interrupt his squad on the road and make off with the bullion.

"I remained in town for a day, meeting with Kirker to refine the plan and then returned to my band—and Carlos.

"The twenty-first of the month arrived to find me flat upon my back with a raging fever from an old wound that has plagued me every so often since the war.

"Thus it was decided Carlos would lead my assigned men out on the raid; this much I agreed to and then went out of my head with that vile fever.

"I took such a bad turn that one of my right-hand men rode full tilt into San Francisco and brought Rosita back to care for me.

"When I came to myself three days later there was many a long face around camp and Rosita was forced to tell me that Carlos had taken his own men and ambushed the U.S. soldiers, killing all but that blue-bellied picaroon of a Kirker, and then worked with him to cache the gold, as it proved much too heavy to carry away in a hurry.

"The following day after raid, Carlos and his bunch rode back to the site of the hidden bullion only to return like a pack of whipped dogs—for Kirker had come out ahead of them with pack mules and fled the country with a king's ransom. It was as simple as that!"

After my visitor finished there came a lull, while I began to cipher the best way to answer a question that was just about bound to come up. And while I rubbed my chin, staring at the ceiling, at my toes, and even over the bandit chieftain's head at the half-closed shutter, the wind, that had been whining around the tavern, began to buffet and bang that shutter and I could hear raindrops pecking at the window frames.

"Rather like a certain day, not long ago, when I was luckily near enough to pluck you out of that wolves' den you were galloping into, is it not so?" Joaquín leaned forward again to light up a long cigarro from the sputtering flame of my dwindling candle, while he cocked his head at the rattle of the rain. "My poor mount out there will be getting a fine wetting from this storm, but he's used to hard knocks, the same as his master."

I could catch the jingle of bit and the thud of hooves as the great gray stallion moved about in the downpour and shook his head.

"Well, I certainly thank you most kindly for that act of neighborliness."

And I yawned, wishing this dangerous young gent would take the hint and leave the same way he'd come—through my window.

"Oh, I was most happy to be of service." Joaquín clasped one knee over the other and blew out a thin ribbon of smoke. "Your kindness to many of the poor folk of the area has not gone unnoticed by some of the more observant. *Sí,* even if Rosita had not sung your praises, it would have eventually come to my attention. I have friends *very close to you.*" He laughed quietly, tapping the ash of his cigarro into one of my boots. "But I must remark that such generosity was also bound to come to the notice of *one other!*"

Suddenly his eyes narrowed, for another sound was threading through the muted hush of the rainfall. A horse was coming down the road at a good clip.

Joaquín sprang from the bed with the swift grace of panther, deliberately knocking over my candle stump as he passed. I could hear him slowly push open the shutter and caught a glimpse of his dim silhouette as he peered out into the rainy night. All at once he gave a sharp exclamation and turned back in the hazy darkness. "That is one of my company. Don't make any sort of sound. I'll return." He was gone before I realized it.

I didn't cause any commotion but wasted little time getting my six-gun out from under the pillow.

Then I waited—*and waited.* He was absent for less than a couple of minutes, but they seemed more like two hours apiece.

All at once, though I scarcely heard a sound, he was back in the room and striking a lucifer to light up the bit of candle. "Take this and put up your pistol. Here is a Spanish musketoon loaded with double buckshot. That *idiota* of an alcalde and those accursed night riders have gone and hung all three of those poor devils at the *calabozo!* There will be pure hell to pay if Carlos Hechavarría comes this way." He slapped the rain from his sombrero and wrapped himself in a serape he'd been carrying. "When you get out of here in the morning, hie yourself to San Diego and warn that madman brother of yours to guard himself well, for he's a dead man if Carlos ever gets near him!"

Young Almada was back through the window and mounted upon his big gray before I could poke my head out into the rain and thank him.

"Next time we'll talk more of Kirker's gold!" Then he and his heavily cloaked companion were gone into the black night with a thunder of hooves.

XVI

I was up at dawn, having spent an uneasy night on the lumpy straw mattress with nothing in my arms but Joaquín's musketoon. There'd been no trouble during the hours after the bandit's departure, and either the tavern keeper was a mighty sound sleeper or he certainly knew how to keep his jaw clamped, for he fetched around my horse from the stable without the slightest expression on his wide brown face. He also seemed to ignore my extra weapon, though I thought I saw a glint of recognition as he noticed it in my hand. I also caught him looking at the scores of hoofprints in the soft, rain-damp earth about the tavern door.

Paying my bill, I was on my way as the rising sun spangled shrubs and grass with thousands of ruby-red and glittering-golden water gems, covering the miles into San Diego as fast as I could without harming the beast. And as we galloped along, I kept an eye open for any strange riders, for, as on the day I'd wound up tax collecting, I felt the nearness of unseen horsemen. I had to believe that Rosita's brother, for his own reasons, had again given me free passage through another chunk of Murieta country.

By the time I finally pushed my lathered mount down into the plaza, the entire town seemed up and in the streets. All was a great hullabaloo over the lunching of the *calabozo* prisoners by unknown riders. Some called out that it was Sánchez himself who'd again fetched in the victims —this time from a nearby cypress grove on the coastal road, where'd they had been discovered around dawn by a peddler.

I had dismounted and was tying my horse to one of the hitching rails on the east end of the plaza when someone poked me in the ribs. "Señor Roy, here is one mighty big trouble!" It was Sheriff Salazar, his big sombrero rumpled and mighty dented and his duds covered with dust. In a few words he told me that he'd arrived about an hour earlier on his way back from below the border and headed north. He had come down with second thoughts on the way back from Mexico and decided to stop at San Diego and pick up his two young horse thieves. "But by the infernal secondhand bugle of San Gabriel! I had myself a feeling that something like this might happen!"

He pointed out the three bodies, wrapped in serapes, lying over on the south side of the plaza under a pepper tree. "They died along with that villainous Murieta's man! *Sí*, young Roy—whoever strung up Pico took along those two boys and killed them to keep them from talking. There's murder here in this little town, by hell!"

While the crowd milled around, voicing their opinion of the dark deeds of the Men of the Night, some cursed the act as brutal and downright cowardly, but others only laughed and shouted out that it was *bueno* and the only way to handle all such rascals.

I noticed Diamond Dick Powers, the gambler, laughing and joking with a group of saloon regulars, as well as with Sánchez himself. Josh's deputy strutted around tugging at his long mustaches and seemed to be almighty pleased with the excitement—and himself! Yet when someone in the crowd jostled him in passing, Sánchez blanched and slapped a hand onto his gun butt. So it seemed pretty plain that the alcalde's law dog was on edge and as jumpy as a tarantula on a hot rock.

"Where's my brother?" I hadn't seen anything of Josh in all the milling crowd, yet he should have been on the street in his capacity as headman of San Diego. I started off for the alcalde's casa on foot.

"Hold on there, young Roy! Your brother and several of the leading citizens have rode out to the woods, near Alcalá Point, to look at the site of the crime. I was going out there but decided to wait for them to come back—and you might as well wait with me." Salazar looked down at the wicked little weapon in my hand. "For the everlasting love of Santa Cecilia's brass-bound harp! Where'd you come by that? The last time I saw such a murdering gun was when we shot one of Murieta's rogues, Black Bonito, out of his saddle at Placerville!"

"And what happened then?"

"What happened?" Salazar wrestled off his flapping hat and beat the dust out of it while the morning sun gilded the top of his vanished scalp. "You mean what sort of a revenge did that bandit king extract from us? Well, I'll tell you! Not one damned thing!" He squinted at me and slowly pulled on his headgear. "I know what you mean. *Sí!* This Murieta has often threatened those who've slain or interfered with his rascals, but a mighty few times has he ever carried out such threats." He stared thoughtfully at the swaggering Sánchez. "Of course, there might come a time when—"

I was about to ask just what he was driving at when shouts broke out in the crowd, and here came Josh with several sober-looking gents, among them Señor Bandini, all riding into the plaza.

"Come along. Let's see what your brother has to say." Salazar pushed his way through the throng and I followed, still toting my little man-killer of a gun.

Josh sat there on his horse, his fancy clothes all rumpled and misfitting, and from the look of him he hadn't been to bed at all. When his blood-shot eyes focused on Salazar and myself, he sort of stiffened in his saddle and just waited for us to come up to him.

"Well, here's Roy and Salazar. So you're both back. This is one devil of a thing, isn't it? You can ride pride just so far and then you're apt to get bucked off damned good and hard. To think we've lost those three prison-ers—even if they were a batch of lowlifes!" He wheeled his horse and started up the street toward the alcalde's casa, while the other riders rode off through the crowd, all as mum as oysters.

Two hours later, when the bells chimed for noon, Josh was still talking, and Salazar and I were still listening. My brother rattled on and on about the "infernal outrage" as if he couldn't stop. He ranted about the jailor's lack of common sense, that fat old man who always seemed more than half asleep. He deplored the absence of any of his deputies during the night, but then turned around and excused them by saying they all had word that Murieta or some of his gang were said to be prowling the outskirts of town, ready to break out Juan Pico and setting up some sort of ambush for any overambitious lawmen.

Josh just about pulled his hair to think he'd been so deep in his account books and ledgers, preparing a report for the headmen in San Francisco, that he hadn't been thinking straight. "I'm as big a blockhead as any of my men—and now I'm paying for it!" He rambled on, figuratively kicking himself in the tailbone, so that in spite of myself I was just about con-vinced Francisco Almada had made a mistake in my brother.

But I could sense that Salazar himself wasn't completely sold that some-thing wasn't wrong, though he couldn't put a finger on it yet. But when we finally got away from Josh and walked uptown for a drink at the American Flag, the little Mexican sheriff spilled his thoughts good and strong.

"I tell you, Roy, there's something about this affair that has a strange look—something odd like!" Salazar hoisted his glass, then sat it down as if he'd all of a sudden lost his thirst. "*Sí*, I don't want to say it, but, by damn, your brother does what your Señor Shakespeare has one of his characters say about another—*that he protests too* mucho!"

"Josh is covering up something?" My neck began to prickle. This fat little Mexican law dog wasn't half as sleepy as he looked No, he was mighty wide awake!

Salazar picked up his beer and downed it with gusto, then ordered another round. "I tell you that listening at all the alcalde's words, words, words, has me dry as a chunk of old adobe. Drink up, young Bean! I guess you've got an idea or two as to what's been going on around here. And I myself have learned a thing or two since the time I pinned this on!" And he tapped the nickel-plated little pie plate of a badge with a broad thumb.

Then, for a spell, we just sat there over our drink. All of a sudden, be damned if Salazar didn't come at me from away around Robin Hood's barn. "Señor Roy, that gold you had when we first met back on the trail, the gold you told me was for a business here—you remember that?"

"I sure guess I do."

"Have any of it left?"

"Well, that's a mighty unusual sort of a question." I gulped half of my beer and wiped my chin. "Sure I've still got it. We just haven't had a lot of time to speculate for likely business prospects."

"*Sí,* and I guess there ain't too much doing in the way of business in such a place as this." Salazar sipped at his beer and then turned his head slowly to look at me. "Maybe you ought to come up toward San Francisco and put some of that gold into some sort of business thereabouts. I tell you they're still making money hand over fist, and not just in the mines. Things ain't as loco as they were a year or so back, but even with old Sam Brannon's stores around the diggings there's real opportunities for young fellows like you, with all your Yankee get-up-and-go. Flour ain't eight hundred dollars a barrel anymore, nor eggs three dollars each, but boots, picks and shovels and suchlike still fetch some mighty fancy prices, and there's no risk of running into *bandidos* like Murieta and Pancho Ruiz if you stay put in town and do your trading." Salazar, for some reason, had got to rattling on just like Josh. "Speaking of Murieta, where'd you say you come by that little murdering gun? Wasn't one of the alcalde's?"

"No, it wasn't!" I said sort of short and sharp like and decided to change the subject. "What d'you know about the girl you came down on the coach with week before last? You know, the one who was in that Comanche wagon train raid with you."

"Only what I've told you before, young Roy. We were both in that terrible set-to and escaped only by the grace of all the holy angels!" Salazar crossed himself hurriedly. "I still carry this decoration, as you see"—he tapped his vanished scalp—"and the young señorita—"

"Yes?" Here could be some more information about the daguerreotype girl, or maybe her folks.

"Poor creature—she carries her own scar, where no one can see."

"You mean she was hurt bad somewhere?"

"No, young man, I mean that her scar is here, in the *espíritu*—the soul! That young girl, she will never be quite as other girls. And that is something for you to consider. At least that is what I believe."

The sheriff stood up, clapped his disreputable sombrero back on his head. "The day grows shorter and I have *mucho* to do before I start on up the road—a report to take down from that black coyote of a Sánchez, and another word or two with the alcalde." He pushed out his hand, and we shook.

As I sat there trying to cipher out what Salazar had meant about Dulcima, the sheriff paused at the saloon doorway. "By the way, young Roy, were all of your gold eagles minted in 1848?" Before I could do more than give him a surprised nod, he'd stepped on out of the shadowy barroom into the golden afternoon and was gone.

Next morning I still hadn't thought of a way to tip Josh off about Joaquín's warning. I didn't fancy my brother digging away at me as to where I'd come upon such information, and I didn't feel like letting him know I'd had suspicions of him being in cahoots with those blackhearted cowards—the men of the night.

At breakfast I made a try at getting something out of him about the lynchings, but he ignored me and began to harp away about the upcoming elections that were due to replace the temporary alcaldes with regular bona fide mayors.

"Just about a month, Roy, and I may be out of a job. Some damn fool politician back in Washington had a brainstorm and my job could be gone up—so why pry into things that don't concern you? I know the better class of folks, Bandinis and others, feel that such jailbird rascals need to be taken care of any way possible—so drop it! Remember what old Aesop said—uh, something about not looking at things too close."

I saw that Josh was so wrought up he couldn't even steal himself a secondhand saying. "I don't give a damn in a bucket for Aesop or any other blowhard! I'm asking you straight out if you ever had anything to do with any of these necktie parties. You might as well answer, for you're sure in one hell of a lot of trouble if you did!"

By now I was so riled up with Josh that I didn't care what came out. My

Bean temper was at the boiling point and I was ready to knock some sort of sense into him or go down trying.

"Trouble? Trouble from who?" Josh stared at me as if he thought I'd up and gone completely loco. Then he lounged back at the breakfast table and began to fiddle with a fork. "You've gotten to listening to some of that penny-ante gossip at the taverns, eh? I've heard that tinhorn Dick Powers has been making a heap of wild talk to all the rounders. It's either got to be that or this interfering galoot of a Salazar has gone and pumped you full of balloon gas! You ought to up and remember, Roy, that plenty of these Mexicans are born troublemakers—and Salazar had lost out on the reward for that bunch of prisoners, Pico in particular. He was supposed to bring them up to San Francisco alive—and you know what happened!"

Before I could answer that, Abraham slipped in from the front hallway and, after a mighty curious look at me, whispered in Josh's ear. My brother got up from the table in such a rush that he knocked over his chair. "Come on, Roy!"

I followed Josh on out at a dead run to the stable behind the casa. As we saddled up, he told me what had happened. Some traveler, riding down the Camino Real from San Juan Capistrano, after taking the flatboat over the river, had passed by the San Diego de Alcalá woods and found another corpse swinging in the sea breezes—and at nine o'clock in the morning! They couldn't turn up Sánchez anywhere, so the fat old jailer, Manuel Boronda, had come huffing over to the alcalde's.

"Another present from the Men of the Night?" I shouted at Josh while we lashed our horses up the street and pounded out the sandy roadway toward the woods two miles away.

"The devil should I know!" Josh snarled back at me, and from the expression on his face, it looked as though he was telling the truth.

Galloping up a gravelly ridge and through a great patch of yucca fringing the road, we flushed out a flock of brown quail that exploded right into our faces. Fighting to keep my mount on the road, I heard Josh give a choked sort of shout and saw the body of a man dangling from the bough of a huge old cypress at the wood's edge.

We both slowly rode up to the suspended corpse, staring into its face. In spite of the shade there was no doubt but that Josh had lost himself a deputy. Sánchez hung there, glaring at us with bulging eyes.

"*Murieta!*" Josh looked over his shoulder, but we three were alone except for the wind keening through the cypress grove.

XVII

Two days after Sánchez's unlamented end, the Bandini girls arrived, traveling in from the rancho in Rosita's surrey, along with Señora Bandini—and Dulcima.

I happened to be in the plaza, lounging in the shade of the pepper trees, gossiping with some of the locals, the talk revolving about the lynchings and the murder of the alcalde's deputy. Abraham, Josh's servant, was also there, having stopped on his way to the town's butcher shop. Though he had no more to say than usual, I felt he was almost as uneasy about the subject as I was, and I think both of us welcomed the appearance of the Almada conveyance.

As it rolled past, Lucia Bandini called, "Here we are at last, and now you've no reason for neglecting us, Señor Bean! And we insist on beginning our daily rides again."

"You are especially invited to our home tonight," her sister echoed. "Just come by at eight and we'll have a surprise ready for you—the three of us. Just see if we don't!"

Dulcima, who sat by the señora, smiled at me and waved gaily. She'd changed considerably from the quiet young lady who'd gotten off the Los Angeles coach so recently. I supposed her sudden blossoming was helped by close herding with that bouncing Bandini pair. There were few folks who got near those young pepper pots who didn't feel the better because of it, if only for the time being.

I went back to the alcalde's right after that, feeling pretty lively myself, but had no sooner crossed the threshold than I was in a roaring Donnybrook with Josh. I could tell at a glance he'd been tackling the jug, for his hair was wild-looking, and his eyes were a watery pink.

"Dammit, Roy! What's this about you financing half of the Mexican community with our gold?"

Someone had spilled the beans, all right and here was my brother landing on me with both feet. But I had some questions of my own that he was going to answer before I obliged him. "Wasn't your gold by a damn sight! And seeing you're so almighty eager to jaw, what's the truth about your infernal night riders?"

Josh glared at me, then tossed off a glass of whiskey neat and shook his head like a mossy-horned old steer. "None of your business, you whelp!" Suddenly he reared up from the table, scattering papers and tipping his beloved ledgers onto the floor with a bang. "What in Hades is this all about, yourself? Where'd you come by enough golden eagles to bail out all those worthless Mexican trash?"

"What d'you care? You got your infernal collections in—and that's what counts, according to you. And where'd you hear, anyway?"

"Sánchez!" Josh reached for the bottle and I thought he was going to heave it at me but it was too full to waste and he fell back into his chair and took a long, gurgling snort from it.

"Sánchez? Well, at least they stretched one neck that needed it!" I pulled up a chair, kicked a ledger out of the way and slapped my sombrero onto the table hard enough to send the rest of the alcalde's official papers sailing. "And you had to wait until you had a snootful before you tackled me about that tax money? Now—back to neck-stretching! You'd best fess up right now, for I'm just about riled enough to whip it out of you!" My Bean temper was up good and plenty.

Josh gave a howl like a sore-pawed wolf and flung that bottle right at my head! I ducked and glass splintered against the adobe wall as I lunged across and got in one good punch. Josh flew out of his chair to come up off the floor swinging for all he was worth—but he was on the wrong side of the furniture.

Before I could get around the table and oblige him, Abraham came rushing in from the back of the house, followed by the Almada hack driver. *"Señores! Señores!* For the love of the saints don't kill each other. Don't do this thing!"

Josh, who'd gone and yanked a hideout gun from his waistband, glared around the room, then shook the hair from his eyes. "Hell! Roy and I were just having a brotherly difference of opinion. Like they say, a little storm always clears the air." He stuffed the Derringer back, wiped the blood from his chin, and folded up back onto the floor—out cold!

"A little too much firewater before lunch," I told Abraham. "Get him off to bed, if you'd be so kind."

While the little Indian and Rosita's old servingman lugged Josh down the hall, I picked up the papers and ledgers, then sat back down, thinking.

That night at the Bandinis' was one of the most enjoyable for good-natured fun I'd ever seen—at least the first part of it.

I left Josh still sleeping it off and walked over to the Casa Bandini on Calhoun, wondering just how Abraham happened to be so friendly with old José, the Almada servingman.

When I arrived at the gate of the Bandinis', the girls were on the lookout for me in the starlight. They let me in, and with Estrellita on one arm and Lucia on the other, they led me through the hallway of the big old house and out onto the patio. The whole outdoors seemed to be lighted with colored Chinese lanterns, as usual. Both Señor and Señora Bandini were seated in easy chairs before a low wooden platform placed between a small pair of orange trees. A beautiful patchwork quilt, stretched on a wire, hung over the little platform doing the duty of a curtain. Dulcima wasn't in sight, and both sisters vanished immediately behind the billowing patchwork curtain.

I greeted the parents and took a seat near them only to find that I wasn't the only guest. A couple of young second lieutenants from the fort, plus Diamond Dick Powers, lounged on chairs near the impromptu stage. Powers was particularly nobby in a cream-colored suit, checked vest and highly polished boots. All nodded pleasantly at me and Powers unbent enough to ask after my brother.

"Understand his official duties are keeping him pretty busy, eh? Haven't seen him around much lately."

Powers had a smile I didn't care for, but I was a guest and so made some piddly small talk about the weather and let it go at that.

Suddenly a banjo rippled away from behind the colorful curtain and three fresh young voices were raised in a caroling ditty:

> *"Ruberii, de cinnamon seed, seed de Billy hop jis' in time,*
> *Juba dis, Juba dat, round de kettle of possum fat,*
> *A-hoop-ahoy, a-hoop-ahoy, double step for juberii,*
> *Sandy crab, de macreli, ham, and a half a pint of Juba—"*

The patchwork curtain jerked back and there were the Bandini sisters, and another girl with a banjo, who had to be Dulcima. All of them black-faced and patting juba in their raggedy dresses like a regular trio of minstrels.

In the midst of our applause, Dulcima, her blond tresses hidden under a frizzled black fright wig topped off with red ribbons, stepped to the front of the rough little platform and bowed just as brash and perky as the sassiest colored gal on the whole plantation.

"Lady and Genman. De Sam Diego Grand Confabulation and Plum Gum Sassisity presents an ebening of de best of ballads of de day and de day after dat!" She gave a ringing ripple to her strings and both Bandinis sprang forward and broke out:

> *"Uncle Gabriel play de fiddle,*
> *Zip Coon he made de riddle,*
> *Bone Squash in de middle—*
> *And we's gals we's play de bones,*
> *While de banjo and triangle*
> *Wid de cymbals jingle-jangle,*
> *And de big drum neat we handle—"*

And on and on, all three black-faced imps cavorted and warbled while Dulcima beat on the strings of her instrument with all the force of a young virtuoso.

To say the very least, I was surprised at the talent of the daguerreotype girl, and I could see that the audience was as flabbergasted as I was. The sisters were very good with all of their fresh, youthful energy, but Dulcima was clearly the professional of the trio.

The only person remaining calm and unmoved by the surprising show was Powers. He sat with folded hands and a standard poker face, as if he'd just caught an ace for his hole card. And gradually I got the idea that he was aware of Dulcima's talents.

The little performance rolled right along as the sisters produced some bones and, stepping to the side, accompanied Dulcima as she strummed her banjo and sang one number after another:

> *"Before we left we danced two reels*
> *De holler ob his foot was back ob his heels!*
> *I played de banjo till dey all begun to sweat,*
> *Knocked on de jawbone and bust de clarinet!"*

Now, as I listened and stared, I forgot all about everything and everyone else—including Rosita. Because here in this unusual little person there was a quality oddly balanced. She was both sturdy and yet delicate, full of a surprising rowdy air, yet somehow aloof like, and her clear voice was filled with a vibrant sort of fire that even Rosita herself might have envied a bit.

> *"I can play de banjo, yes, indeed I can!*
> *I can play a tune even on de frying pan*

I holler like a steamboat, 'fore she gwine ter stop
And I can sweep a chimbly and sing right out de top!"

When she'd finished the last song, spinning the instrument around in
her hands like the flashiest of minstrels, we were all on our feet applauding
—even the old folks and Dick Powers.

Lucia rushed out to me. "What did I tell you? Isn't she just perfectly
wonderful?" Then she turned and all three of the little pickaninnies
darted away into the house.

They were back, all changed and furbelowed in their fanciest dresses,
with their hair set to rights and the burnt cork washed away, by the time
the Bandini servants had finished serving refreshments.

Taking up a couple of glasses of wine, I got to Dulcima before Dick
Powers. "Let's take a bit of a stroll, if you'd be of a mind." I led her off
through the orange grove under the glowing moon while the two young
officers tried an encircling movement on the Bandini girls, leaving Diamond Dick to sit chatting with the señor and señora and glare at me.

"Now where in the name of tunket did you ever learn all that jiggery
blackface nonsense?" I laughed as we seated ourselves in a rustic bower
out of sight of the patio.

"Did you like—me?" She smiled slyly up at me.

"Tell the whole wide world, I'd say so! But I'll bet my poke you never
learned such monkeyshines at your finishing school. Does your aunt know
of your musical talents? Seems she'd be almighty proud of you."

At the mention of Rosita her expression changed ever so slightly, as if a
shadow had passed the shining face of the moon. Her blue eyes darkened
and she looked away from me. "No, Rosita doesn't know—many things."
She gave a short, odd little laugh—musical and yet somehow tinged with
harshness. "No, Señor Bean, Rosita is only aware of what interests her at
the moment."

"Seems to me that your aunt—" I stopped short at her frown. "Your
adopted aunt, then. It seems she's got your interests at heart. Why she—"
And I pulled up short again, about to remark on Rosita's request that I
keep an eye on her "niece" and Mr. Diamond Dick Powers off the prem-
ises as much as I could.

She sipped at her wineglass without a word, then looked up at me.
"And it seems to me, Señor Bean, that you know even less about Señorita
Almada than you know of me. I can answer your questions right enough,
but you'll have to speak to Rosita herself of *her particular interests.*" And
here her voice took on that same hard tone for an instant.

While I was chewing that over, I saw that damned gambler had gotten himself loose from the older Bandinis and was sauntering toward our bower, his thumbs in his checked vest, for all the world like an overgrown white tomcat out prowling.

I saw that I had to make some sort of move before Powers got to us. When he was out of sight behind some of the trees for a moment, I took the empty glass from Dulcima, sat mine down, and grabbed her up to me, giving her one of my best Bean hugs—the sort that had never failed to jolt the señoritas right off their feet.

For an instant I thought she was going to slap me right in the eye. Her face flushed, her eyes narrowed, then they blazed with a strange light and she returned my kiss with a fervent zest, sending a like fire burning right through me.

I'd been on my best behavior ever since coming out to Josh's bailiwick, but now I knew I'd been without the wonderful touch of a woman too long. I'd felt the same near Rosita—but Rosita wasn't near now, and this was somehow different!

Before I could go any further, that pestiferous gambling man was looming over us, and we broke apart, both breathing rather hard and fast.

"Why, Mr. Powers," Dulcima smiled, all cool and collected, "I thought you were having a nice little visit with the Bandinis." She sat up, patting at her hair and fussing a bit with the front of her gown as if everything was completely regular, when he could see something rather unusual had been going on in the grape arbor.

"I came to see—Mr. Bean here." Powers was a barefaced liar, and he saw I knew it. Anyone with half a glass eye could tell Diamond Dick was wishing I was in Hades or Hong Kong—anywhere but sitting side by side with Dulcima.

"That so?" I got up and shoved back my coat, letting him view the pistol in my sash. "Well then, let's us take the air and not bother the young lady, eh?"

Powers gave Dulcima a quick, sharp glance, then shrugged. "Good enough." By now he'd flipped his own coat open and I saw he was packing a pair of six-shooters in holsters.

Dulcima, looking from one of us to the other, with her own poker face, rose and placed a hand on my arm, smiling slightly. "Señor Bean, now isn't the proper time to finish our interesting chat. Perhaps we can continue it a later time."

"I expect the girls will be planning another horseback jaunt shortly. Why not plan to come along and we can talk—without so much interruption?" I bowed and kissed her fingertips to show the gambler that he wasn't the only one around San Diego with style.

But Powers stood off ignoring me as he lit up a stogie and scowled at the moon as it drifted on behind a pack of stormy-looking clouds.

Before I could say another word to Dulcima or Powers, Lucia, wrapped in a shawl and carrying another, came toward us. "There you all are! Sister's gone and taken herself a chill in this night air and Mother's ordered her off to bed this instant. It's a wonder that the three of us don't come down with something; this pretty imp here drove us so hard, preparing for our little musicale." She placed the shawl over Dulcima's shoulders, then looked back over her own shoulder. "And here come both of those pesky young officers. Now that Estrellita has bowed out of the scene, I imagine that it's up to Dulcima and myself to entertain them; at least Papa says we should. They haven't been to the casa before and Papa wants to remain friends with the Army," Lucia chattered on. "There'll be enough unrest hereabouts when the elections commence next month, so he says."

"That's all right. Mr. Powers and I were just about to take our leave," I said, repeating my *caballeroso* performance again with Lucia's own pretty fingertips, while Diamond Dick, without a word, shook hands with Dulcima.

"You don't mind, Roy?" Lucia wrinkled her pretty nose at me anxiously. "It was really great fun, wasn't it, and besides we are going for our ride tomorrow, aren't we?"

"I'll see you tomorrow afternoon at the usual time." And I walked off, with Powers stalking along at my side.

When we met the two young shavetails as they ambled toward the grape arbor, Powers muttered, "Too damned many folks around who don't know their place!"

I'd have answered him but we had to take our leave of Señor and Señora Bandini, both of us asking after Estrellita, and laying it on with the old folks about the fine time we'd had at the musicale.

Once outside the gate, I turned on Powers before he could open his mouth. "I heard your remark about folks not knowing their place and I just about locate you right in the middle of such a tribe! In other words, I'm warning you to keep your ugly face away from the Casa Bandini and Miss Dulcima in damn particular!"

Powers made a motion toward one of his holsters, but I stood my ground. I was close enough to crack him on his pointed jaw before he could draw a weapon. As the alcalde's brother it didn't behoove me to get into any sort of a brawl with his business rival, but the next minute, damned if the hothead didn't try to pull a gun on me anyway!

And half a minute later I was helping him back to his feet and dusting off his pretty white suit. I kept his six-shooter in my left fist, while I set about getting him steady on his pins.

I must have hit him mighty hard because he stood weaving in the moonlight like a poleaxed steer and blinking his eyes.

"What'd you sandbag me with?" he muttered, rubbing his jaw and waggling it from side to side. "You hadn't ought to have done that. All I was going to do was make you eat a little crow; I'm no dadburned killer, you know."

He stuck out his hand for his weapon, but I shook my head. "No dice, Mr. Powers! I tend to believe you might have just gotten enough grit to pull that trigger on me."

"Grit!" Powers back off and flipped open his coat. "By hell, I'll show you who's got grit. I never was afeard of the devil himself from the time I could walk." He shook a fist at me. "Put that pistol of mine in your fancy go-to-meeting sash and we'll just see who's got the sand!"

"No dice again! I hear you're a bearcat at fighting, but this is not worth going to war about." I turned my back on him and started off, half expecting to hear him slap leather.

"You Beans are all alike—crawfish cowards! Your fine brother plays hide-and-seek with those damned bandits instead of trying to run down such rascals as an alcalde's sworn to do. Well, election is coming and we'll see how he makes out then. But that's got nothing to do with you trying to lollygag around with Red Rosita's precious shirttail niece!"

"The way you've been trying to do ever since she came to town!" I'd spun around and had my hand on the butt of the Colt Navy. "And while we're trading insults, let me tell you there never was a Bean hatched that couldn't take on half a dozen tinhorns like you at once!"

Powers made a grab at his left-hand gun, but I had the pistol out and pointed straight at his midsection before he could take a breath.

"Bean, I haven't taken to you since I first caught sight of you, and the same goes for your redheaded gasbag of a brother!" He shook his fist at me again. "Now let me tell you one thing. I knew Dulcy before you did—and knew her mighty well!" He gave a dirty laugh.

"Where you knew her or when is none of my affair," I snapped, while my neck began to burn to think of this slippery sport and Dulcima. "There's just one thing for you to remember and paste in your fancy hat, and that's to keep plumb away from that young lady from now on. It's not just me talking, either. Señorita Almada orders you to stay in your own pasture—*comprende?*" And I kept the six-shooter pointed right at the middle button on his pretty vest.

Powers stood stock-still and then with a snort turned on his heel and stalked off toward his saloon. "Tomorrow we'll finish this and you will hear from me; don't forget it," he shouted as I shrugged and went on to my brother's casa.

The moon overhead was drowning in a sea of dirty silver clouds. "Well!" I thought. "Here's a devil of a way to end an almost perfect evening."

XVIII

"Got yourself into a hassle with that sidewinding Dick Powers?" Josh held his head and managed to get down some black coffee, served up by a silent but watchful Abraham.

I sat across the breakfast table from him in the alcalde's low-beamed dining room and looked seriously at Diamond Dick's personal Cold Navy as I polished it with a napkin and checked it over. "Where'd you hear that?"

"I took the liberty of mentioning it, Señor Roy." Poker-faced Abraham stepped up and poured some more Arbuckle for both of us. "It's all about town this morning. It seems Señor Powers has already inquired of the señor alcalde's new deputy, Agostín Haraszthy, for permission to hold the *duelo*. Such has been allowed, from time to time, hereabouts as an ancient Spanish custom."

"Confounded blackleg should have come to me for any permission," Josh grumbled, pecking at his flapjacks. "And that Haraszthy's already got his eye on my job—if those damned elections come out the wrong way."

"Seems to me you're more concerned with your job than my skin!"

"Never mind that. I've already sent word to Agostín I wouldn't allow any such fool thing in my town. So you needn't get a chill about it, anyhow."

"We'll see," was all I said. I was thinking of Dulcima and her sweet lips, and last night. If I punctured Diamond Dick just a little, it would show her who was cock of the walk and make him sing small for a change. It would also be a way of keeping him away from Rosita's ward—damaged! I recalled what Salazar had said about Dulcima, that she wasn't like other girls, and never would be. Her performance at the Bandinis' was some kind of proof of that, all right. She was certainly one amazing and talented young lady. But it bothered me that she had such strong, almost resentful feelings, toward Rosita. It could be a family matter, I supposed—a young filly just balking at being saddled and bridled at a strict finishing school, when she really just wanted to kick up her heels a bit and run free. I also found myself wondering what she actually knew of Rosita and particularly

Joaquín! Then, finally, I got to ciphering just what Diamond Dick Powers had been driving at when he bragged of knowing *Dulcy* before—and so blamed well.

Josh, who'd seemed to have forgotten all about that thump on the jaw I'd given him, held out his hand as I got up and thrust the pistol back into my sash and pulled on my jacket. "Where are you going, now?"

"Just up to the plaza."

"I felt we should talk some about those gold eagles you've been spreading around the country."

"Later!"

"Well, stay away from that tinhorn Powers; he'd do anything to put me in a bad light through you—and he's rattler-mean."

"I'll cut his rattles for him, but all in due time." I grinned and went out the hall and slammed the front door.

Twenty minutes later I had myself a private talk with the skinny, mournful-looking Agostín Haraszthy at the corner of Mason and Calhoun. Some folks were saying that as the successor to Sánchez, Agostín had enough to worry him, but he seemed to come by his gloomy air naturally.

"Well, señor, I guess if the alcalde says he's changed his mind, then you are at liberty to accept thees Diamond Deek's challenge. He has given me this to make it legal." And the deputy pulled out two folded slips of paper. "One is for you and the other for my records."

"Why didn't he send one to the alcalde—or to me?"

"He says that he is not on such good terms with either of you señores, and so delivered this to me to pass on to yourself." Haraszthy stared sadly at me, while I read the note, which was short and sweet.

I, Richard T. Powers, as the affronted party do hereby challenge one Roy Bean, known to be a hanger-on about San Diego, and a relative to that corrupt local official who calls himself Joshua Quincy Bean. The said duelo to be conducted with pistols on horseback at noon two days hence on the streets adjacent to the plaza of the Village of San Diego, California!

There was also a pencil scribble at the bottom:

Bean, I intend to take your hide in full view of the local populace, and a certain young lady, who shall remain nameless! Dick Powers.

Early in the afternoon I stopped by the Casa Bandini to see if the girls were ready to take a horseback jaunt along with Dulcima, but the old señora sent word down to the gate that Estrellita was still under the weather and all three young ladies were at siesta.

It looked as though she'd gotten wind of the upcoming fracas with Diamond Dick and had penned up the señoritas until things were over.

When I walked away, I caught sight of one of the girls at an upstairs window, waving a handkerchief and dabbing it at her eyes. I lifted my sombrero, giving the house a low bow, as I thought to myself that the señora would have herself a high time keeping those headstrong fillies close herded, Dulcima included.

I sauntered back to the Casa Lopez and got out my horse, saddling her up without being noticed by Josh. Abraham came sidling out into the adobe barn.

"Señor Roy rides out with the señoritas Bandini?"

"They're not riding out today. One of the señoritas is just a bit under the weather."

"Then the señor plans to ride toward Rancho las Fuentes?" Abraham proved right there that he was a first-class mind reader as far as I was concerned.

"Think it's dangerous over that way?" I asked as I led my roan out of the barn and swung up into the saddle.

"No, Señor Roy. I believe the roads are safe enough, but—"

"*Adiós*, then!" I gave my mount her head and we loped up the alley leaving the little Indian, a white blur in the velvety blue shadows.

When I racked past the plaza, turning the corner of Calhoun, I saw Diamond Dick Powers and a pair of his flunkies lounging in the shade by the Crossed Muskets. They only stared until Powers made some smart remark, then laughed with nasty expressions. One, a big, overgrown pug-ugly Hidalgo Montano, who was about the least likely Mexican in the whole of California to be confused with any genuine *hidalgo*, yanked a dirty thumb across his neck and lolled out his tongue; then I left them covered with dust and was gone.

Outside of town the day was fine for late summer as great curdled white clouds drifted eastward from the ocean and hundreds of birds continued to sweep up out of the scrub and grass ahead of us. Over in the shimmering, lavender distance, where the Lagunas bulked, several pairs of dark wings hung motionless in the fleece-spangled blue, as if painted there, and I recalled Salazar cursing out the thoughtless selfishness of the prospectors who'd killed such monarchs of the heavens in order to get their wing-tip quills to tote their gold dust.

If Rosita would really level with me about Kirker's hoard and I could locate that huge pile of gold, then we'd need a lot more than a flock of California vultures' wing tips to transport that treasure.

And wouldn't all that glittering gold open up Dulcima's pretty eyes about as wide as they could be? There were a couple of flies in the ointment, of course, such as Francisco Almada and his murderous sidekick—that other half of Joaquín Murieta, Inc.! I'd have to make some sort of deal with them, if it came to that, or keep as far away from them as possible. I knew one thing, though: it wouldn't be with that loco Carlos Hechavarría if I could help it.

So on I rode at a brisk clip, keeping my eyes open for any sort of trouble, but I had a mighty good idea that Abraham had his own way of knowing if there were any outlaws in the area. He seemed to know just about everything that went on, in and out of the Almada rancho.

The countryside was peaceful and lonesome, but I did see a column of dust coming up from the south around two o'clock, and finally a party of men, some on mules and a few on horseback, but kept my distance. From the racket they were making, I guessed them to be another bunch of half-drunken miners on their way back up to the northern diggings. I noticed they were traveling on one of the wagon roads that bypassed town, and guessed they'd heard of the San Diego alcalde's hard-nosed attitude toward rowdy mobs passing through his bailiwick.

They were bawling the ditty about Joaquín running off with the mules when they ambled out of sight beyond La Cañada de los Coches, and I wondered what they'd really do if they should come headfirst onto Joaquín himself!

Racking on between the brush-covered Lagunas and then wending through the Valley of the Old Women, I still kept an eye peeled for any sort of ambush, for I was certainly right spang in the middle of Murieta country, if ever there was such a place. All remained calm as cream, with the breeze riffling the scattered willows and black oak into green-and-yellow shimmers of colored light and sending little golden dust devils dancing along in front of us.

Once rounding a blind curve, a beautiful mountain lion burst out of the roadside brush on the lope, hard on the heels of a scrambling wild hog. My mount reared and plunged, but the big cat gave us just one quick, green-eyed stare and was gone into the scrub after his squealing dinner.

I fought the mare to a standstill, wiped the sweat from my face, then really put the steel to her and left that place in a hurry.

Within the hour I was passing little scattered farms with their small flocks of sheep, and skirting the humpbacked bulk of Mount Selix, now beginning to flame with masses of Indian paintbrush and the last of the season's poppies. Another hour and I came out on the Allison's Springs road, turning to the northeast at the tavern where I'd waited for Rosita Almada and wound up spending part of the night with Joaquín Murieta.

Riding on, I soon crested the last hill and sat breathing my mount, and looking over toward Rancho las Fuentes. The long yellow wall fronting the buildings was still spangled with vines but the roses of summer were withered and gone, while the woods behind the place seemed more lonely than ever. The surrounding orchards were now brave with the fruit of peach, pear and apple, yet somehow the entire establishment had an oddly deserted look.

I kicked up the mare and rode across the mesa to the rancho, and dismounted before the wall. Standing at the arched gate, I tugged the bell rope. The chiming of the bell inside mingled with the lacy whisperings of the fountains, yet it also seemed muffled and subdued. Tying up the roan at the hitch rail, I heard the groaning creak of the gate and turned to find the same ancient little servingman, José, standing in the archway.

"Señor Bean—"

"Would you tell Señorita Almada that I've come out to talk with her."

"She has gone, señor." The old man bowed crabwise as he motioned me onto the flagstone path. "Please to come up to the ranch house. I have a message from the señorita."

I sat in the big armchair on the porch and read and reread the letter that José had fetched, while the splash of the fountains echoed through the empty courtyard.

Señor,

Pardona for this hasty note, but circumstance has so dictated. I am forced to close up the rancho again, and travel to San Francisco.

My brother suffers, from time to time, the effects of a wound taken in the war against the Yankees. This now demands an immediate visit to a proficient physician at Yerba Buena. I shall accompany him, along with some of his retainers.

Dulcima has been sent funds and instructed to proceed back to her school by the first of the month. Now, I beg of you, see that fellow Powers stays away from her! I've recently learned some unsettling facts —and shall deal with her when I am able.

Again, pardona for such a greeting, and believe me when I assure you that I planned to visit Casa de Oro that night but Francisco

preceded me—and I was then forced, at the last moment, to bring him
a most urgent message!
   Another time, perhaps?
   P.S. Have no fear of J.M. All have gone northward.

I lounged back, looking at the courtyard. Here and there a stray, wind-blown leaf scuttled and scratched along the flagstones, a solitary butterfly hovered near a tattered rosebush and a bird or two called from the neighboring trees. But it was all so different from that merry moonlit night of not so long ago. For another moment I watched Rosita's empty hammock swing gently in the shadows, then got up and bade goodbye to old José.

There was a long, lonely ride ahead back to San Diego, and a noonday meeting mañana with a gent called Diamond Dick.

I had a hard time settling down that night, though I tried to read a new yellowback, *The Prisoners of the Aztecs.* Josh was out until way past midnight, meeting with the Bandinis, the Torreses and other influential Spanish-Americans, plotting out his campaign for the upcoming elections.

When he did get home and opened my door to stand staring at me and pulling his chin whiskers, he growled like a sore-tailed bear. "So! You confounded lunkhead, you went and let that tinhorn Powers finagle you into a crazy duel after all! And I hear tell you've told my feather-brained deputy Agostín that I said it was all okay. Well, just one thing—" he gave his whiskers a violent tug—"you'd best shoot danged straight, because that jasper is known to be black death with a pistol!"

"I thought you'd kibosh things if you heard."

"No, it's gone too far now. It can't be said that I've got myself a blamed coward for a relation!"

"Might hurt your election hopes, eh?"

"No such damned thing! Just you see that you don't do more than wing him good, though. If anybody's killed, I'd have to put the other in the *calabozo* sure as sin." Josh glared at me and then slammed the door behind him, only to reopen it again. "Now, you know full well, Roy, that I'm behind you all the way. Hell, you're my kid brother. But for the love of Lazarus, watch yourself tomorrow!" He shut the door easy that time.

I blew out the lamp and rolled over. For a while I kept seeing Dulcima's face in the dark, but it kept changing into that of the wistful little girl of the daguerreotype who had been Dulcima. Presently, for some reason, Rosita swept into my drowsy half dreams, with her curves, brilliant eyes and masses of flame-tinted hair blowing in a cloud about her sensuous features. Then hard-eyed Dick Powers crowded before both girls, swaggering through the darkness with a big deadly pistol in each hand. For a long moment a strange chill crept in waves over me, and then I seemed to loose my clutch on existence and dropped away into empty nothingness, and slept without another dream to my name.

XIX

I got up late next morning cursing out Abraham for not waking me earlier. Scrambling from my rumpled bed, I washed and shaved carefully, then dressed in the very best duds I owned. The black velvet trousers and silk shirt I bought up at Los Angeles, were topped off with a gold-embroidered vest set with a swarm of small shining pearl buttons in several different patterns, including that of an eagle, or perhaps a California vulture, in full flight across the back of the garment.

Looking myself over in my washstand mirror, I decided that maybe I wasn't the caballero to end all such dudes, but I still came pretty close after all!

Strange to remark, I wasn't one bit edgy, but when I sat down to a late breakfast and heard the old hall clock boom out eleven times, my cup of coffee began to try to hop from my hands. I attempted another sip, then gave it up as poor business.

"Where's the alcalde?" I asked Abraham, waving off the little Indian and his coffeepot. "And by the way, why didn't you tell me Señorita Almada had closed the rancho and left the territory?"

"I'm right here." Josh came into the room, dressed to the nines in his very best alcalde get-up: gold-encrusted jacket, green waist sash and flaming orange pantaloons, with his largest golden ring in his ear.

"Where'd you come from? You look like you're just in from some fandango, or been selling snake oil."

"Never you mind about that! And I think somebody's said to beware of the sort of enterprises that demand new clothes," snapped Josh, "so it looks as though we're both mighty stylish for a funeral. I hope to high heaven that it won't be yours. But you remember what I told you about any actual killing." He tugged at his goatee, a sure sign he was on the prod. "And what's this about that hellcat of an Almada gal? She's gone and cleared off?"

"Yes." I was short with Josh. I didn't take kindly to his language. "I'm going out to saddle up. It's getting on for noon, and I'm not going to be late for that sidewinder of a diamondback!"

Josh followed me out back to the adobe barn, behind the casa, and pitched in with Abraham to help saddle up my mare. "Here, take this." My brother handed me his personal silver-mounted pocket Colt with pearl handles. I stuck it into my sash, along with Powers's Navy. The gambler's pistol was a .36 caliber, while Josh's was only a .31, but two hands were better than one—and maybe two six-shooters!

When I rode down Mason and turned into Calhoun toward the plaza, my eyes really opened up. The entire plaza and the streets around it were decorated fit for a fiesta! Red and blue banners looped across the streets between buildings, bunting drooped from the trees and a big American flag flapped lazily in the fresh breeze, humming across from the sparkling waters of the bay. The streets were crowded with natives and visitors from out in the country. Peddlers wandered through the chattering crowds selling tortillas and meat pies, and both saloons seemed to be doing a brisk business, from the drunken shouts and catcalls echoing around the plaza. There even was a four-piece band in the plaza itself.

The bells in the old mission, down by the fort, were chiming the noon hour as I pulled up my mare and looked around for Powers, but the first person I recognized was Dulcima. Dressed in a flame-red gown, with a brightly colored mantilla, she stood under one of the pepper trees, both Bandini sisters at her side. All three fluttered handkerchiefs and called to me, but the off-tune brass band had begun to blare out some Mexican polka. I lifted my sombrero, then turned to find Agostín Haraszthy at the side of my horse, looking more down-in-the-mouth than usual. "Just over there, señor, I've had these next street roped off, from Twiggs to the next corner of these plaza. Señor Powers awaits you there. Let us go over and get this thing finish!"

When we got to the other side of the plaza, Diamond Dick, mighty somberly dressed in a coal-black broadcloth suit and dove-gray sombrero, was standing beside his beautiful white stallion, White Lightning.

A pack of his hangers-on were grouped about the roped-off street shouting boasts at all and sundry who'd placed bets with them—and there'd been one devil of a lot of wagers placed, according to Haraszthy.

"Here are the rules, Señor Bean," Haraszthy began as the uproar grew and the infernal band, squealing and thumping, came marching over to our side of the square, leading more onlookers, including the girls, who must have outtalked Señora Bandini.

"The rules say," the deputy doggedly went on, "that when I fire my *pistola*, you both shall ride to opposite ends of the roped-off street, and on my second shot, you shall ride toward each other, firing as you please. But only at each other. If anyone else should be struck, and some of these folks seem bound to get in the way, then I must halt the affair and take the one responsible for the shot to our *calabozo!*"

I nodded and rode back to my end of the street after Haraszthy had lifted the ropes aside. Powers was mounted now and galloping back to his end of Twiggs, for all the world like some funeral director on horseback who was in a big rush to get on with the services.

I made up my mind right there that he wouldn't be around to attend my services, if I had anything to do with it!

Bang! went the deputy's six-gun while the crowd whooped, flags fluttered in the freshening sea winds and the band snarled into some sort of a Mexican bullring serenade; then the second shot cracked out.

I put the spurs to Brown Bess and charged toward Powers on his big white horse, while half a dozen mongrels cavorted along at our heels. Just about when I was halfway to Powers, who still sat with hands on his pommel, I caught the flash of something metallic on the roof of one of the nearby buildings. But I kept on the lope, Navy in my right fist and my reins in my left.

Whack! Whack! Where Powers had gotten those guns so fast I never knew, but he was coming at me like a white-lightning bolt, firing as fast as he could with both pistols, reins in his teeth.

We thundered past each other, cracking away, and were halfway down the street before either could rein up in a cloud of dust and gravel. The ringing air was suddenly jammed with silence, then the crowd whooped, all shrilly meaner than ever, like a bullfight mob on the lookout for blood!

Again we were headed for each other, as fast as we could spur the horses. With just one shot left in the Navy, I rammed it back into my sash and grabbed for Josh's .31 peashooter. It was about all I had left, and I knew I had to get close enough to do any damage. *Whack! Bang!* And there came Diamond Dick, eyes glaring out of his poker face. The last of his shots snatched off my sombrero with a blow on the scalp, carrying all the punch of a sledgehammer! Blood poured down my face as my head whirled, but I still snapped two shots as we flashed past again, and I got him!—for he swayed in the saddle, grabbing at his shoulder and dropping a pistol, then made a wild attempt to haul in his mount as both crowd and band shrilled like infernal maniacs.

Wheeling my horse and scattering those blamed curs, who seemed as hot for excitement as anyone in the clamoring crowd, I was headed back to my end of the street when I glimpsed that flash again—a gun barrel on the roof!

That rifle boomed from atop the building and a bullet slammed the pearl-handled Colt from my hand, plowed through the saddle and my mount's spine. I hit the dirt as Brown Bess rolled over stone-dead, and yanked the Navy from my sash. Another rifle ball bored the ground at my feet, throwing grit and stones into my face, but I got off my last shot and saw a man stagger to the roof's edge and plunge headlong into the roadway!

Before I could wipe the blood and dust from my face, Powers had recovered and was coming full tilt at me, gun in his left hand and aimed straight at my head. But he pulled up short as Josh broke out of the silent crowd with the musketoon Francisco Almada had left me at the Casa de Oro!

"Back off, Powers!" Josh poked the mean little weapon right into the gambler's face. "This is loaded with fire and brimstone, all set for you." He jerked his head at the body of Hidalgo Montano where the no-good lay facedown, with that pack of frisky mutts sniffling him over. "You've had your duel and you've lost the pot—including your back-shooter!"

"Yeah, you've had your infernal *duelo* right enough, Mr. Diamondback," I said, rubbing the blood and dirt out of my eyes. "And I guess its your own hide nailed to the barn door, ain't it—along with your pet skunk's?"

I'd have said more, but Agostín Haraszthy took my arm and tugged me through the cheering, hat-tossing crowd. "Come along, Señor Roy; like I tell you, if you shoot each other that's your business. But anyone else, even such a one as these Montano, then it's my business."

I stared at Josh, who was following us, along with a mighty soberlooking Abraham. "What's this? Are you going to let him pull me in for trying to save my neck?"

"Go along, Roy," Josh fingered his scrubby goatee, but kept that deadly little blunderbuss at the ready. "I'm sworn to uphold the law, and I've got to back up my officers as well as my relatives. Go along and I'll handle matters."

"Handle matters?" I stared at him. "I get it! The old politics again. Well, go by your blamed book if you want, but I'm just about fed up with this town and you both!"

I gawked around for Dulcima and the Bandini sisters but couldn't spot them in the milling crowd, and guessed the old señora had herded them back to the casa. Powers wasn't in sight at all, nor any of his bigmouthed gang.

"I'll be back, Roy, so just sit tight." Then Josh and Abraham also made themselves scarce—and mighty soon *I was sitting tight,* right in San Diego's *calabozo!*

I was so frazzled from being knocked out of the saddle and from my scalp wound that after I was bandaged up by the jailor I stretched out on the canvas cot in my cell without even shucking off my boots. So there I lay, tossing and turning and even shivering, for it wasn't every day that I shot and killed another human, even one so low-down as Hidalgo Montano. At last I drifted into an uneasy sleep.

I don't know how long I slept, but something jolted me out of a deep slumber—a crash, then another shuddering crash that shook the whole building. Muffled shouts and curses exploded out front, along with the thudding of many feet and jangling of keys. Raising myself up on one elbow, I saw a batch of torches flaring their way toward me down the dark hallway.

"Come on, Bean! Come out of there, you damned killer! Here's your midnight date with the rope!" And there loomed a knot of figures, bulky and misshapen in white sheets and robes pulled over their heads.

But their hands were free and filled with weapons; one of them unlocked the barred door to my cell. One hooded rascal reached out for me but staggered back, cursing in gasps from a well-placed boot in the breadbasket. Then that masked mob fell on me and began to drag me from my cell, muttering muffled threated and curses.

As I was lugged through the echoing hallway, kicking and punching at my faceless captors, their sputtering torches flung a pack of goblin shapes along the walls until it seemed I was hurried hellward by a batch of the devil's own.

They'd just shoved me headfirst out into the jailor's office when another bunch of masked men charged through the front door, guns in hand!

Caught flat-footed, my abductors froze in their tracks, dropped weapons and torches, and hoisted hands roofward without a mutter.

"That's right, you white-sheeted coyotes! Down on your ugly faces and grab yourself some sleep! You're already in your night shirts, ain't you?"

I scrambled up and took a good look at the four masked strangers in the torchlight. All wore range clothes and used bandanas for masks. The one doing all the talking was just over five feet in height—the Flea! His taller companion was also definitely Army—Corporal Bates! And the other pair, I recognized at once despite the old clothes: Josh and Abraham!

XX

"Come on, Roy!" Josh shoved me toward the doorway. "Let's get out of here, pronto!" But he stopped to bend over one of the figures on the floor, yanking away its hood.

Diamond Dick Powers lay there grinding his teeth with pain and pure rage and clutching his bandaged shoulder, eyes glittering in the torchlight.

"You were so damned curious about the Men of the Night, eh? Well, take yourself a good look at their blamed captain!" Josh gave Powers a boot in the ribs, then signaled the Flea and the others to get to work. In less than five minutes each member of the lynch team was hogtied with their own rope and roughly rolled into a corner of the room.

"What about them there?" The Flea indicated the jailor and deputy, where they lay bound and gagged in an opposite corner of the office.

"Use what you call a brain," Corporal Bates snapped. "They're th' law here, and once loose they'll be askin' questions—like who are you and who am I; then that bunch of killers on th' floor will have some more scalps to go after!"

"Right!" Josh muttered. "Leave now. We'll send help later."

While Abraham stood at the door, with a torch in one hand and a pistol trained on the trussed-up prisoners, we went out to the hitching rail in front of the *calabozo*. The night was still crisply brittle with stars, while a fitful breeze drifted in from the bay to whisper through the trees. I looked over the lineup of horses, recognizing Jack Dolan's gray, Carlos Castro's paint and even Diamond Dick's great stallion, White Lightning—all midnight mounts of a lynch mob, made up of the gamblers, plug-uglies and hangers-on from Powers's Crossed Muskets.

Bates tossed over a bedroll, while Joshua Quincy unstrapped his six-gun and handed belt and pistol to me. "There's a change of clothes in that roll, along with a duster and some money." He peered narrowly at me in the starlight. "I take it you haven't much of that gold left—or have you?"

"Mighty little." I strapped the six-shooter on and then tied the bedroll behind the saddle of Powers's White Lightning.

"You may not have the hang of stayin' out of trouble, but you sure know how to judge good horseflesh," snickered the Flea, emerging back from the *calabozo* with an armload of weapons.

"I figure that diamondback in there owes me one good horse," I said, adjusting the stirrups and untying the reins before swinging up into the saddle. "What now?"

"You make yourself good and scarce! Light a shuck for Los Angeles or farther north, then we'll see what happens." Josh fingered his goatee.

"I don't want that horned toad of a Powers to think he ran me out of town," I said, gentling the great horse as it sidestepped nervously with a strange rider on its back.

"It's not like you haven't been chased out of a town before," Josh snorted, but I could see that he was restless for me to take to the tall timber. "If you stay here, it's right back into the pokey until I can get us a lawyer; my jurisdiction only goes so far. That pea brain of a Haraszthy thinks he's got an iron-plated charge against you for plugging Powers's pet coyote, and it'll take some doing to get it dismissed. And, in spite of catching Diamond Dick red-handed, he can still stir up a heap of trouble for you—and me."

"That slippery sidewinder'll go and claim he's a bona fide vigilante and wriggle out of it somehow," volunteered Bates.

"And you and I won't get out of anythin' ourselfs if we don't get our tails back to th' fort," the Flea said as he dumped the raiders' weapons into a rain barrel. "They change guards at five and that blue-bellied Brown would just hone to get us on report for bein' off post!"

Already a pale thread of light was inching out across the eastern mountain gloom as the stars' luster dimmed.

Josh ordered Abraham from the *calabozo*. "High time for us all to scatter." He lit a lucifer on his bootheel and inspected his watch. "Four o'clock!"

Bates and the Flea shook hands before forking their nags for the fort, the Flea calling out his parting shot: "Next time, plug the right skunk and save us our sleep!"

"My hat's still in there somewhere," I told Josh, who motioned Abraham back into the jailhouse. The little Indian returned with his hands full of sombreros, which he handed up to me one by one. After the third try, I settled for a grey Stetson with a fancy silver-mounted band.

"I thought that one would do." Abraham gave one of his fleeting smiles.

The sombrero was Diamond Dick's!

"Seems you always know more than you let on," I said. "Like what's happening at Fountain Ranch and *who's coming and going!*"

While Josh unhitched his black mare from down the rail, Abraham stepped up to my horse's head. "Señor Roy, I was Captain Almada's body servant during the war, and am still loyal to Don Francisco and the señorita, though I have never been faithless, in principle, to your good brother. He has always treated me like a white man!" He unhitched his bay and stood waiting for Josh's commands.

"Let's get a move on, Roy. I'll ride out with you a piece." Josh guided his mount up beside us. "And you best ride over to Señor Bandini's and roust him up, Abraham. Say there's been a hell of a commotion at the *calabozo*, then skin for home!"

Abraham sat his saddle for a moment; then as I nudged my new mount up Wallace after Josh, the little servingman raised his hand in farewell and rode across the shadow-filled streets toward the Casa Bandini. And it gave me a stab, sharp as a stiletto, to think I was leaving that lovable pair of scapegrace sisters over there—and even more, Dulcima! I knew that I had myself two goals to gain: Kirker's gold and the daguerreotype girl.

"I'll go out with you as far as the river ferry," said Josh as I spurred up on Diamond Dick's great stallion. Then we clattered down the empty streets headed for the Camino Real.

A night bird or two called sleepily and the breeze, which had been complaining among the trees, began to grow as a storm commenced to crawl in from the ocean. Sheet lightning flashed crooked fingers through the drifting cloud banks, but the thunder's mumble was lost in the drumming of our horses' hooves.

By the time we'd loped out of town and were heading toward the woods, where Sánchez had met his end at the hand of Murieta, the east was daubed with crimson bars and the first shreds of amber were beginning to pour over the fading wall of night.

We reined in the horses at the edge of the timber and sat breathing them for a moment. "Shouldn't be anyone on your tail for a spell," said Josh, staring up at the cloud wrack sliding on toward the land. "Fact is, I told Abraham to report you as headed south for the border."

"He's a pure wonder," I said, watching the blazing rim of the sun bulge up over the distant mountains, then suddenly spill a golden flood across the dark horizon as another day was born.

"He's surely all of that. And it was his idea to get Corporal Bates and that sawed-off pardner of his out of Fort Stockton. How he did it I couldn't guess—but that's Abraham for you."

By now the storm was drifting off to the south as the thunder growled away into a muted mutter, while the lofting sun burned into the wind-driven clouds until they seemed turned into peaks of pure molten gold.

"Looks like the weather'll be passable," said Josh, squinting at his watch again. "But this here's not the best place to be catching a body's breath." He stared over at the twisted old tree where Sánchez had dangled in the lonely winds.

"I wouldn't bother much over Sánchez—or Murieta."

"And how'd you know?"

"Just a feeling," I answered, then changed the subject. "How in the world did Sánchez get mixed up with that gang of lynchers?"

"Oh, Sánchez was always too damned eager to heave his weight around, and I guess Diamond Dick got to him and made him feel a lot more important than he was. The whole thing had to be Powers's doings. He knew that I was a hard-nosed law-and-order man; in fact when he first showed up I had to warn him about crooked moves with the cards and dice. Then we were rivals in business, so I guess he thought that if he could make out that I was unable to handle matters or control the midnight riders—and I've got to admit that I pulled out my hair more than once—it would smear my name worse than mud when the elections finally came around." Josh tugged at his goatee with nervous fingers. "Yep, Diamond Dick's one fellow who likes to plan ahead. Shouldn't wonder, in spite of last night, or maybe because of it, that he announces his candidacy when the time comes!"

"But I'd have thought that his plans had backfired for good."

"No, you don't know that rattler, even now. He'll claim to be a real public-spirited citizen, like Corporal Bates says. And it'll be his word against mine—with you on the scout."

"That takes care of the question I had for you," I said, fishing out Kirker's gold eagle from my vest pocket and flipping it over to Josh. "Guess I owe you one in return."

"What's this?" As my brother held the coin up to the sunlight, it flashed with a glinting fire all its own. "Thought you were stone broke."

"It's the last of what took care of your tax money—but also the answer to where there's a thundering lot more of the same—if I can figure out exactly where!"

Then I proceeded to tell my brother the story of Jeff Kirker and his secret hoard, leaving out any mention of Rosita or Francisco Almada.

Josh's eyes took on some of the coin's gleam as he inspected the little gold piece. "You know where?"

I reached out and took the coin back, studying the cryptic, manmade inscriptions again for the thousandth time. "No, I said I didn't know—yet. But I surely intend to. Tell you what, when you fold your tent down here, come up to San Francisco and join me," I enthused. "We'll form an expedition to locate the cache. And split right down the middle, fifty-fifty."

"I'm not about to fold any tents yet," Josh bristled and then stiffened in his saddle. "By gobs, there come some riders from town. Could be that fool of a Haraszthy or someone. You get along from here, and I've got to get myself out of sight in a hurry before they spot me!" He pushed out a hand and grabbed mine. "When you find a roost—Frisco, you say?—drop me a note from there and then, just maybe, we can go out hunting your bullion later on—providing it's still there. You're not figuring that Murieta would be looking for his own gold, are you?"

"I can chance that, I guess," I said, shaking his hand as I took myself a fast look at the approaching dust. The horsemen were too far off yet to see us, but it was time to be on the fly.

"Adiós!" I put the spurs to White Lightning and we leaped up the road, crested the hill and started down toward the river ferry.

"Get in touch with Salazar," Josh called. "He'll give you the lowdown on that place and the rest of the country up there." Then he turned off into the woods and was out of sight.

I rode down to the riverbank and looked around for the flatboat man, then saw there'd be no use waiting for him to go to work, for the old Mexican lay out under a tree with a pair of empties beside him, snoring the mosquitoes away. It looked like he'd also had himself a bad night.

Behind me the riders were in plain sight now, loping down the sloping road and whipping up their horses. I caught their distant shouts, though I couldn't yet make out the words.

Before me the river stretched wide and jammed with sandbars, but it was down considerable from the lack of recent rains. So when I heard that first shot crack out, I didn't waste a second!

With the second slug already keening by my head, I kicked White Lightning into the river, and we lunged and thrashed our way across the stream, scrambling up over a shoal of gravel and sand, then back into deeper water on the far side, coming, at last, to the steep cutbank. Here the great horse really showed his mettle, for, though he was somewhat winded by the struggle, he only snorted, shook his head and pawed his way up the treacherous incline onto solid ground, to unloose a triumphant neighing salute at both horses and riders across the river.

"*Alto! Alto, Señor Bean!*" And be damned if it wasn't that long-faced Agostín Haraszthy and another Mexican named Chávez. Apparently they'd trailed me north instead of toward the border. Haraszthy was a sleepy sort of a fox after all.

"You want something?" I yanked out Josh's pistol and held it where both lawmen couldn't miss the weapon glittering in my hand. "I leave something at the *calabozo*, when you so kindly let in those murdering coyotes to lynch me? I'm sorry but I just don't have time to sit around parlying right now."

"No, señor, you didn't leave anything, even yourself. You know, you still got to stand court for shooting Hidalgo Montano! We just got to be all law-abiding about these sort of business." He started to hoist his six-gun, then thought better of it, as I threw down on him and his pardner. "An' it won't do much good to resist, señor. You only make it bad—for yourselfs and your honorable brother, the alcalde!"

"Hey there, you sure got yourselfs a hell of a horse all right," Chávez yelled, with a big grin, as he tried to stay in my good graces, in spite of the fact that he was more ready and willing than able to get the drop on me.

"That reminds me," I shouted back, "where's that slippery low-life who used to own this poor horse?"

"Back at town, senor," the deputy bellowed. "An' he's swearing out the warrant for taking off his horse there, so there's gonna be two charges now. You better come back and straighten them out!"

"Haraszthy, you're even dumber than you look. I don't know what Diamond Dick pulled to wiggle out of his law-abiding raid on the jail, but I'm not about to come back to your flea bite of a town—" And I was about to add more when someone opened up on the pair from the woods. Three bullets clipped through the sunlight, shrilling away with screaming ricochets. The bay and black reared and plunged with alarm, almost throwing Chávez, while Haraszthy only stayed aboard by dropping his pistol and grabbing leather to his bosom in a desperate clutch.

"Too bad," I yelled across at the deputy and the deputized. "Looks like Murieta's right on your tracks! Guess you're next to decorate that tree back there!"

They gave their frantic horses their heads and plunged off toward the river mouth and nearby beach, out of sight and gone for good.

I gentled the big stallion, looking back up the hill toward the woods.

There rode out both Josh and Abraham, the latter lifting a long rifle in a last salute while Josh waved his sombrero.

I threw up my hand, then turned White Lightning and headed up the Camino Real through the brilliant sunlit morning.

XXI

Heading north along the Camino Real, I stared back toward San Diego, but there wasn't a single soul on the empty roadway. The river willows had dwindled from sight below the gently rolling land, and far beyond them the storm, so threatening in the early morning, was just a dirty-gray patch upon the sunny blue stretching over Mexico. And once again gawking backward, I saw a faint flash of lighting, no more than a flying spark struck from a distant cloud, its thunder less than a rusty whisper.

So that was the way my troubles were fading, I figured. Plumb fizzling away. And here, at last, I was on my way toward that hidden bonanza. Riding onward, I dwelt on that golden hoard with all the downright pleasure of some skinflint miser, counting it and fondling it around in my mind until I lost all thought of just how that sort of gold came to be out there in the northern wilds. I completely forgot those dead men who'd perished because of that gold—the six unlucky troopers, and even that likable but treacherous Jeff Kirker himself!

Sometime later, when my road bent toward the coast, I came out of my daydreams and took a last look in the direction of San Diego—and my brother Joshua. Well, I told the sea breezes, that would be the very last town they'd run me from, for there'd be a new sort of Roy Bean around, shortly—a young man of very ample means. Just as soon as I could discover those means!

Then I gave up all woolgathering and, putting the spur to White Lightning rode on so briskly, even loping right past El Ruiseñor, the roadside groggery, that I arrived in time for dinner at the Santa Anna.

After the meal, while I waited out front for my horse, a nattily dressed, middle-aged fellow in a hard-boiled hat sauntered out from somewhere in the tavern just about the time the hostler fetched up the great stallion.

"Magnificent animal, sir." This gent, who spoke with an Irish brogue, took off his hat, lifting it in a sort of salute to the horse. He replaced the lid and leaned back on his gold-headed walking stick.

I allowed that I certainly was aware of my good choice in horseflesh and put a foot into my stirrup, when the stranger's next comment kept my feet planted on the ground.

"If I mistake not, I've beheld that noble brute before." He tugged at his drooping red mustaches and leaned over for a closer look at the flank of the animal. "Ah, *Diamond-A!* Why, sir, I've seen that steed many times upon the very streets of San Francisco. A well-known sporting man, the owner—"

"Diamond Dick Powers?" I eased my hand down near the butt of my Navy Colt. I didn't know what this gabby jasper was up to—and I wanted to be on my way, but not with a horsethief posse behind me.

"Ah, yes! A strong patron of the arts, Mr. Richard Powers. And the very person who fetched that dazzling young Lorette La Fonte to our establishment." He waved an appreciative hand at the sky. "You see me here, awaiting the next down stage to San Diego. Stopped off here at San Juan Capistrano yesterday to break the journey and conduct a bit of business." He pointed to several gaudy posters affixed upon some of the tree trunks and stuck on the sides of the building:

> The McGuire Traveling
> Opera and Theatrical Company
> Featuring
> The Famous Julia Deane
> The Incomparable Caroline Chapman
> Will Soon Be Appearing
> In Your City
> Along with That Dynamic Talent
> Lorette La Fonte!

"This Miss La Fonte wouldn't be known as Señorita Dulcima Almada?"

"Exactly!" The man lifted his hat again. "Permit me? I'm Major Thomas Mulcahey McGuire, sole proprietor of the world-renowned Jenny Lind Opera Theater at San Francisco—and San Diego is where I expect to meet with Mr. Richard Powers in an attempt to gain the full services of his protégé, Señorita Dulcima, otherwise Mademoiselle La Fonte!"

"Roy Bean." I lifted my sombrero to the fellow. "When you meet Mr. Powers, you might mention that I thank him kindly for the loan of his horse. But this La Fonte business, how'd that come about?" I still couldn't see how this Irish showman and Diamond Dick were about to get Dulcima away from her legal guardian, Rosita.

"Really quite simple." McGuire proudly pointed his cane at one of the

gaudy green-and-orange posters. "Powers had heard that our young Lotta
Crabtree was down sick and fetched Mistress Dulcima around to try out
for her part." The showman smiled and wagged his head at the recollection. "The girl was nothing short of a smashing success. Took to the songs
and patter like a duck to a puddle. I had a short talk with Powers right
after that weekend at my theater on the outskirts of the city, the McGuire
Palazzo."

"But?"

"But she vanished, and after Powers had told me his young thespian
had wanted to work at the theater full time! But I went ahead with plans
for a road company—traveling shows to the hinterlands and the camps."

"And you included this Miss—La Fonte on your handbills, along with
the other ladies?"

"Exactly. I took a flyer, you might say. But she'll make a champion turn
if I can get her. The girl's so versatile. She sings, dances, and can act with
the very best of them."

"I know!"

"Ah, you've caught her at another theater?"

"More or less."

"Well, it's worrisome, for I've built up a good reputation in the past
couple of years, but I think I can track her down through Powers, and
then you'll see if she doesn't become a great favorite. Even better than
flashy Lola Montez or that fancy Red Rosita! Ah, there's a pair of fiery
fillies for you—" He was about to rattle on, when the down stage from Los
Angeles heaved into sight and I got aboard White Lightning.

"Come by the Jenny Lind when you're in Frisco and you'll see a great
show!" McGuire handed me a couple of passes before hustling back into
the tavern for his luggage.

"Thanks. I'll take you up on that—especially if this Miss La Fonte is on
hand," I called after the Irishman, and, giving White Lightning his head,
I went racking up the road toward Los Angeles.

An hour or so later, with the tang of the ocean filtering through the
wind, I came to the same point where Salazar and I had sat our horses and
stared out across the limitless Pacific. I turned off the main road, guiding
my mount down the same little sandy lane, past the clump of cypress and
over the hill. And there it was, somehow different from the stretch of
water at San Diego. Here the wild sweep of emptiness again brought to
mind all that lonely vastness of the great grass ocean I'd wandered over
not so long ago, blown along by the never-ceasing winds.

For a spell I watched the tall white clouds lofting along the glittering horizon like towering mountains of snow and wondered if they had sailed from as far as China or those distant Sandwich Islands. It would be fine to visit such places, I thought, and made up my mind to do such traveling. And I planned to do that just as soon as I got my hands on that secret hoard. I'd be doing the jaunting to such places with Dulcima, of course; I had not the slightest doubt!

The slanting sun was already tinting those clouds peaks with glints of gold and flaming orange as it began its downward surge toward the Pacific. It was high time to get under way, and I turned White Lightning back onto the Camino Real, settling down to the serious business of making time.

There were few people abroad as I neared Los Angeles in the purple haze of the twilight. A train of woodcutters followed a small herd of beef cattle, the patient little mouse-colored mules ambling along in the dusty wake of the bawling steers. I passed all such travelers with the rush of the wind, as my horse seemed to take a pleasure in leaving everyone, animal and human, far to the rear of our dust. Now I could see how Diamond Dick had gained such a reputation for his long riding. With such animals he was a match for even Joaquín himself.

A big fall moon was drifting over the eastward mountains as I rode past the first of the haciendas fringing the pueblo of Los Angeles. For a long minute, as it hung in the silvery blue of early evening, it looked for all the world like a huge, glowing Chinese lantern and I thought of the night I'd first met the Bandinis and the last time I'd sat out on their tree-bowered patio under such Chinese lanterns. That had been the night the daguerre-otype girl had become the dashing and delightful Dulcima herself.

I turned down a side road toward the town's center and found myself riding through the shabby Calle de los Negros, with its roughs and lowlifes who still lounged in front of the lantern-lit gambling dens in their battered sombreros and tattered serapes. Most of these folks seemed in low enough spirits or were too drunk to bother taking note of my passage, except for one down-at-the-heels fellow who howled out in Spanish that if I was looking for a proper thrashing he was just the rooster to do the job. I'd had enough scrapping to last me for a good long spell and kicked up my horse and rode on through the alley.

Dismounting in front of Wagner's Saloon, I stood looking about myself. It was now quite dark and the sperm-oil lanterns, mounted upon posts in front of every other place, flickered away like little yellow moons, while the moon itself, now high over the hills, was pouring its light down into

the dusty streets of town and silvering the hulking ramparts and outbuild-
ings of old Fort Gillespie on its pine-strewn mountain west of Los Angeles.

In the pale light, the cathedral's twin towers quietly lofted into the
gently shining sky like two translucent hands reaching toward the heavens.

Los Angeles seemed just then about as peaceable as its jawbreaking
name: *El Pueblo de Nuestra Señora la Reina de Los Angeles de Porciúncula*—or in plain Yankee lingo, the Town of Our Lady the Queen of the
Angels of Porciúncula.

I tied up my horse in front of the saloon where Salazar and I had
stopped when first we got to Los Angeles, and went in for a dust-cutter
before supper. Pushing through the batwings, who should I meet coming
out but old Sheriff Persifer? He looked me over and then caught sight of
White Lightning.

"Well, now, Mr. Bean, ain't it?" He stood in the doorway, shook my
hand and then took another gander at the hitching rack. "And, if I don't
mistake, that'd be one of Dick Powers's animals. Am I right?"

"Right! Powers insisted that I borrow one of his horses so I wouldn't
need to travel by stage. I'm on my way up to San Francisco on business for
my brother, the alcalde." It was a mite thin but it was all I could come up
with in a hurry, and the old lawman seemed to swallow it down.

He clapped me on the back and went on down the steps without seeming to give White Lightning another thought.

I changed my mind about that drink, unhitched the horse as soon as the
sheriff turned the corner, and rode over to the National Hotel on Los
Angeles Street. There I took my meal in the bar and then stayed put in
my room for the rest of the night.

It was scarce sunup when I checked out, got my horse from the stables
and was on my way from town—without breakfast. I didn't intend on
running into any more folks who seemed to pleasure in small talk about
Diamond Dick's horse—and lawmen in particular!

Threading our way through the crooked, ungraded streets in the growing light, I saw that Major Thomas Mulcahey McGuire was a man who
believed in backing his spoken word with the printed variety, for I
counted near a dozen bills pasted on adobe walls and tree trunks, pro-
claiming the approach of McGuire's Traveling Opera and Theatrical
Company.

A few of the bills were different from those I'd viewed at the Santa
Anna Taverna. The one that caused me to pull up staring was a gaudy

pink and yellow—with the full-length portrait of a flashy young lady who wore skimpy tights and little more than a wide smile. And it was no one else but Dulcima!

The artist seemed to have worked from a recent tintype, and I wondered just how and where it had been taken. Without her aunt's permission or knowledge, I'd be bound. No doubt the doings of that underhanded rascal Diamond Dick Powers. Small wonder that he'd bragged of having known that young lady before she lit in San Diego!

I reached over to the tree trunk and pulled the sheet off, folding it and placing it in my pocket. I'd take a closer look at it as I rode along. I still didn't want to spend much time in getting on up the Camino Real.

By early afternoon I was as hungry as a lobo wolf when I stopped at a roadside tavern, the General Lopez, twenty miles north of Los Angeles. I sat at a rough table, under a vine-covered bower, outside the establishment along with a half dozen Mexican drovers, all of us filling up on the excellent tamales and local beer. The cattlemen were on the way back down to Los Angeles to pick up another herd of beef cattle for the San Francisco markets.

Between mouthfuls, one of the good-natured rancheros remarked that his trade was booming, with cattle bought on the hoof at fifteen dollars a head fetching upwards of fifty dollars each at San Francisco.

"These gold diggers, they come down from these hills, and they want the best—eat and drink like a pack of loco coyotes!" The round-faced ranchero shook his head. "That is one town, señor, like no other. You been there?"

I informed him I was on my way and hoped to stay there for a while, once I got there.

"You go to hunt for these gold?"

"I might, but I'll wait and see."

"Good thing you go now, and not last summer. You heard?"

I'd read about that June-time commotion in the *Alta California* but hadn't given it much thought beyond comparing the San Francisco brand of justice with the ruthless night riders of San Diego.

"Some vigilantes?"

"*Sí!* Not some, but damned plenty. Before these vigilantes got done, they up and hung a corralful of fellows they called these hounds, and run off a thousand more. And all of 'em *americano* no-goods, or these Australian bad hombres!"

"Vigilantes can raise a thunder of a lot of commotion, all right."

The talkative ranchero polished off his bottle of beer and sighed. "But that is not all, señor. As soon as these vigilantes got done wiping up the streets with these *yanqui* badmans, they chose themselfs a bunch of real bad *hombres* to get chasing some of the really bad gangs!" He rose up, wiping his mustaches, settled his scarlet sash more comfortably around his middle and started to join his fellow drovers out at the hitching rack.

"Just who is chasing who?"

"Well, they got themselfs a *yanqui bandido* hunter named Harry Love. He's riding around in circles after Joaquín, who's said to be back in these north. And there's that Salvador Salazar, Sheriff of Alameda County. Salazar's one *bueno hombre-cazador* (man-hunter). He's already run down Three-Fingered García, and Manuel Soto! These Captain Love and Salazar are now in and out of town with their posses, busy looking for Joaquín." He pulled on his sombrero, then wagged his head. "But I bet you they never catch these Joaquín. He's one foxy *hombre*, all right!"

Mounting up, I thought that drover really had no idea at all of just how foxy Joaquín Murieta really was. If this Captain Love or my old *amigo* Salazar ran down Joaquín, I only hoped it would be the *right one!* In spite of the trick young Almada had played on me that night at the Casa de Oro, I still kept a sneaking liking for him. Besides that, he'd once chased some of his rascals off my neck—and he was Rosita's brother!

The remainder of the day I made good time on the road and lay over for the night at a clean little *taverna*, the Bunch of Grapes, on the south slope of the Santa Inés Mountains about ten miles south of Santa Barbara.

The following morning as I was nearing the great bay that rimmed the town of Santa Barbara, I came upon a mighty odd *carreta*, driven by a hulking, one-eyed Negro dressed in a pair of old army pants and a seedy-looking yellow coat. I rode up alongside the cart and passed the time of day with the black man, who told me he'd come out to California with the first batch of gold hunters. When he'd gone busted as a miner, he went back to his old trade as a barber, making himself ten dollars a shave, day after day.

"I'se always got an eye out for oppotunity," said the man, who'd introduced himself as Peter Biggs. He blinked that good eye at me with a knowing sort of wink, while the paler of the two stared straight up the road past his gray mule's drooping ears. "Onc't I almos gobbled deh market in aigs up along ol Featheh Rivuh. Aigs wuz goin' at moh dehn three dolluhs each, when you could get'm. I give ovuh my barbuh woik, took evey blame cent I could lay hands on and went up and down deh Sacrementuh Rivuh a-buyin' aigs, aigs, aigs. Plumb clean out all of ol' Sam Brannum's penny-ante stohs, until I had ebbry aig in dat end of deh hull territory. I spen ovuh twelf hundred dolluhs, but I was King of Aigs!" He touched up his mule with a limber switch and the cart creaked ahead more briskly, while some kind of infernal growling eased out from under the wagon's patched and wrinkled canvas.

Before I could inquire as to what in tunket that noise was all about, Biggs winked again. "Oppotunity!" He motioned for me to ride nearer and pulled aside one section of the faded canvas.

From their wicker cages under the wagon bow, dozens of cats glared out at the daylight and myself. Yellow cats yowled, black cats spat, brindle and spotted cats hissed, striped cats as well as fat cats, lean cats and in-between cats fumed, raved and swore at the world and all its inhabitants in every sort of cat language and dialect—when they weren't cussing out their nearest neighbors.

"What—?"

"Like I tole you Mistuh Bean, oppotunity! Rats sometime gits big as hosses up at Frisco. Some of dem rats even tote off stray dorgs when no one's lookin'. Frisco folk plum honin' foh cats, so I done rustle up ovuh a hundred cats from around Los Angeles and points south. Dis is my fustest load. I'se gonna peddle dese cats at one hundred dolluhs per cat—and gonna git it, see if'n I don't!"

I could only stare at that bale of cats and nod. "But—what about those eggs?" I had to say something.

Biggs smiled sadly as some memory seemed to smite his broad black brow. "Went at it too hefty! Yassuh, dun ovuhstock! When I finally got dat flock of aigs toted to camp, all nice and easy, on a pair of slow-steppin' mules, with 'em all wrapped like diamonts in bales of sawdust from Mistuh Suttuh's mill, half de minuhs in all of Featheh Rivuh was a-waitin', dere tongues jus' hangin' out for an aig."

"And what?" I pulled off a bit from the wagon as a pair of fiery-eyed cats were doing their utmost to reach out and spur up White Lightning.

"I had me a hundred dozen aigs if'n I had one. Only one thing wrong, though. Blame aigs all done gone bad. I think ol Brannum bought hisself mighty ol' aigs and den saw to it that I got deh oldest of deh hull lot."

"And you lost your shirt in the deal?"

"Bettuh dat den my neck! Dem boys was mighty upset and plum chase me and my mules right outa sight. I took deh hint and went on down to

Los Angeles befoh I quit travelin'." He looked sideways at his fuming feline menagerie, then brightened. "Anyways, now's I gonna make it back. For no mattuh how long I keep dese heah cats penned up, ain't none of 'em gonna spoil. Deh may be a bit mad like, but when we gits to Frisco, rats look out!"

Wishing that dark speculator the best of luck, I rode on down into the village of Santa Barbara. From the looks of the place, the oncoming Peter Biggs could make a pile in peddling his cats to the natives, for whole streets of adobes, roofs gone and walls tumbling, gave Santa Barbara a used-up, gone-to-seed appearance. The palm trees were mainly dead and the olive and fig trees dilapidated and shabby. Even the old mission by the seashore had seen much better days, and the same thought struck me when I looked over the few folks on the dusty streets.

The sun was still over two fingers high on the horizon, and so I wasted no time in getting on out into the open country again.

We'd gone another half dozen miles before the red disk of the sun at last sank into the purple edge of the Pacific. Darkness swept in on broad, velvety wings while great flocks of geese stretched their wavering vees overhead, flying southward to the green marshes of old Mexico.

For an hour or so I navigated along by starlight, for the moon was still under. The Camino Real ran on ahead, a pale ghost of a road that led straight through a peaceful, starlit world.

Though I'd begun to think I might be forced to spend the night alongside the roadway, I presently noticed a gleam of light in the distance. It vanished as the road dipped down into a hollow and then reappeared when the road climbed upward. Then I caught the sound of a guitar and a voice singing a familiar saloon ditty.

"Looks as though we'll have ourselves a meal and a bed mighty soon," I told the great horse. White Lightning could tell the whereabouts of any nearby stable and tavern as well as the two-legged *vagabundo* upon his back and let me know it by laying back his ears and picking up his gait.

The road slanted off into another hollow but I could still recognize that song drifting toward us from the *taverna*.

> "Once I loved a yaller gal, her name was Suzy Brown,
> She hailed from Alabama and the fairest of her town.
> Her eyes so bright—they shine at night,
> When the moon's done gone away . . ."

Warbling the same song I'd sung many a time back in the Army, I spurred up from the hollow and came near riding headlong into a body of horsemen blocking the road in front of me. A dark knot of shadowy shapes.

"Halt! Throw up your hands!" someone sang out. There was no mistaking *that* tune, and I hauled in White Lightning and reached for the stars!

XXII

"Here now, let's see what we fetched in our loop!" The big, heavy figure of a man bulked in front of me as he scratched a lucifer on his saddle horn and, bending toward me, stuck the fluttering blue flame at my face.

I caught the glint of hard eyes in a beefy red face before the light sputtered out.

"Who're you, and where are you off to on such a night?" someone asked from the shadowy cluster of horsemen.

As it was a mild, starlit evening, it struck me as one damn fool question, but I was in no shape to debate its merits. "Bean's the name and I'm on my way to San Francisco for the San Diego alcalde," I answered, adding, "Who are you-all to be stopping folks on the highway?" Somehow I had this bunch figured for some sort of posse. One thing certain, they weren't *californios*, for they'd have shot me from the saddle and then hailed me.

"Humph!" The big man motioned me to lower my hands and growled out some sort of orders to his henchmen. "All right, Mr. Bean, we've heard of your relative, though we don't know you from old Adam. We're a legitimate law force out after bandits, and that black devil of a Murieta in p'ticular. I'm nobody else but Captain Harry Love of th' State Rangers, and seein' as you ain't up to no devilment, I'd admire you to come along and join us for supper. We're just about to put on th' old morral and feed some."

He drawled another command at one of the shadowy riders, who remained on picket duty at the hilltop, while I, along with the rest of the rangers, loped up the road to the tavern.

Once we'd arrived, the musical ranger was parted from his guitar and sent back down the highway to join his lonely friend on guard.

Now, if I was a hand at cracking jokes, I'd have to say that the supper at the Del Monte Tavern was just a humdinger of a "love feast," for by the time the drinks came around there was no one more satisfied with the California Rangers than the rangers themselves.

First and foremost, Captain Harry Love was the most satisfied of all, and he told the entire barroom just exactly why, with each speech punctuated by approving yelps and applause from the six assembled rangers, all of them mere greenhorns. Later in the evening I found them to be a collection of store clerks, bank tellers and the like, all out for a lark away from their jobs, and following Captain Harry Love. Love himself turned out to be an ex-policeman, ward heeler and small-time rancher from Texas, who'd talked the San Francisco City Council into forming a body of ninety-day rangers.

"Nobody nohow was ever able to catch a holt of sech confounded rascals as that José Carrillo and Tiger Juan Flores until we hit th' trail after 'em. Carrillo, he's a-pushin' up cactus while Flores is locked away at that there new *juzgado* at Point San Quentin," drawled Love, tugging at his black oxhorn mustaches. "And yours truly, with my bloodhound rangers, done it!"

"Pequeño pescado," one of the gray-bearded rancheros in the corner muttered to a friend, where they sat puffing their pipes.

"Oh, I heered that," Love shrugged and called for another round for the whole house, including the skeptical rancheros. "Small fish, *mebbie,* but 'tain't only small fish we're after, but some mighty big ones—sharks even. Well, you can tell the hull wide world that Harry Love's in th' field and he ain't comin' back, except for supplies, till he runs down that gol-dummed Murieta!"

"And we'll gobble him long afore that slowpoke of a Sheriff Salazar gets halfway from Frisco," said a skinny young hide salesman and ninety-day ranger. There were approving shouts and the rattle of six empty glasses.

"This here Salazar jest ain't got th' knack of trailin'," Love told the barroom. "Back in th' old Lone Star, even before th' war, I used to hunt me an Injun or a Mex before breakfast just to keep in practice. I been at this business since Nero was a pup!" He looked at me narrowly, red face flushed with liquor, but his words were steady. "I'm not prejudiced but y'gotta recollect that I'm a God-fearin' Yankee, leastwise a Texan, while this here Salazar's a greaser same as this sidewinder Murieta." He shrugged. "So it don't take no blind man to see that there sheriff's not gonna move too briskly after his own sort, now does it?"

I got up. "Mr. Love, I happen to know Sheriff Salazar pretty well, and his one hope in life, aside from growing back a new scalp, is to get his hands or rope affixed onto Joaquín Murieta!"

Then I bade the entire bunch *buenas noches* and got to my room before I found myself mixed up in a barroom fight with that whole lot of California Rangers—shoe clerks and all.

Next morning, when I took breakfast in the bar, I was glad to learn that

Captain Almighty Love and his men had lit out at daybreak. I felt somehow sorry for those young fellows, and even for that red-faced blowhard
Love, for he had stood me to my supper and drinks. But if those California Rangers ever got near either Joaquín, I truly feared for the whole
posse's continued existence.

The rest of my travels up the El Camino Real took White Lightning
and myself a total of six and a half more days. From time to time I'd meet
or pass such run-of-the-mill travelers as peddlers' carts, occasional stages,
mine supply wagons and, once in a while, small herds of beef cattle, as
well as restless groups of miners, going from camp to camp as they headed
toward that "better strike." But there were no more such curious folks as
Peter Biggs and his cartload of fighting-mad cats, or odd characters like
the swell-headed Captain Love and his squad of amateur *bandido* extermi-
nators.

At about eleven o'clock on the twentieth of October, after riding fifteen
miles from the comfortable Mansion House, where I'd spent the night, I
reined in my white stallion on the crown of one of the hills that ringed
San Francisco from the south, east and north. There I sat breathing the
mount and peering downward toward the great landlocked harbor, but
there was little to see at the moment. The entire city below lay hidden
under a shining sheet of vapor, shimmering whitely as it swayed and
rippled in the freshening sea breeze, for all the world like the curtain of an
immense theater that was about to rise to reveal the latest melodrama—
or, more likely, comedy.

The thick grass among the scattered chaparral, flanking the roadside,
now turning a paler green, flared and tossed about in the Pacific winds.
Somewhere in the distance a pair of mourning doves called to each other
from a knot of pine saplings, while a suddenly swooping marsh hawk,
diving after some rabbit or gopher, scared up a flock of valley quail. The
unexpected thunder of wings spooked my horse and in the time it took to
head him back into the road and somewhat gentle him, that foglike vapor,
spread across the city, had parted leaving silvery shreds and billows to drift
off over the northern hills.

There the entire panorama lay, all shining before me, as the arching sun
gilded rooftop and steeple of the first truly Yankee city I'd viewed for
many a year. New York, I supposed, could be no finer.

Slowly the vista widened and I saw the steep little city climbing up its
sandy slopes, surrounded by rings of barren hills, now all golden green,
clustered in a crescent, and stretching downward to a waterfront where

what seemed like half of the world's shipping rode at anchor. Bright flags fluttered or stood out stiffly in the winds. On an inclining sandy cliff to the north, called Telegraph Hill, the gaunt arm of the signal semaphore was etched blackly against the bright blue of the sky as it waited to point out the arrival of the graceful, snow-white-winged clippers. Here and there one of the little river steamers, down from the Sacramento, trailed a threadlike banner of smoke as it crisscrossed the wide sparkling bay. The Long Wharf, at the water's edge, looked like nothing less than a narrow watery village strung along the forest of masts that speared up from the busy waterfront.

Far up from the hodgepodge of the dock area, I could see dozens of little crooked streets, winding along like a series of footpaths among the block upon block of little white-and-gray frame houses, and just about make out the scallops of wooden trimming along their eaves. Beyond them, iron houses perched upon the upper slopes, while dozens of canvas tents, of all sizes and colors, flapped farther up the windy heights. And in the very heart of the crescent-shaped city, rising tier upon tier, there lofted the massive buildings of Portsmouth Square. These, I could see, were built to stay of stone or painted plaster, and all trimmed out with wide balconies and finely wrought railings. Those, I found, were mainly the gaming houses and theaters, along with four-storied hotels, for ever since the gold rush the sporting life had become a part of San Francisco's existence.

Somewhere down there I'd find Dulcima sooner or later, maybe at one of the theaters—and Rosita, though I'd not thought of her much lately. But that fiery señorita was bound to be off there somewhere in the foot-hills, with her brother. And beyond those foothills, and the open country, there waited—Kirker's gold!

Thinking on such things, I lingered upon the hill, while all that distant sound of voices and the rattle of carriages and carts and footsteps, echoing up from the wooden-planked streets, blended with the shrilling of the winds through the grass and shrubs. At last, jolted from my reverie by the approach of hoofbeats, I turned in my saddle to discover the dusty approach of one of the San Francisco-bound coaches.

I lingered no longer but gave my horse his head and went pounding down the steep road, leaving the coach far in the rear. We shortly came to the outskirts of the city, loping past low, rambling warehouses and various sheds. As the road curved on toward the waterfront, I began to meet the traffic of a busy city. Here on Montgomery, a carelessly planked street that had taken over from the broad El Camino Real, I passed between crowded

shops and stalls. Again and again I had to pull aside to keep from colliding
with the many red-and-white hackney coaches. These conveyances, filled
with miners on a spree, dashed past at full tilt, barely missing the swarms
of sailors who came clambering up from the boat stairs, as well as men of
every color and hue who hastened up and down the narrow street or
leaped cursing from under a hackney's wheels.

White Lightning shook his head and jingled his bridle chains at the
ungodly racket and confusion but kept on along a street that now climbed
toward the city's center. And as we clattered through the noisy throngs, I
saw more than one stranger pause to watch us go by, though I knew that
he was admiring the great white stallion and not the linen-duster-clad
vagabond on his broad back.

Crossing Jackson and heading toward the haven of Portsmouth Square,
where, a passerby at the waterfront had told me, "everything happened in
San Franciso," I passed shops filled with mining implements that over-
flowed out upon the wooden sidewalks. Some stores displayed the newest
in miner's togs, while others were filled with the latest in tailor-made
fashions from Paris and New York; everything seeming to have something
to do with the acquiring of gold and the spending of the same.

I had a view of San Francisco's new wrinkle in transportation when I
pulled up at Kearny Street to let one of the new Yellow Line's canary-
tinted omnibuses roll past on its way out to the Mission Plank Road on
the city's outskirts.

When I rode into Portsmouth Square I seemed to have arrived in the
middle of a regular Arabian Nights masquerade. Reining in and looking
around for some sort of inexpensive tavern or hotel, I could only stare at
the noisy spectacle. Here transplanted Yankees were playing Spanish dons
to the hilt as they strutted along in their sweeping sombreros and black
velvet capes or, equipped with serapes and glittering spurs, walked some
mighty passable horses around the square. Scores of red-shirted miners in
town to celebrate a strike or forget their troubles strolled from building to
building, each armed to the teeth with low-slung pistols and bowie knives
stuck in their boots within handy reach. And there was no mistaking the
gambling fraternity in their tall, silky stovepipe hats, dapper suits of both
somber and gay colors, all with snowy-white, fancy-frilled shirts set off
with diamond studs or glittering gold breastpins—each fancy outfit
topped by a nobby neck stock of flashy patterns.

But the gamblers, miners and plain citizens all beat a hasty retreat
whenever one of the brightly painted carriages, lined with red silks and

drawn by pairs of spirited horses, dashed out from one of the side streets to add to the noontime bedlam.

Noticing a likely-looking hotel on the north side of the square, I dismounted, tugged off my duster and handed the reins to a ragged bootblack while I went into the Parker House. I came back out almost at once and took the reins back, tossing the urchin a coin. Twenty dollars a day was just too rich for my blood.

I was directed over to nearby Washington Street by a passerby, where I landed a room on the third floor of the San Francisco House at the more reasonable rate of ten dollars a week.

With White Lightning safely housed in Bryant's livery on Clay I took lunch at a nearby saloon-restaurant and went back out into the brilliant fall sunlight to enjoy the afternoon. Walking back down to the square, I stood outside the lavish Bella Union, looking over the parade.

It seemed that the same crowd, or one like it, was continuing its march about the square. Dapper gamblers passed in and out of the various halls, along with rougher miners, well-to-do businessmen, and just plain folks of about every nationality, including fuzzy-headed Kanakas from the distant Sandwich Islands, raggedy Negroes and, by their lingo, Germans, Italians, French and even British, along with scores of pigtailed Chinese. The Chinese women in particular were delicate of build but bold of eye, and all were coming and going upon their private errands—or just loafing around with the rest of us, watching the excitement of an average day in town.

From the gaming houses' open windows came the sound of flutes, fiddles and banjos, as well as the shouts of laughter of the winners and the sharp outcries of the losers. From time to time, one of the women within, who dealt cards or turned a wheel, would lean from an upper window to smile down upon the crowds, drumming up some trade while the room behind her sleek head blazed with candles to rival the golden afternoon.

Coming up to this three-ring circus from the easy, usually soft-going atmosphere of San Diego made me realize mighty shortly that all of this was going to take some sort of getting used to.

It was a good thing, I thought, that I had plenty of time, for I needed to hole up for a spell and do some serious planning in laying out my campaign.

I had to get in touch with Josh, tell him where I'd lit, then wait and see how his election prospects panned out. I also had to try to find Dulcima, then fit my projected hunt for the gold into our future. As for Rosita, she was always there, somewhere in the back of my mind, and vaguely bothering me, for some reason that I couldn't quite pin down. Perhaps it was because she was Dulcima's guardian, though only a few years older than the "niece" she'd threatened to deal with when she had the time—and perhaps it was because of her connection with the Kirker loot and Murieta.

I returned to the hotel at sundown, having stayed out of the gambling halls all afternoon by a great effort of willpower, and had myself a decent meal of steak and potatoes at a nearby restaurant. Then I picked up the latest copy of the *Alta California* and went up to room 303.

After I'd shucked down to my underwear, lit the cracked spirit lamp and piled into the creaking wooden bedstead, I took out the handbill with Dulcima's picture and spent some time looking at it. It got me plumb fidgety thinking that she might come to town almost any day. And what if she showed up with that low-down Diamond Dick? That circumstance could be explosive to say the least. Well, Mr. Diamond Dick Powers was going to find himself playing some mighty poor hands—if I could deal them. And I was downright set on getting Dulcima, and keeping her— right along with his horse!

But Dulcima was anything but a china doll. She certainly had a mind of her own. I'd seen that. So neither Diamond Dick, nor Rosita, nor even Major McGuire himself was going to do any thinking for her, I was certain. At least I was pretty certain.

Finally I put aside the handbill and, taking up the paper, read of the discovery of the largest nugget since 1848 out on the American River, and of the arrival of such flash clippers as the *Sea Witch* from Bristol and the *Surprise* from Boston.

Reading along the columns I ran across a certain James King, who seemed to be having a run of bad luck. He advertised for the return of his prime riding horse, Bolívar, lost, strayed or stolen from his barn out on Jackson. He also asked help in recovering a runaway house slave named Champ. He offered one hundred dollars reward for the mount and fifty for his black man, probably because Bolívar had four legs to Champ's two.

Jackstraw's Pharmacy on Sacramento was proud to announce that they'd just received the latest shipment from back East of Dr. Wheeler's Universally Celebrated Balsam of Moscatello: "The most valuable vegetable preparation discovered for the cure of cholera morbus and the dangerous effects of drinking cold water when overheated." They also stocked Phoenix Blue Bitters, claiming it as "the most effectual remedy extant for the cure of each and every disease to which man is subject!"

That made some mighty compelling reading, but what really made me sit up and put my feet on the floor was an item at the bottom of the second page announcing the grand reopening, after previous fire damage, in just two weeks of "the Celebrated Jenny Lind Theater, at the corner of Washington and Kearny on the Square."

The story went on to state that Colonel (he'd promoted himself) Thomas Mulcahey McGuire, proprietor of the theater, in addition to sending out several companies to entertain the outlying camps and districts, also planned opening the local season with the appearance of several outstanding thespians. These included "the great Junius Booth, as well as the brilliant Caroline Chapman." They were to be featured in the opening production of *All That Glitters Is Not Gold,* which had its first showing in New York just six months earlier.

But that was not the least, for Colonel McGuire also promised: "To make the evening absolutely tip-top, that newest young sensation of the stage, Miss Lorette La Fonte will also appear in several delightful songs and sketches!"

All this made my mind a bit tipsy, so, as I often did, I got out Jeff Kirker's ten-dollar gold piece from my money belt and inspected it again for the hundredth time. Again I wondered at the odd markings on the coin. They had to mean something, but cipher as I might, I still couldn't puzzle it out. Well, as the Spanish had it, there were always plenty of mañanas around. And in just about a dozen mañanas Dulcima should be right here in San Francisco. I put away the coin, blew out the lamp and lay in the dark. Just as I was drifting off, there came the rumble of thunder, another racketing clap much nearer, then more rolling out over the hills beyond town. I was nearly asleep by then, but was still aware of a velvety rushing downpour. The first of the fall-time rains had begun.

The rains slackened next morning and up and quit by nine, so I got White Lightning from the livery and rode up Stockton and out Columbus to get away from the noisy bustle of the city and do some thinking.

North San Francisco had the same hilly makeup as the southern section, but it seemed to have more sandy beaches and sheltered coves. There were also fewer houses out past the sand hills, and I soon came to an elevation overlooking the shining stretch of water between the two peninsulas they called the Golden Gate.

There seemed to be a couple of miles of open water across to the steep reaches of the Marin Hills to the northwest. Several small sailing ships were moving out through the gate, and as I sat White Lightning I saw the new propeller steamer *Kangaroo* on its way eastward across the great bay to San Antonio Landing, which was getting to be called Oakland. The

Marin Hills themselves cradled a small fishing village, Sausalito, which in the distance looked about like a pinch of white gravel tossed onto a green pillow.

I'd heard there were several wide-open gambling dens and cathouses at Sausalito, but San Francisco had plenty for me—and the whole of California, for that matter.

I had counted my money that morning and found the cash Josh had stowed in my blanket roll was now two dollars less than two hundred. It was plain to see that I'd best keep my nose out of any games, unless I felt mighty lucky.

Though I gave myself plenty of time to think things over, about all I came to decide was that I'd walk mighty easy around Powers when he showed up. I didn't want to get into any more shooting scrapes when I was this close to the gold—wherever it might be—and even more close to Dulcima. But if Diamond Dick showed fight, I'd not back down one iota!

On the ride out to the point and back, I did manage to draft up a short letter to Josh in my head. When I returned to my room after dinner I got pen and paper and wrote it down:

Brother Josh,

I'm here at the San Francisco House, having arrived in one piece yesterday.

I've not run across Salazar yet, but most talk has him and a tinhorn vigilante, named Love, out beating the brush for Murieta. But not together!

This is one jim-dandy city, over 40,000 and growing by leaps and bounds. If your election doesn't pan out, you ought to come up here.

Tell Abraham, Bates and the Flea mucho thanks for their help. It goes without saying that I surely thank you most of all!

Hope to hear from you shortly. Be sure and give the Bandini family my best.

Your brother Roy!

There was no use in sending greetings to Dulcima. She'd get them in person, mighty shortly!

Though the next day was Sunday, no one without a calendar would have guessed it, except for the fact that the visiting miners seemed to be wearing their best red shirts. While there were more miners in town than ever, the supply of professional gamblers seemed to be equal to the red-shirted invasion.

Reminding myself that I was out to spend some time and little money, I visited a good half dozen of the most fancy halls with their great glass chandeliers and wall-to-ceiling mirrors. There in the Empire, the Arcade and the Mazurka I found most of the dealers to be Frenchwomen in mighty low-cut gowns. These handled the faro banks and roulette layouts, while their slick-looking male partners sat around in boiled dickies and fancy frock coats, dealing blackjack and poker. These gents seemed to be mainly French and Italian, with a scattering of Yankee gamblers.

Most of the places stuck to a pair of squeaky violins, an out-of-tune guitar and an asthmatic flute, but the Bella Union offered a Mexican string quartet with two harps, two guitars and a handsomely played flute.

Sabbath or not, the halls kept up to twenty tables running full blast. Mexicans sat absolutely motionless, except for eyes and hands, winning or losing a thousand dollars on the turn of a card. Sober-faced Chinese played at low-stake craps with scarcely a sound, except for the rattle and snap of the "bones." But most of the assembled Americans, miners, stage drivers and sailors, whooped, bawled and cussed at the top of their lungs—and seemed to have the very time of their lives.

Finally I left the last hall with its pretty but cold-eyed Frenchwomen dealers and walked down to the Fontine House, a small but tidy restaurant at the corner of Kearny and Sacramento. There I blew myself to a Sunday dinner of grizzly bear steak, which tasted right close to good lean pork. Like other better eating houses around town, this spot offered a whopping bill of fare at all seasons. There were such items on the menu to make any back-East swell hold a debate with himself before ordering: elk, deer, antelope, turtle, hare, partridge, quail, wild geese, brant, all sorts of ducks, snipe, plover, curlew, cranes, salmon, trout and other fish, along with oysters!

The meals ran around two dollars and only three with a good bottle of wine thrown in—and that wine straight from Paris.

As I sat there in the small group of diners, men of all sorts and trades, who kept their mouths shut except to tie into the vittles, I got to thinking of my recent troubles and "retreat" up the territory when a face began drifting through my thoughts. It wasn't Dulcima, Corporal Bates or one of the Bandini girls; then I remembered it was a face I'd seen in San Francisco, the face of one of the Mexican gamblers who'd sat at monte in a corner of the Alhambra.

As I thought over the last hour or two, I recalled how my eyes had met those of a handsome, quietly dressed young Mexican. The fellow had been coldly polite. Though he hadn't known me, I was certain, as I'd walked

through the crowd, he'd bowed his head an instant and then turned back
to his game of monte.

It was *Hechavarría!*—the man who'd killed Sánchez *and vowed to kill
Josh!* Hechavarría, alias Joaquín Murieta, or one of the two Joaquíns. And
here he was in San Francisco!

I was positive as I thought back on it, and I'd have bet all of Kirker's
gold that I'd seen his portrait as a young officer on old Señor Hechavarría's
dining room wall not two months back. *Carlos Hechavarría!*

Still mulling over Hechavarría's appearance, I paid my bill and stepped
out into a foggy evening. As I slowly eased down the wooden sidewalk
toward my hotel I got to wondering if, somehow, I could reveal myself to
the bandit, without a fight, and square Josh, explaining that my brother
was innocent of the midnight lynchings at San Diego.

Thinking about it, I stopped on the corner of the next street, trying to
get my bearings in the hazy light cast by streetlamps where they glowed
through the chilly fog in a palely fading chain that seemed to vanish into
nothingness half a block ahead. Everything was subdued by the drifting
fog. Even sounds drifting down from the roistering gambling houses were
muffled and subdued.

Suddenly through the distant shouts and wavering twang of guitars and
whining chirp of fiddles came the clop-clop-clop of horses pulling an approaching vehicle.

For an instant I couldn't see the oncoming carriage, then it floated out
of the swirling silver, a dark blur carried toward me by a ghostly team,
whose heads bobbed in and out of the mists, horses without bodies or legs.

I stepped back against the front of a building, waiting for it to pass, but
the carriage halted under one of the streetlamps and I could see the
motionless driver upon his box, swathed in serape and slouch hat.

The vehicle's curtains were closed, but as I watched, ready to move, a
woman's pale hand appeared at the near window and slowly pulled aside
the blind.

That hand beckoned to me, and as I leaned in toward the carriage,
hand upon my pistol, I could make out the face of a woman, all but
hidden in the half light.

"Roy, acercate mi querido amigo [approach, my dear friend]!" And it
was the voice of Rosita Almada, calling to me out of the night!

XXIII

I got into the carriage, hand still near my pistol, and then at Rosita's quiet laughter settled myself beside her on the leather seat.

She gave an order to the man on the box and we rolled out through the foggy night. For a spell neither of us spoke as the hazy yellow circles of the streetlamps drifted past, and then were gone in the darkness. We seemed to be heading down toward the waterfront, then our course changed and the horses began the long pull up toward Telegraph Hill.

"Here!" she called to the coachman, and at last the vehicle rocked to a stop. I'd been content just to sit beside her and feel the soft warmth of her hip against mine. But Rosita Almada always knew just what she was about, always seemed in complete control of events, and I knew she'd not just suddenly appeared out of the fog to swoop me off for a secret buggy ride.

After a polite word or two had been swapped about each other's health, she got down to business! "Did you know that Carlos Hechavarría is here in the north—and it could be dangerous if he was aware that you are in the city?"

"I saw him just tonight in a gambling hall; recognized him from that painting at his father's rancho. But why dangerous to me?"

She placed a firm little hand on my arm. "He's sworn to kill your brother, or anyone connected with him. He's determined to wipe out the dishonor of Joshua Bean's lynching of his men. And as you know he's made a start by getting that ugly deputy of the alcalde's!"

"And he'd get rid of me if he knew who I was?"

"Yes, he's had some plans go wrong lately, and now he lashes out at anyone he has *la ojeriza*—the grudge—against." She leaned toward me, and I could sense her warmth and the sweetness of her breath. "I have a certain regard—no, more than just that, a certain *afición* for you." She paused, then continued. "You, in your *americano* way, have become quite dear to me. And, perhaps, I am bold and shameless as ever to say this." She gave her husky laugh. "But *I am Red Rosita!*"

In that moment, when she was so close to me, I was also mighty close to grabbing her—and kissing that sweet, laughing mouth; then there came a sudden thought of that little stiletto!

"Josh had nothing to do with those lynchings," I muttered, just to have something to say. "It was that shifty sidewinder of a Dick Powers!" Then I told her of the escapades at San Diego, my head-on clash with Diamond Dick, and my escape from jail. "Before I left, I found that my brother's servant, Abraham, had been a part of your family's rancho for years—and the pipeline to Murieta—your brother. Why didn't Abraham let you know that Josh was innocent of those midnight raids?"

"He did, from the start, though he'd not discovered who was guilty. But there was such suspicion and rumor among the gang members that Carlos refused to believe that anyone but a powerful man such as Joshua Bean could be directing the brutality."

She stopped suddenly and lifted her hand. The serape-clad driver had bent down and whispered something. Then I caught the thud of hoof-beats.

Rosita gave a hasty command, and our carriage wheeled into a side road, behind a clump of trees. There we waited until the strange riders had passed on into the darkness, then the carriage turned back toward the hazy dots of light marking the city.

"Things have been dangerous—for some time. My brother and Carlos have exchanged many hot words, for Carlos is bound to carry out some sort of raid upon the Fort Smith Armory at Benicia, across the bay, and gain enough weapons to begin an uprising."

"Uprising?"

"*Sí,* but you must promise not to inform the authorities—yet. My brother still recovers from his old illness in a secluded place, and he could find himself in much peril, with the officers swarming the hills!"

"But you're talking of a real double-barreled rebellion. That could raise holy hob hereabouts! Now, I know you and your brother are—"

"We do wish the return of our country and the vast lands that your so-called United States plundered from our people. Though there are many who might join Carlos, it would bring more trouble than it would ever be worth—blood and destruction! We've had enough of that!"

The coach rocked back down the incline of the hills, and before I could fetch Dulcima into our conversation, it had pulled up before the dim outline of my hotel.

"You even know where I hang my hat?" I was surprised the driver had navigated right up to the front door of the San Francisco House.

"I knew the hour you arrived in town. We have many friends in many places, you see. I even watched from a distance the first day you rode to the point on your magnificent horse." She held out her hand. *"Adiós,* and I beg you to be most careful. Warn your brother the alcalde to stay away from San Francisco while Carlos Hechavarría is near!"

I got out of the carriage and taking her slender hand raised it to my lips in my best caballero salute. I found myself wanting to see her again, in spite of Dulcima, which was downright confusing.

"When will I see you again?"

As the carriage rolled away into the night gloom, her voice drifted back: "We'll meet again, when the time is right."

Next morning I got off a short note to Josh, telling him there was good reason to suspect that Joaquín Murieta was close to town, and that he'd been known to have made more threats against him. I advised my brother to remember what Murieta had done to his deputy. But, knowing Josh's bullheadedness, I had my doubts that it would make him change any of his plans.

Though I revisited the gambling hall, where I'd seen Hechavarría, I never got another glimpse of him, either there or upon the crowded streets. Rosita had also vanished again, and I found myself puzzling over her warning of the planned raid on the U.S. Armory at Benicia, and wondering just what should be done about it.

For the next two weeks I had plenty of time to think, while I waited for Josh's answering letter—and for the opening of the new Jenny Lind Theater. With little to do, I took my horse out for a canter each morning, and played some small-stake poker afternoons at the Águila de Oro, just off Portsmouth Square. The game there was run by a pleasant young gambler with sharp black eyes, recently arrived in town like myself. Charley Cora had worked many of the mining camps and already had himself a reputation for a feisty temper, but I had no trouble with him, and I usually managed to walk away from his table with as much cash as I had brought to the games. And, sometimes, a bit more.

At last came the reopening of the Jenny Lind, and I joined the crowds filing into the theater and got a tingle up my backbone as I saw the name of Miss Lorette La Fonte on the showbills outside the large, handsome building.

I had to hand it to "Colonel" McGuire, for the Jenny Lind's interior was positively lavish. Carved pillars supported the first tier of boxes, while rich draperies of red and gold, along with dozens of bright lamps, turned the auditorium into a dazzling showplace. There was a pit, a parquet and even a gallery—and, to top it off, a towering gilded dome at the ceiling beamed the glowing radiance back down upon its gawking audience.

As I took my seat along with the noisy but orderly crowd of businessmen, gamblers, sailors and miners (all in their best togs), I wondered if Dulcima knew I'd be out front waiting for her appearance. I also looked over the packed house on the off chance that I might spot Powers, for I knew that underhanded rascal had to be somewhere about, but I saw no one who looked like Diamond Dick.

We hadn't long to wait, for suddenly the little pit orchestra struck up a lively march, with its trumpets, fiddles and drum; the big painted curtain, shimmering in the footlights, rippled, then slowly rose upward, helped along by a rousing burst of applause . . . and the show began.

All That Glitters Is Not Gold was a wonderful drama, at least I thought it was, with a detestable villain, a stunning heroine, played by curvesome, red-haired Caroline Chapman as Kitty LeRoy, and Junius Booth as Frank Sinclair, the stern but handsome young hero.

Each scene won its share of applause, compounded with whistles and much stamping of boots, but it was Dulcima (as *Lorette La Fonte*), bursting out from the wings between acts, who completely bowled over the audience.

She came dancing out at the end of the first act in a long-tailed green coat, knee breeches and a tall green hat, to do first an Irish jig and a reel, then cut loose with her darky songs. She sang three minstrel tunes, one right after the other. I'd heard the first at the Bandinis' but the other two were new to me, and each as funny and lively as the first.

At the end of the second act, while the audience was trying to decide if Junius Booth (Frank Sinclair) would ante up enough money to save the old farm from the villain, Dulcima reappeared. Now dressed as a miner in ragged pantaloons, neat little boots and the usual flaming red shirt, she outdid herself with a trio of parodies on the life of the miners.

The song getting the most applause told of the escapades of McDougal, a well-known fellow notorious for getting himself into rows and coming out the worse for wear. It went in part:

> *"For shame, oh, fie!*
> *Maguire, oh why*
> *Will you thus skyugle?*
> *And curse and swear*
> *And rip and tear*

The unfortunate McDougal?
His wind's bereft—
About you've left
Enough to blow a bugle!
But now you've smashed
And almost hashed
The form of poor McDougal!"

And how the miners, in particular, whooped and howled about that song!

At the play's finale, with the old homestead won away from the villain, and Kitty LeRoy and Frank Sinclair all set to wed, the cast took their curtain calls. Then Dulcima returned for her own finale.

Dressed in a plain white frock, she stood motionless at center stage, lifting her pure, strong young voice in a medley that began with "Lilly Dale" and ended with a brand-new song, "Woodman, Spare That Tree."

She received a regular standing ovation, and I could see many a rough customer wiping his eyes as the audience filed out into the foggy night.

As soon as I could wriggle through the mob, I hustled around to the dark alley and knocked on the stage door. It was flung open immediately, and I was looking at Diamond Dick Powers.

Before Powers could shut his mouth—or the door—he was staring into my pistol muzzle. I wasn't taking any chances!

"Roy!" Dulcima darted to the doorway, still in her white frock. "Oh, I'm so glad to see you came tonight. I wondered if you were in town, and Dick—Mr. Powers—said—"

"Put away that weepon, you hothead, that's no way to come visiting my players," a voice boomed from the shadows. "Colonel" McGuire stepped into the lamplight, shaking his walking stick. "So, you've seen our *Miss Lorette?* Now I recollect you from down near San Diego. And how'd you like the show?"

"Forgot your passes, but it was money well spent." I holstered my Colt, seeing Powers kept his hands strictly away from his sides.

Dulcima crowded in front of Diamond Dick and McGuire, holding out her hand. "Roy, I'm staying down the street at the old Oriental Hotel. There's a rehearsal in the morning, but come by in the afternoon. We've a lot to talk about!"

I shook her hand without another word but gave Powers a long look before turning back into the foggy alley, as McGuire hurriedly barred the door from any other stage-door Johnnies.

XXIV

The very next morning I had an answer in the mails from Josh, short and right to the point:

Brother Roy,

Much thanks for your warning, but it's somewhat too late. We've had a special election here on last Monday, rigged up by Dick Powers, who seems to know as many ward heelers at the capital as I do! But it didn't do him one lick of good, for San Diego up and elected no one else but your old friend Haraszthy!

My term is up anyway at the end of the month, and as I've roped in a buyer for the saloon, you can look for me shortly.

Josh!

That certainly gave me something to chew on along with my dinner, until it was about time to go down to the Oriental Hotel and ask for Miss La Fonte. But before I could settle myself in the Oriental's lobby to wait, Diamond Dick Powers came strolling down the staircase.

"Hold on there, Bean!" Powers flipped back his expensive checkered coat to show me he was unarmed. "I know we haven't had much use for each other in the past, what with all our run-ins, but I'm through with pistol fights. The odds are too tough!" He stood at the bottom of the steps watching me. "I grant you that little *hazing* at the *calabozo* sort of got out of hand, but, after all, you wound up with my favorite horse. So I'd say we just about stand even."

The man's brass dumbfounded me, and I just stared at him.

"I've been up to see Miss Dulcima, on business. She'll be down right shortly." He lifted his sombrero, turned on his heel and went out.

While I was trying to decide what to do about that slippery thimblerigger, Dulcima herself came down the stairs. She was turned out in a dark blue gown, with a wine-red waterproof over her shoulders and a chipper little black straw bonnet on her golden curls, looking every bit the young lady of quality.

"Roy! There you are." She handed me the day's copy of the *Alta California*. "Now just see what they're saying about our show—and me!"

Standing there in the lobby, watched with envy by all the lobby loungers, with Dulcima holding on to my arm, I glanced over the article:

Lorette La Fonte has proven to be a very comet of dynamic talent; and we plan to watch her course with the same emotions that we would follow the brilliant movements of a shooting star, flying through space, alone, reckless and still undestined!

"Well, they seem to think you're a regular theatrical comet," I said, folding up the paper, and turning with her to the door.

"Oh, isn't it just wonderful? You know they hardly said a thing about the play itself, not that young Juney Booth isn't a dream, but now I think that Colonel McGuire, and—others were right in wanting me to kick over the traces and come into the theater on my own!"

"Others, like Powers? I guess that reporter hasn't guessed that you're not quite as unguided as he thinks." I didn't feel it was the place to mention what *Aunt* Rosita would have to say.

By now we were outside in the watery half light of a gloomy day, watching the busy street traffic of drays, hacks and dodging humans.

"Oh no, it's mainly the colonel. He could see Caroline Chapman isn't up to holding on to her audiences anymore, even in a brand-new play from back East. And that's why he wanted me in the company, to liven up the shows." She pulled the waterproof over her slim shoulders and turned toward an oncoming group of people. "There comes old lady Chapman now," and she pointed out a tall, dark-haired woman approaching. "We've another rehearsal this afternoon, but say you'll come back tonight." She stepped close and lowered her voice. "And if you want to—talk, when we've time of our own, leave a key for me at your desk, and I'll come visiting, sometime after midnight."

All I could do was try to keep my jaw clamped and nod my head, then the black-eyed, well-rouged Miss Chapman was upon us. There were introductions and the two were soon on their way down Kearny toward Washington and the theater.

Looking after them, I noticed that before they reached the next corner and were lost in the swirl of traffic that a pair of gentlemen joined them. The shorter of the figures was one of the actors and the other, Diamond Dick.

That evening was a repeat of the performance of the night before. The Jenny Lind was positively jammed, with scores standing at the back of the house, but I'd purchased my ticket early and was well down front where I could view the whole show. And Dulcima was just about the whole show as far as the audience was concerned. They gave each act of the play a sufficiency of applause, but kept the majority of its boisterous enthusiasm for Miss Lorette La Fonte!

Never repeating a single number from her past performance, Dulcima romped through a dazzling series of minstrel songs, banjo numbers, breakdowns, jig and reels, winding up with a tearful little ballad that threatened to bring a wave of sorrow throughout the audience, but ended her sparkling routine with a song that fetched a roar of laughter and waves of applause:

> *"I've been out to Califony,*
> *And haven't found one dime!*
> *I've lost my bloomin' health*
> *And a powerful lot of time!*
> *All I've left is spade and pick*
> *And if I felt quite brave,*
> *I'd surely use them there things*
> *To dig myself a grave!"*

And each moment, as she was swirling around the stage, I sat there, positively glowing to think that before the night was done Dulcima could be mine!

As soon as the show ended, I made tracks for the San Francisco House. Leaving a key for a "lady visitor," I went up to my room and waited, and read the paper, and waited. At last it was past midnight, and still I waited.

Finally, as I'd often done, when time crawled along, I put my mind to work on some problem. I got out Kirker's gold piece and studied it over and over. By holding it at an exact angle to my lamp flame, I found that I could make some sort of sense out of those scratches on the coin.

After looking long at the inscriptions, I took a stub of a pencil and the back of Josh's letter, and sketched what seemed to be a crude Roman numeral. Turning the gold eagle over, I traced down the other marks, a sort of lopsided circle balanced between the points of the letter M. Under the letter M were three tiny half circles, cut off at the middle and sitting on a line with the round parts facing upward. The middle circle, or hump, was marked with a tiny cross.

The more I studied the coin's two sides, the more I was positive that the stretched-out letter M represented twin mountain peaks, with the tiny half circles standing for a trio of big rocks or possibly boulders. That

Roman numeral IV must indicate a date, probably a month—the fourth month, April!

I stared at my drawings and cussed to think how long I'd been blind to the meaning of those hen tracks.

That lopsided circle was meant for the sun. And in April that sun would be rising or setting between those twin peaks, with the treasure just waiting for me under that middle boulder, all marked neat and tidy with an X. *Somewhere!*

Suddenly I was swimmy-headed, and as sleepy as if I'd been up for three nights in a row. I decided, then and there, that I'd better take myself a catnap to be ready for Dulcima when she arrived.

I tossed the coin onto the dresser and stripped down to my long johns, put the paper under my pillow with my pistol and turned down the lamp. Then forgetting the excitement of the answer to the coin's conundrum, I was dead asleep in twenty winks.

Sometime late in the night, something roused me. Still half asleep, I heard something moving in the dark. I was reaching for my pistol when I felt someone near and caught the odor of perfume.

I started to speak when a woman's hand brushed my face, and a woman's fingers stilled my lips.

My own hands went out in the darkness, encountering a warm, bare shoulder as the visitor slipped into bed beside me. A bit more investigating, and I knew she was smoothly, invitingly bare—all over!

Then I began to burn with pure joy, and more! I wrestled myself out of my underwear and was back under the covers pronto. As I groped for the girl, a pair of eager arms wrapped themselves about my neck and pulled me to her rounded form. Then our lips met and with that meeting we were joined with a wonderful completeness.

I'd not been close with a woman since Chihuahua, and that, plus the fact that I'd wanted this girl from the first time I saw her, turned the empty darkness into a blazing dream.

Once, as we lay resting in the shimmering velvety night, her soft curves tight against me, I began to talk—but her hand, again, covered my mouth and then it was my mouth covering hers, and more!

It seemed we just couldn't get enough of one another and were both set on proving that beautiful fact over and over. But at last I sank back on my pillow, with an arm about her, her perfumed hair in my face, and drifted off to sleep.

When I next came to, it was stark, broad daylight. I reached for her— but my arms were empty, and so was the bed.

I rolled out, feet on the floor, and stared around the empty room.

All was the same as the night before, except for a little golden stiletto pinning a note to the wall over my head.

Then I knew that, somehow, Rosita had taken Dulcima's place in the night. Pulling the dagger from the wall, I sank back down on my creaking bed to read her note.

XXV

After a long look at that wicked little stiletto, I read Rosita's penciled note. And reread it as I dressed.

Friend Roy,

Last night I found that obstinado *Dulcima entering your hotel, and am sending her away, again. That the girl is greatly talented, in several ways, I would be the first to admit. However, she's much too young for such actions.*

Though unable to keep a previous evening's appointment in the weeks past, I hope you will not have minded my little charade. I found it, and you, all I hoped it might be.

We leave this part of California for the present, as Francisco seems to have recovered in fine style.

Now, if you are still of a mind to warn the authorities of Carlos's plans, he is determined to carry out his raid on the night of December 2nd.

We are still devoted to our country's freedom, but not at the cost of so many lives!

Rosita

It was only after I'd put the note away in my pocket that I found my sketch of the map to be missing, though Kirker's coin still gleamed up at me from the bureau.

Rosita had traded her golden dagger for a golden map!

That afternoon, when I went down to pick up a ticket at the Jenny Lind, a notice outside the theater informed all and sundry that, though the drama continued, Miss Lotta Crabtree was appearing in place of Mlle. La Fonte, who was temporarily indisposed.

The evening's performance was as good as ever, though I'd learned most of the lines by heart, and Lotta Crabtree seemed to be a lively young filly, with red hair and plenty of spunk. But I don't think she matched Dulcima in voice or looks—and neither did most of the audience.

I knew there was just no use getting in the way of Rosita and Dulcima's differences, and that, sooner or later, the niece would shake the aunt and be back in town. So I lazed around playing poker with Charley Cora and biding my time. Then by Wednesday, I'd made up my mind to hunt up Salazar, and rode down to Diamond Point in the afternoon, stabling White Lightning at the small livery, and took the propeller steamer *Kangaroo* across the Bay.

Docking at San Antonio Landing at three o'clock, I trudged up the drowsing main street to the ramshackle, vine-wrapped town hall. There I found Salazar out of town, "somewhere northward at the mines," chasing bandits. As he was not expected back under a week, I left him a note, telling him that it was mighty important that he reach me at the San Francisco House before the first of December.

I caught the same *Kangaroo* back at suppertime, along with a bunch of visiting miners. As the steamer only made the bay crossing twice a week, I figured that though I'd missed the sheriff I was lucky to get back to San Francisco in one day.

It was a good thing I did, for Josh arrived on the next morning's stage and came hunting me before I was out of bed.

Still deep in pleasant slumber, I was again about to clasp Rosita to me. And even more satisfying, I was now able to see all of her lovely charms, but just then some fool began to pound away on a drum and shout muffled threats, while Rosita faded from my straining grasp!

Barely half awake, I propped up on one elbow, hazily wondering why I dreamed of Rosita—and not Dulcima. At last I roused enough to recognize Josh's bellowings in the hallway.

Piling onto the floor, I staggered to the door and let in my brother with his armload of carpetbags.

Then for the next hour, Joshua Quincy Bean, late alcalde of San Diego, sat on the edge of my bed and filled me in on his business and political shenanigans.

As soon as he got around to Diamond Dick, I found out why Josh was in such high spirits, despite a long and bone-shaking coach trip.

"That tinhorn Powers might have finangled me out of office, but he didn't get in himself for all of his thimblerigging," chortled Josh. "And when he let himself get caught redhanded at the *calabozo*, his connections with those midnight lynchings came to the surface. So now he's under a bond to appear before the Los Angeles magistrate in May!"

Josh leaned back, lit up a stogie, blew a great looping billow of blue smoke and grinned like a contented cougar. "Y'know, I don't think Diamond Dick cares too much for yours truly after I swore out an affidavit holding him responsible for those murders. Best part of all is that he had to sell his dive in San Diego to raise that bond and pay off his lawyers! Here, have a cigar."

I told my brother that I'd run into Powers twice since coming to town but didn't mention Dulcima. "Powers surely has that poker face, for he never mentioned you, nor his hard times."

"Well, an honest confession is good for the soul, they say—but tough on the reputation," grinned Josh, ringing in another of his old saws. "But Diamond Dick's got more to trouble his soul than that: I also plagued him good and plenty up here, too. With all his law problems, he couldn't raise enough money to make a down payment on a champion little gambling saloon over here at 920 Sacramento that we'd both heard about." Josh twiddled with his goatee and snorted. "I went over and signed the papers this morning while you were still sawing wood. So we're in business, Roy —until you can lay hands on that danged treasure trove. Yes sir, I guess Señor Richard Powers had best think twice before he tangles with any of us Beans again!" And Josh waved away any more talk of Diamond Dick, along with our wavering rafts of cigar smoke. He'd also brushed aside thought that Murieta would be able to do him much harm in the middle of the bustling city of San Francisco.

I'd held my tongue, covering up my knowledge of the upcoming raid at Benicia, in the hopes that Salazar would be able to put the kibosh on Carlos Hechavarría for good—providing he was able to get to me in time.

By the middle of the month, Josh and I had the new place, which we'd renamed the Golden Nugget, humming. We had ourselves two bartenders, one Shanghai Bender, an ex-sailor with a wooden leg—and the other, that dusky businessman and cat importer, Peter Biggs.

Bender came by his name from the fact that he had been sandbagged at least three times down on the waterfront and toted onboard one of the many clippers plying between California and the Far East. After losing his leg to a shark out in the Sandwich Islands, Shanghai worked his way back to San Francisco and hung about the dockside saloons, swamping and washing bottles and glasses, until he was as proficient at the bar as the next man. About a week after we opened, he came stumping into the Golden Nugget. Josh hired him on the spot after watching Shanghai deftly divest himself of his wooden underpin and use it to subdue a big drunken miner who was trying to start a war in our saloon.

I ran into Peter Biggs about the same time where he was hanging around the El Dorado, looking much the worse for wear and trying to keep his good eye out for some sort of "oppotunity," as well as a place to sleep. I braced him and found that he'd made a tidy fortune peddling his feline rat fighters but had turned around and lost every cent "bucking the tiger." As I'd been acting as super to Shanghai, as well as dealing some of the games, I fetched Biggs back to Josh and he was hired as assistant to Shanghai behind the maghogany. Thus we had ourselves a pair of bartenders with a grand total of three eyes and three legs, but we still needed a professional dealer.

It seemed pretty fortunate at the time when Charley Cora sauntered into the saloon one evening. "So, this is why you haven't been around to butt heads lately! Heard someone named Bean bought this place, but didn't think of you."

He smiled slightly and shrugged when I asked him to step up to the bar for a drink. "Fine, but I can't buy one back very easy." He went on to tell us that a high roller named J. J. Bryant, who'd toted a hefty grudge against him for all of the faro games of Bryant's he'd busted back on the Mississippi, had landed in town the week before. The first thing this Bryant did was to buy out the establishment where Charley worked and have him tossed out on the street. "And to make matters even worse," Cora shrugged, "be damned if an old girl friend from Natchez hasn't showed up and is on my trail to marry me. Knowing Arabella Ryan, I'll bet a dollar to a plugged peso that she finds out some way to corral this here child!"

"Never bet on a sure thing unless you're able to lose," said Josh. "You need to get to work to take your mind off your troubles." And then and there he hired Charley Cora to handle our tables.

So the days ran along, with Josh and me staying at the San Francisco House, taking our meals at a little restaurant on Sacramento and putting in long hours at the Golden Nugget. Charley Cora dealt the pasteboards, and handled the faro bank, with Peter Biggs tending bar, while Shanghai Bender had advanced to bouncer, owing to the lurid gossip about his "deadly" wooden leg, which put more fear into possible troublemakers than the pair of murderous little Derringers that Charley kept tucked in his vest.

With such a team, the place ticked away like a Waterbury clock, and the money came in hand over fist.

To get shed of the saloon grind, I'd taken Josh to several of the local theaters, including the brand-new Metropolitan, where we saw the Starks and their company give smashingly good performances of *The Rivals*, *Much Ado* and *Pizarro*, along with a couple of rollicking comedies. But I always seemed to come back to the Jenny Lind, where the two Edwin Booths, father and son, were bowling over their audiences in their production of *The Iron Chest.* Little Lotta Crabtree was still on stage during intermissions and winning herself a strong following, while Lorette La Fonte became a fading name.

I'd inquired of Dulcima's whereabouts several times, but "Colonel" McGuire, who looked down-in-the-mouth about it, could only announce that she was still "indisposed." I took that to mean that Rosita's express orders kept her under lock and key at her finishing school. The "Colonel" had not had a word from Powers either, and Josh and I figured that Diamond Dick was lying low trying to beat his indictment.

There'd been several items in the papers concerning Captain Love and his expeditions, but actually little to report beyond the fact that "the gallant officer remains on the trail of the Murieta Gang as well as other dangerous law-breakers." At ten cents a mile, Love and his flock were not doing too badly, whether they ever caught up with anyone.

On the last day of November, I had a visit from a real law dog at last when Salazar himself stumped into the Golden Nugget out of a drizzling rain about suppertime. After shaking hands with Josh and myself, he tugged off his flopping sombrero, which looked more like a damp mushroom than ever, and sat down at a table with us.

Declaring himself mighty happy to see us, Salazar looked over the noisy room and made small talk until Josh got up to tend to some business at one of the tables, then he tackled me. "Well, young Bean, and what's all this business? For, let me tell you, by St. Lazarus's spotted pups, I only got back from the American River half a day ago!" He picked up one of the beers that Biggs had fetched over and lifted it in a quizzical salute.

Keeping my voice down, I let Salazar have both barrels. *The place! The time! And Murieta!*

The little sheriff's eyes about stuck out of his head with excitement, and the top of his vanished scalp positively glistened as I repeated everything except where I'd come by the information.

Presently Salazar leaned back and lifted his forgotten drink, sipping at it with great satisfaction. "You have done the world and me a great big favor, young Bean. But I notice you do not say how you came by the welcome news." Then he shrugged. "Well, it is *non importante*, for I know you to be—how do the *anglos* say?—the straight shooter! This I also knew when I heard how you put a hole through this low-down *picaro* of a Powers!" He tugged at his oxhorn mustaches and smiled broadly. "And I have heard some other things. Among them that you ran away with his horse while rousting that rattle-headed Haraszthy, and that you may have tried to do the same thing—running away with Powers's little *niña-amiga!*"

Before I could start to defend myself, I stopped, for if it came out that Dulcima had been bundled out of town, the talk might turn to Red Rosita. So, I only kept my jaw clamped and ordered another round of drinks from Biggs.

"And to speak of that little beauty Señorita Dulcima, I behold you still have the eye for the ladies, and by all the pretty angels, there's one over there dealing cards!" Salazar nodded his shining head in the direction where Charley Cora's curvesome brunette girlfriend dealt poker to a grinning group of sailors and miners—winning as usual.

"That's Belle, Charley Cora's girlfriend. He convinced Josh that we needed someone to dress up our games, and she was hired a week ago." As if she knew we were talking about her, Belle glanced over, flashing one of her wide red smiles, then turned back to trimming her customers.

"*Sí!* Now I know her! She and this gambler, Cora, got into a row at the mining camps along the Sacramento not long ago. Señorita Belle, as you can see is *mucho bella!* And this Senōr Cora, a devil at faro, is also the very devil when jealous. He shot a bullet through the leg of one of the señorita's admirers and the pair had to leave that camp in a hurry. That Belle! She'll get that young man hung yet!"

Presently Salazar arose, thanked me again for my information, donned his serape and shapeless sombrero, shook hands with Josh and went out into the rainy night.

"Now, what in tunket was that about?" Josh wanted to know. "I thought he could be here to haul you in for horse theft. You know, that little sawed-off horned toad never wastes much time or effort!"

"Just a friendly visit," I said, looking a bit more closely at Charley Cora where that gambler sat keeping one eye on his game and the other on his buxom girlfriend.

The next thing we heard of Salazar was a front-page story in the *Alta California* four days later, on December 3:

MURIETA THWARTED!
SHERIFF SALAZAR SAVES ARMORY
BANDITS DRIVEN HEADLONG FROM BENICIA
MANY SHOTS EXCHANGED

Acting upon reliable information, Sheriff Salazar of Alameda County, and a number of his possemen, laid in ambush at the Benicia U.S. Armory, north of Oakland (San Antonio Landing), on the night of December 2nd, and attacked the Joaquín Murieta Gang, when those rogues attempted to gain entrance into the Fort close on to midnight.

After hailing the goodly body of brigands, who'd come equipped with two wagons to haul away their proposed plunder of weapons and ammunition, Sheriff Salazar opened fire. The ball was immediately begun, and the entire Gang, under California's most notorious Bandit Chief, returned the Lawmen's fire with a will, before, at last, abandoning their rolling stock and fleeing for their lives into the western mountains. It is estimated that over a hundred shots or more were exchanged in the darkness.

One bandido was cut from the saddle and later identified as Pío Hidalgo, one of the most brutal robbers. Two of the sheriff's group were slightly wounded. It is not known the exact extent of the damage inflicted upon the ubiquitous Joaquín, aside from the obvious thwarting of his grandiose plans to arm some of the dissatisfied villains, who still lurk in the wilds.

Well, that put the kibosh on Carlos Hechavarría for the time being, but I had a feeling that if he ever found out who tipped off Salazar, it would go mighty hot for both Rosita and myself. And it was more than likely that Carlos (Murieta) had gotten word that Josh was in San Francisco.

I surely wished that Salazar and his bunch had shot straighter!

XXVI

As if Salazar's stand-off with Carlos Hechavarría at Benicia wasn't enough, Josh had himself a falling-out with Charley Cora at the end of that week, and practically heaved him out of the saloon, along with his girlfriend after Cora had stuck one of his pet Derringers into the face of a high roller who'd tried to get fresh with the bold-eyed Belle.

"Think I did right, Roy, tossing out that hothead and his calico cat?" Josh fussed while we sat at supper. "Can't have him throwing down on someone every time they pat his tootsie's rear. There's just bound to be a shooting, sooner or later!"

"Charley's a good man," I said, "just about the best I ever saw with a faro bank, in front of it or behind it—but we don't need any more rumpus. I've got enough on my mind as it is."

Josh looked narrowly at me, and wagged his head. "I guess you're just champing at the bit to get out after that gold cache, and I won't be a bit downhearted if you find it," he mumbled, between bites of pie. "But, like you've said, there got to be dozens of twin peaks out there. Looks like you got yourself a gold needle in a haystack of mountains."

I didn't have the heart to tell my brother I wouldn't be the only one hunting for that *needle,* and wondered just where Rosita was—and Dulcima. I knew both might turn up at any time, for both were a mighty hardheaded pair of young fillies.

Then Dulcima suddenly did appear in town two days before Christmas. And Diamond Dick was with her!

I discovered this when the hotel clerk handed me a note as Josh and I came down to breakfast:

Mister Roy Bean,

Friend Roy, here I am back in San Francisco, for a moment. But go out with Colonel McGuire's touring company in the morning, in order to be at Rabbit Creek for our Christmas performance. We have Mart Taylor, Mrs. Sinclair, and several other live wires. Colonel McGuire agrees that Mr. Powers, who has been through some bad times, should

be our manager. If you still wish to see me, I'll be at the same hotel,
the Oriental on Montgomery, for most of the afternoon.
Dulcima Stevens!

I went over to the Oriental in early afternoon and sent up word that I
was in the lobby. In a few minutes the porter brought down a message for
me to go up to room 200. And I didn't waste a moment in climbing those
stairs.

When I knocked, the door opened immediately, and there stood
Dulcima, in a fancy embroidered yellow dressing gown, golden hair piled
upon her head—and with a drink in her hand!

It would have been perfect, save for the fact that Diamond Dick Powers, dressed in a flashy checked suit, flaming red necktie and polished
boots, lounged in one of the two easy chairs.

"Ah there, Bean." Powers stood up and, reaching for his ulster and
wide-brimmed hat, crossed the floor to the doorway, as I stood aside,
without a word to him.

"Host of things to do for the busy manager." Powers waved a hand at a
pile of luggage in the corner, all strapped and bound up with rope and
cord. "I'm on my way to check with the rest of our company. Have to be
on the road at first light." Then he was gone out, shutting the door behind
him—and I was alone with Dulcima.

"Now, I know you haven't much use for Dick—ah, Richard—but he's
been a lifesaver for me, Roy." Dulcima wavered slightly as she walked over
to the dresser and, without asking, poured me a stiff drink of whiskey.
"Here, you can drink to our forthcoming triumphs out in the wilds of
California."

I took the glass, sat down in the chair vacated by Powers and looked at
her. Dulcima's eyes, always blue as the summer skies at midday, were
sparkling with a different light, and her mouth was—mighty inviting. But
I downed some of the drink and waited for her to speak.

She crossed back to the bed and sat down on its edge, tipped up her
glass and drained it like an old soldier. "You know that hellcat, that so-
called aunt of mine? She had me kidnapped again and carried back to that
hateful Salinas finishing school—that two-by-four prison for little milksop
females!"

I nodded and downed the rest of my whiskey to keep her company, as I
noticed Dulcima's pretty knees appearing through the edge of that fancy
gown—and even more! I felt like I needed another drink then and there.

"Roy, you must know that I'm old enough, nearly eighteen, and I'll live my own life, in spite of that flashy *perra!*" She stood up again, and marched back to the whiskey, poured herself another glass, then came over to me. As she bent with the half-empty bottle, her dressing gown slid open, and I could see that it was her sole bit of clothing! "Here, let me fill up your glass."

"How long have you known Powers?" I rasped, trying to get the drink down and smooth out the dryness in my throat. "He says a long time!"

Dulcima belted away half of her drink with the ease of an old toper, then sat the glass down on the carpet, dressing gown falling half off her shoulders as she did. "Ever since the first time I ran off from that old hairpin Miss Granville and her silly little school and came up to San Francisco. I hadn't any money to speak of, and Dick Powers found me on the streets and was very kind. He bought me a meal, got me a room and when he found out that I wanted to go on the stage, had me in to Colonel McGuire's little theater at the edge of town. She smiled shyly as she settled her robe about her again. Then she frowned and shook her finger. "I know you think Richard is more—than a friend. Well, that's neither here nor there, is it?" Her soft red mouth hardened somewhat. "He's helped me get where I want, in spite of Rosita—Red Rosita Almada—and Joaquín Murieta!"

I gaped at her, then gulped down the rest of my whiskey.

"Yes, Roy, I know a good many things. I discovered Rosita's brother was the bandit, and that her pretty hands, those perfumed little fingers, were not any too clean at that." She leaned over to recover her drink and her gown fell from her—completely, revealing young, swelling breasts and deliciously dimpled body. But she paid no attention. "I knew all this five years ago, when I heard them plotting at the rancho. Rosita must have suspicioned what I knew, for she sent me off to that school at Salinas—and kept me there as much as possible."

I stood up, weaving a bit myself from the warmth of the room and the alcohol. "Does Dick Powers know this?"

Dulcima also arose, completely childlike in her nakedness, looking at me innocently with her blue eyes, now a bit out of focus from drink. Then she shook her golden curls. "No, I know enough to keep certain things to myself, Roy; do you?"

She came to me and put up her arms. "Remember when I told you that I meant to come visiting?" Those slim, rounded arms were about me now, her smooth curves pressed hard against me, and her golden head buried against my chest. "Well, I did—only that she-cat came in the night and had me thrown into her closed carriage!" She raised her lips. "Did you miss me?"

I picked her bodily up and toted her back to the bed. And mighty shortly I was showing her just how much I'd missed her.

Dulcima was mine at last! When I left her, I was walking two yards above the wooden sidewalk, as I recalled all the things we'd said—and done. There'd just been no way that I could have kept from telling her of that fortune out there—somewhere. And we'd planned that I'd search the country for it while she toured with the "Colonel's" company.

I spent a good share of the next day, December 24, thinking of her sweet embraces and her promise to wait for me until I'd found Jeff Kirker's gold. Diamond Dick Powers was just a back number now!

Around suppertime that Christmas Eve, Josh came to where I was running the faro layout for a cheerful mob of celebrating miners, sailors and Mexicans. "If you can stop mooning over that little piece of calico long enough to keep one eye on the game and the other on the place, I'll go up the street and take some supper. We're just too busy for the both of us to feed at once."

"Wouldn't need to double up like this if you hadn't heaved out Charley Cora," I growled, not meaning it, but irked by Josh's reference to Dulcima.

He stood for a moment looking over the busy, smoke-hazed room, one thumb in his vest and the other twiddling with his goatee, as he always did when pleased with himself. "Well, that nigra Biggs does a mighty fair job handling the dice game when Shanghai takes a turn at the bar. And you have the makings of a first-rate gambler yourself."

My brother had left his overcoat at the hotel to have some buttons tightened, so he pulled on his hat and my own ulster, then lingered to talk to me, between deals, of our family back home and wonder if Ma and Pa would still be having the same sort of big Christmas they used to have when we were all young-uns.

"Sometimes, Roy, I wish I'd gone back to old Mason County after the war, and not stayed way out here. I think brother Sam showed better sense staying put in New Mexico after you two flew the coop out of Chihuahua City."

I nodded and kept dealing, still out of sorts. And that was the last time that I saw my brother Joshua Quincy Bean alive!

He'd left the Golden Nugget and was walking through the gently falling drizzle toward our favorite restaurant when someone stepped from an alley off Sutter and fired two pistol balls into his back at such close range they set his coat on fire—despite the rain!

A gambler from the Red Rooster, who'd seen Josh fall into the street, caught a glimpse of someone in a serape and sombrero run up Sutter and fade into the night, then he beat out the flames from my brother's clothing and began to yell for a policeman.

They fetched Josh back to the saloon and laid him on a poker table, while our customers and employees stood around in stunned silence. After we shut the place, Shanghai stumped back to the bar and brought over a couple of bottles, and we sat down and drank to Josh. The police had already been in, looking for any possible motives for my brother's assassination, but I could only say that Joaquín Murieta was known to have made threats, and that Charley Cora and Dick Powers had little reason to wish Josh any too well. I didn't mean to throw suspicion on either gambler, but it had to be said. A young reporter from one of the shabbier weeklies named Ridge who'd been tagging the police around heard me, but I didn't think anything of it.

"Shot by a person or persons unknown," said Coroner Riley, who then began to jot down the cost of a funeral in his capacity as part-time undertaker.

As I sat there, drink in hand, looking at Josh laid out in his muddy clothing and thinking what a hell of a Christmas it was going to be, I recalled how glad he'd been to see me when I'd arrived at San Diego in the summer just past. Yes, it was just one hell of a jolt.

Then I got another jolt when Riley, long red face creased in unaccustomed thought, spoke up again. "Y'say your brother there was a-wearin' yore overcoat? Well"—he took a healthy belt of whiskey—"could be they was tryin' for you!"

XXVII

We buried Josh the day after Christmas out south of town at Potero Hill, where a small cemetery had been in use since the early days of the Rush. It was a peaceful but lonesome spot, with a pair of huge redwoods standing like mournful sentinels at the back of the two-acre lot. Most of the great redwoods around San Francisco had long been felled for the building of everything from ore sluices to lumber for slap-up housing.

There weren't many folk in the funeral party, preached at graveside by the local Methodist minister, a tall, stoop-shouldered old fellow named Ashworth. A few of our regulars came out in one of the three hired hacks, as did Peter Biggs and Shang Bender. Sim Watson, the local marshal, was also on hand, along with Salvador Salazar.

After the short service was over, a chilly December rain began to fall through the hazy sunshine, and we piled into the hacks for town, following the empty hearse. Salazar rode with me, while Shanghai drove and Peter Biggs sat up front with him, wiping away at his good eye.

I'd sent Josh off in as good a style as I was able, dressing him in one of his fancy alcalde get-ups, and with one of the very last of Jeff Kirker's gold pieces in his vest pocket—to show St. Peter that he'd left the game standing pat.

"I seen that you place the *moneda de oro* in your brother's pocket," Salazar jostled my thoughts—as to who could have back-shot Josh, and had those bullets been meant for me?

"*Sí,*" he went on, tugging at the ends of his oxhorn mustachios, which were now drooping as mournfully as his battered sombrero, "I think that it is the ancient custom, the giving the dead one plenty pesos to pay that old ferryman for safe passage across to the other shore."

I'd a feeling that the little officer meant to twist the conversation around to those gold eagles of Kirker's, as he'd done before, but he remained silent.

"*Muerte—Murieta!* There's an hombre mighty well named, isn't he? Death and a dealer in death," I said, my thoughts jostled onto another trail. I stared back at the redwoods, where they loomed up like a pair of

crimson monuments in the late afternoon, seeing again the coldly handsome face of Carlos Hechavarría. "Where might that damnable Murieta
be by now?"

"The devil himself only knows where such hellfire *bastardos* get themselves off to," grumbled Salazar. "Young Bean, again I must thank you for
your help in saving the Benicia armory—though most of those villains
escaped, as you know! But, like I told you in the past, all gold, in the
ground or out of it, is the curse of our poor land. It brings much sorrow
and death, as you know, poor fellow!"

Wondering again just how much Salazar knew of Kirker's gold, I
switched the talk to the whereabouts of the other murder suspects, Charley Cora in particular, who'd vanished since his fight with Josh. I was
about certain that Diamond Dick was still away in the mining camps with
Dulcima and the traveling troupe.

For all the conversation on the ride back, we'd come to no definite
conclusion as to who'd actually cut down on my brother.

When the hack pulled up in front of the Golden Nugget in the rainy
dusk, Salazar and I got down to stand before the locked door. He took me
by the hand, wishing me well and asking as to my future plans.

"I suppose I'll keep the place open, for the time being," I told him, to
the obvious relief of Biggs and Bender, who thereupon drove off up the
street to turn in the hack at Johnson's Livery.

The little marshal's broad brown face sobered as he lingered under the
gaslight by the saloon door. "I see you pack *la pistola.* I felt that as we sat
side by side. *Bueno!* But guard yourself well, *amigo joven!* It may be that
the cowardly assassin who slew your brother might return!"

We shook hands again, and then Salazar walked off, his squat figure
wavering and fading into the gathering darkness.

Standing before the locked and bolted door of our empty saloon, I made
a vow that not only would I guard myself but I'd see that someone paid for
Josh. And paid in blood!

For the next sixty days, I stayed close to the Golden Nugget, managing
its affairs and taking care of the money, for we'd gained the reputation of
being a straight house. Sometimes I felt as though I had a couple of holes
right spang through me, like poor Josh. One was an emptiness that came
from not knowing just when I'd see Dulcima again, and also wondering
about Rosita. The other gap in my life was the realization that my brother
might still be alive if I'd have stayed away from California.

But other times, when the money came in hand over fist at the tables, and I'd about decided to become a gambling czar, instead of my old daydream of being a merchant prince, I shrugged off all worried and morbid thoughts.

That didn't mean that I didn't watch my back each and every time I went home to the hotel in the late hours, or visited the other rival saloons, on the lookout for either Carlos Hechavarría or Charley Cora. But both of those rascals seemed to have disappeared from California, though I figured that Carlos was off in the mountains licking his wounds after the whipping Salazar had given him, and who knew where that grinning wildcat Cora could be?

I still kept up a haphazard sort of love affair with the theaters of San Francisco. Even with Dulcima no longer in town, I couldn't keep away from McGuire's Jenny Lind, where young Lotta Crabtree was settling down for a long run, starring in *A Loan of a Lover,* playing a pepper pot named Gertrude. A great little trouper, with all sorts of wild jigs and reels, she reminded me, again, of Dulcima and her electric enthusiasms.

The high point of the new year came when the great Lola Montez returned to San Francisco in February, after a two-year tour of the world, and knocked the theatergoing crowds into a cocked hat with her new production of *Maritana* at the San Francisco Theater, where she took three parts herself. Then the dazzling, raven-haired thespian topped that smash with *Charlotte Corday.* And how those packed houses whooped it up when she gave the villain Marat the deepsix between the ribs with her glittering bowie knife!

But as much as I enjoyed the fabulous actress in her triumphs, I only attended two performances, for the sight of that lady's well nigh incomparable looks brought memories of Rosita—partly from the two women's past association and the fact that they were two of the greatest beauties of the day.

By earliest March, spring was easing up the coast. Birds were returning from warmer climes below the border. Jays, larks and magpies swooped about in noisy clusters, while quail and wood pigeon circled the outskirts in great masses. I had an idea that most restaurants' bills of fare would shortly feature roast pigeon as well as canvasback, for the latter were now swooping into the coves and backwaters in thundering gray clouds.

Riding White Lightning out to visit Josh's grave at Potero Hill, as I did each Sunday, I saw California poppies, wild iris and Indian paintbrush stitching tender stalks through the greening grasses, as hundreds of yucca reared their crowns of sword-shaped leaves about the countryside. The oak, manzanita and laurel as well as the rest of the trees in the groves and woodlands were already a tawny green shimmer in their new leafy shawls.

Foxes, coyotes and deer trotted or loped out of my way as I racked along the country roads, and several times I saw black bear lumbering into the shady protection of a neighboring woods. But never did I see any lurking horsemen or suspicious riders, though I met and passed dozens of folk coming and going from the mines or small farms.

The chilling rains had ceased days before and now the winds, forever ranging the coasts, seemed more charged than ever with the unending roar of the vasty reaches of the Pacific—a sound never entirely forgotten, though pushed backward into some corner of the mind.

So it was with Josh, I told myself, as I stood and stared at the low, sunken patch of earth with its raw wooden cross, already weathering into a faded brown. His brutal and cowardly murder and the unseen threat still hanging over me was also something never completely forgotten. It was a situation that filled me with a half-felt restlessness, compounded with such things as the low, distant but insistent booming of the mighty ocean, and the fact that I was young, and that it was spring—and that I had to be on the move. It wasn't yet the time to start hunting for that golden hoard, and yet I had to be on the move—somewhere.

Returning to the Golden Nugget on the second Sunday in March, I made up my mind to ride over to the mining camps, where McGuire's touring company and Dulcima were performing. I already had their itinerary from the "Colonel": Grass Valley, the first four nights; Rabbit Creek, six nights; Taylor's Gulch, five nights; Rich Bar, four nights; Gibsonville, two nights; and Hangtown, two nights. As it was now March 16, the company would be in Gibsonville by the time I could get out there.

Three days later, I was traveling the rough trail leading to the mining camp of Gibsonville in the Bear River Valley. On the way out from San Antonio Landing I'd taken a wrong turn, where the road forked at the old Mexican village of Río Oso, and rode north for near a day before running onto the little mining camp of Bullard's Bar, at Feather River, where I finally got straightened out.

Even though I'd sighted the houses, shacks and mining rigs of Gibsonville squatting along the curving brown river in the late afternoon, it was deep twilight before I got down the steep slope of nearly two thousand feet and was riding up the dusty main street.

Lamps were already alight in the hamlet's two hotels and several saloons, while the sounds of banjoes, fiddles and applause rippled out of the little log Opera House, between the hotels.

There was barely standing room at the back of the stiffling-hot auditorium, but I paid my ticket and watched Dulcima, the Chapmans and the rest of the company go through their paces in the play of the evening, *The Little Detective.*

Dulcima, obviously revelling in the story, impersonated six characters. As one of them, Harry Racket, she came out in a fawn-colored sporting costume that drew waves of applause from the shabby miners. Switching from one role to another as she pursued the obvious villain, she literally brought down the house when she turned up as Barney O'Brien with a blarney-filled repertoire of jigs and reels.

When the threadbare red curtain rippled down upon the performance, she returned and completed her conquest of the laughing, shouting audience with a final, naughty little ballad, "Chaff and Wink Your Eye."

I slipped out into the street in advance of the jam-packed mob and stood to one side, waiting until I was able to force my way back to the dressing room, and saw an old acquaintance, Captain Harry Love, puffing on a cigar, striding along, elbow to elbow with some of his rangers.

Watching Love surging through the crowd toward a saloon, I felt a touch on my arm and turned to find Dulcima beside me.

"Oh, Roy, I felt you were here. But don't ask me how!" Her blue eyes were dim with tears. "I heard about your brother, and I felt so bad for you!" Suddenly she stamped a little boot. "But why did you wait so long to come to me? We could have been together again. I've thought of nothing else."

When I tried to explain, she brushed all aside with a sweep of her hand. "No matter! Dick Powers has changed our schedule. He's waiting for the company at Hangtown, where they've had a big strike. Our coach leaves in less than an hour!"

Late next morning, after an uneasy night at the hotel, I was riding through a pine grove that topped a ridge twenty miles west of the village of Gibsonville when some sound or movement broke in upon my thoughts.

For a moment I pulled up White Lightning and let him take a breather, as I turned in the saddle to stare back down the twisting, brush-fringed trail. Nothing!

As I scanned the empty landscape, all those bitter, anxious words of Dulcima's pounded through my mind again.

I slapped the great stallion's reins and rode on down the steep slope. *Dulcima!* How I'd felt the pressure of her firm young thigh against me when she'd stood so very close in that laughing, jovial crowd while we waited for the evening stage.

"It would be wonderful, Roy, if you could find that money . . . *that gold of ours,*" she'd whispered to me. "But I want us to get far away from this country. I've always hated this terrible land ever since I was a little child—a child those horrible red beasts nearly killed when they burned and destroyed our wagon train!" I felt her shudder. "It was those savage animals and this wild country that threw me straight into the arms of those murderous Almadas, making me the helpless, orphaned ward of a redhanded bandit and a red-haired slut!"

I'd shuffled my boots in the sand to hear such words coming from those softly kissable lips, and asked about Powers's whereabouts on the night Josh was shot. But, according to Dulcima, Diamond Dick had been nearly a hundred miles away from San Francisco, at Murderers Bar, on the Sacramento, that particular evening.

Once more, thinking of the urgent fire of her farewell kiss, I pulled up my mount at the crown of another tree-clad hill, listening. All was still save for the rusty-hinge creaking of a pair of mountain jays and a dismal wind that slipped, whining, through wavering oak and pine boughs.

Kicking up my horse, I'd started on down the next slope when a rifle cracked out from an oak grove to my left, the bullet creasing White Lightning's shoulder. In less than a breath, I'd hit the rocky ground with a teeth-rattling jolt as my wounded stallion plunged off into the underbrush.

I could spot nothing but a faint blue thread of smoke drifting upward, then a second shot banged flatly and the rifleman rode out of the trees, aiming his weapon down at me, where I crouched by a boulder.

I yanked my Colt, thumbing off two shots. Though it was a far piece, I saw the stranger's black sombrero fall off, then up went his arms and he toppled stiffly from his big gray mount.

Stumbling through the brush and thickets after White Lightning, I suddenly heard shouts and calls break out from where the murderous drygulcher lay.

"*Murieta!* Hey, Captain, here's Murieta!" And I caught Captain Love's bass voice baying back exultantly at his men, like an excited hound dog that'd treed his coon!

At last, after a five-minute search, I found White Lightning in a rockstrewn gully, quivering but sound enough except for that bloody gash across his shoulder. I wiped it with moss and water from my canteen, then led him through the tangled undergrowth, and around the hill to where I could mount and ride to hell out of there!

Murieta! Murieta dead or taken! Now there seemed nothing more to worry about except finding my gold!

XXVIII

San Francisco was in an uproar when Captain Love and his bunch made their triumphal return to town. Most of the local papers clamored with any number of wild yarns of the supposed end of Joaquín Murieta. The first story to appear in the *Alta California* might just have been dictated by that four-flusher of a Love himself, as it made my lucky shot sound like a pitched battle:

> *JOAQUÍN CAPTURED, BEHEADED AND HIS BODY*
> *IN THE HANDS OF HIS CAPTORS*
> *It has just been learned that the valiant Company of Rangers, commanded by the redoubtable Captain Harry Love, met the notorious murderer and robber, Joaquín, and six of his equally infamous band, at Panocho Pass, and after a desperate running fight, Joaquín and one of his gang were killed. . . .*

The item went on to relate how the bandit's head had been cut off by Love's rangers and "placed in spirits."

According to Peter Biggs, who immediately took time off from his dice table to view the grisly souvenir, in its place of honor behind the bar at the Crystal Palace on Jackson, it was hard to say just what the man might have looked like "when he had his haid on."

I was still troubled by the dead man's identity. A nagging thought gripped me that I might have shot down Francisco Almada, though I couldn't believe that Rosita's brother would have tried to drygulch me.

Elbowing through the jostling, whooping, hard-drinking crowd at the busy Crystal Palace bar, it was plain to see why the management had outbid a dozen other saloons for a chance to display the hideous trophy. When I finally stood close enough to view the bruised and battered head floating in its glass jar, the only thing I could be certain of was that the thing had two whole ears. It was *not* Francisco Almada!

I stuck tight as a burr to the Nugget for the next week, helping Bender and Biggs, along with a brace of gamblers I'd hired named Ad Pence and

Jack White, trying to stay so busy that I wouldn't have much time to think.

At night, however, in spite of everything, I couldn't get rid of unwanted visions of poor old Don Hechavarría, and what his demented son had done to Josh—and what I'd done to him, in turn. That ghastly head often floated before my eyes, even in the dark.

It was during such dark moments that I truly welcomed memories of Dulcima, and burned to recall all that golden girl's desirable charms. But as often as I thought of Dulcima, Rosita would come crowding into my mind. Where, I wondered, had Red Rosita and her outlaw brother gone since the night she'd traded her lovely, passionate self for a treasure map?

The Almadas might have that map, all right, but a big chunk of the puzzle was still missing. Where were those twin peaks the April sun would be rising or setting between? When I began to mull over the many mountain ranges up and down California, my head ached so that I gave it all up and tried to find some sleep.

As the days stretched on into April, I began to think more, during the days, busy or not. Odd times found me off in some corner of the saloon, studying another copy I'd made of the map, and cudgeling my brain over where Kirker could have hidden his outlaw gold.

Then on the evening of April 16 the last piece of the puzzle fell into place. We'd just closed up the Nugget for the night and were having a drink at the bar, after counting over the take, when Peter Biggs began to harp upon his favorite subject, lost "oppotunities." As neither Pence nor White had heard the sad tale of the King of Aigs's downfall, I nudged Biggs into retelling the story of his sudden abdication and headlong flight from the miners' wrath at Feather River. While he droned out his tale of woe, I was glancing over a current issue of the San Francisco *Herald*, which was featuring the serialization of the reporter John Rollin Ridge's *Brigand Chief of California*, and had just come across the section where my very own brother had been shot down in cold blood by Murieta, when Biggs mentioned something in his ramblings that caught my disinterested ear.

"What was that you said about *Hully Bullies?*"

"Sayed when dem fightin'-mad minuhs tuk an' run me outa camp, through no fault of mine, I wuz so confuse ah mighty nigh come ridin' noath towards them blamed *Yollar Bullies!*" Biggs's good eye winked with alarmed recollection. "Ain't wanter go thata way. Real wile Injuns up dah!"

There was no doubt that he was speaking of Jeff Kirker's *Bullies*. I could still hear Jeff's "Found myself a place where not one damned white man had ever set foot. *She's all hid there—and she's bully!*"

But I'd been mistaken a bit. What Kirker must have said was, *"She's all hid there at the Bullies!"*

It had to be that, for Kirker had traveled over a hundred miles north of the mining country with the stolen gold.

Waiting until Biggs finished his mournful story and Pence and White had gone home laughing, I sat down with Bill and Shanghai to learn something few folks knew. There was a small range to the north of the Russian River, and east of the Eel River country, called the Yolla Bollies. Shanghai, who'd knocked around the coasts had heard something of those ranges, adding that Yolla Bollas was Yuki Indian for "High Snowy Mountains."

At last I had what I needed!

For the next two days I scratched gravel, getting a traveling kit put together and picking up a pack mule at the livery. Kirker had used a pair of the beasts, but I thought White Lightning was big enough to tote his share.

I told the desk clerk at the hotel that I was going off to do some prospecting for a couple of weeks, and put out the same story at the Golden Nugget. Both Bender and Biggs were all for coming along, but I gave them their orders to tend to their own knitting and keep an eye on our new gambling team—as well on each other.

On the very morning I left, April 19, I received a short note from Dulcima, dated from her hotel over on Montgomery, telling me that the company had returned and asking me to call that afternoon.

It was a big and mighty welcome surprise, but I thought I'd soon have an even bigger one for her, so had our swamper take an answer back to the Oriental that I'd be away from town for around ten days.

During the first several days of my trip, everything went well. I'd ridden down to visit Josh's grave, then over to take Wednesday's boat across to San Antonio Landing. Without stopping by to see Salazar, I'd struck on due northeast for the Sacramento. On the second morning I rode past the forlorn wooden fortifications of Sutter's Mill, where so much of the gold madness began in 1848. Just two years later, Sutter's farm and deserted holdings were a shambles, with the captain a ruined man. Ferried over the broad, brown reaches of the Sacramento from Sutter's Wharf, I then headed straight north, leaving the last of the main mining camps.

About the end of the fourth day, I began to have the feeling that someone was trailing me, though I sighted no dust during the daylight nor campfire smoke in the evenings.

Following the rough map I'd sketched out from Biggs and Bender's descriptions, I veered away to the east on the sixth day, placing the jagged white wall of the Cascades looming at my back. I now rode across lush meadows, below the Red Bluffs, where great green prairies, with their countless islands of clustered oak spread onward like the sea itself. All was untouched land, and as I traveled on eastward, toward the lofting Coastal Range, that pleasant, virgin country began to take on an odd strangeness. It was as if I entered a land where the white man had seldom, if ever, ventured—nor was ever wanted. It was just a feeling that I laid to the lonely expanses, and the thought of what awaited me when I got there.

If I were the scribbler of some yellowback, such as *The Prisoners of the Aztecs* or *The Black Riders of the Congaree,* I'd be able to spin a yarn of how I suffered the most God-awful hardships and hair-raising dangers on my journey to the Yolla Bollies, but it wouldn't be so. The trip, instead of growing progressively tougher, was easier than my trek from Mexico to California. There was plenty of water in the clear, winding creeks, and more than enough firewood. And I lived high on the hog, for I'd fetched along some of the very best supplies available.

At last the prairies gave way to rambling foothills and vast hogbacks, and after breakfast on the eighth day, I struck a dim trail at the edge of series of foothills. It wound up valleys, through and across canyons, up and down ridges and along steep slopes. Sometimes the way eastward lay along a bare hillside, but more often through open forests where great, noble trees shot up on every side. Laurel, or bay, trees with fragrant foliage, firs, pines and oak, all mingled in a scene that changed with every winding of the faint track.

Almost before I knew it I was right in the midst of the Yolla Bollies, so gradually had the ancient trail risen. Around me was a sea of mountains; every blue billow a mountain, with deep, shadowy canyons threading through them. Redwood forests darkened the canyons on the west toward the Pacific, while a gray-green carpet of chaparral covered the ridges to the east. Many of the peaks rising upward were very high, some nearly four thousand feet or more.

I sat the broad back of White Lightning and stared around. With all of those towering peaks, where, I wondered, were the Twins?

Riding on down, through the fading light, into a small grove of trees, I unsaddled the horse and picketed him, along with the pack mule, on some decent grass at the trees' edge. The sun was already dying in a silent storm of crimson-gold behind the westward mountains, while the eastern skyline was now a vague, saw-toothed streak of lavender where night drowned the mountain ranges.

With the chill of the high places creeping down the dusky slopes, I hustled to make a fire and get my beans and coffee working.

In the morning . . . !

XXIX

Each night that I'd been on the trail from San Francisco, I'd slept easy, but when I rolled out of my chilly blankets in the morning and began to hunt up dry firewood, I was striding through an ocean of mist.

And my recollections of the night just past were as hazy as the clutching sheets of fog. I'd dreamed something to do with Dulcima and Rosita —and Josh, but it wouldn't come back to me.

Squatting over my small chunk of fire, sipping at my scalding coffee, I saw the mountains to the east looming in giant silhouettes against the yellow inferno of the coming day.

One by one the humps and peaks began to tear their way through the glowing mist, and as I gulped my steaming Arbuckle I came mighty nigh dropping the cup. There ahead of me, a pair of noble mountains swam out of the thinning haze, all rimmed with growing flame. And then the sun, as round and fiery as the biggest golden coin in the universe, came rolling up to balance, for a blazing instant, between the twin peaks. Kirker's twin peaks!

I tossed the coffee, rolled my blankets, stamped out the fire, and rounded up hobbled horse and pack mule. By the time I'd finished and was swinging into the saddle, I could see an entire valley below me that I'd missed on the climb up the plateau, sheltered as it was by one of the many great ridges.

A half hour riding by an easy trail that threaded around shale and sandstone rocks let us down the thousand feet onto the valley floor. It was an enormous valley, stretching mile upon mile to the north and south, and filled with such game as bear, deer and elk, all lumbering and loping slowly away at our approach. Birds of every sort, including quail, grouse and wild pigeon, whirled upward in thundering flocks from the magnificent oak groves. But I had eyes alone for the two towering peaks to the east.

Another hour brought me to the base of those snow-mantled twins, and there at the beginning of the first upsurging foothills where a small, clear stream cut down out of the mountains, I could see a trio of huge granite boulders, just beyond a stand of poplars.

Piling from my saddle, I tied the horse and mule to some nearby cedars, then pushed my way through the underbrush, splashed across the shallow stream and stood panting in front of the three boulders.

The central giant was marked with a lopsided X, hacked into the surface, but there were also several crude paintings that had the look of Indian work. Someone had been at the three rocks, either before or after Jeff Kirker.

I dropped to my knees to claw away the dead grass and brush from the boulder's base—and felt some sort of coarse cloth. Peering down, I saw what looked like at least four gray bags within a deep recess under the boulder.

Flopping upon my belly, I reached into the cavity and slowly tugged, and eased out a canvas bag marked with a faded U.S. It weighed close to a hundred pounds but I staggered up, hugging the chinking sack to my chest with a shout. Then I scrabbled back down onto my knees and ripped at one end of the bag with my bowie knife.

A shining gush of rattling, chiming coins spewed onto the ground. As I sat there pawing through the golden treasure and talking to myself a flock of birds burst up from some neighboring trees and White Lightning wickered once; then as I turned to see what might have spooked them, a chunk of the boulder exploded a spray of granite dust into my face, and the scream of the ricochet chattered off among the hills.

Before I could scramble around the rocks to safety, another shot cracked out. Whoever it was, was mighty damned close!

Kirker's old Tige rifle was out of reach on my saddle, but I had my Navy Colt and fired back at the white smears of gunsmoke curling out of a stand of timber, forty yards down the creek.

That unseen marksman put two more shots close to my head, the balls screaming off from their shattering impact with the boulders. Then at least four muskets began to slam from the brush-covered slopes above us.

For over five minutes the second bunch kept their fire directed at that unknown rifleman in the trees. He answered back several times but suddenly quit.

All at once there came the shrill, wildcat squall of an Indian war whoop, then another, and four half-naked braves, so close I could see their fancy tattoos, came plunging down the grassy slopes, heading straight for the man in the timber.

Then a high-powered rifle snapped off, from higher up on the slopes. There came the whipcrack of another. And again, both ripped out. One of the running Indians leaped into the air and came down in as neat a somersault as a circus acrobat. But he stayed put, hitting the ground stone-dead, while the others veered off into the brush and vanished.

I couldn't spot the party on the hill, and as they failed to show themselves, I wriggled out, got the ripped gold sack and stuffed it back under the boulder.

All was still save for the movements of my animals off in the distance and the ever-rippling rush of the little mountain stream.

I waited, and waited, but nobody moved. So I did!

Colt in one fist and bowie knife in the other, I slipped quietly along the edge of the stream bank and ghosted into the little wood.

Two people were on the ground, near a large oak. One sat hunched over, head on knees, while the second lay beside him. A twig crackled under my boot and the man looked up. It was Diamond Dick. There was a rifle at his feet but he made no move.

"Bean! God, I thought it was those bastard Indians!" Powers lurched to his feet, a perfect scarecrow. His clothing was ripped and stained, and his face, smudged with gunpowder, was streaked from tears that had creased his cheeks.

Then I looked at the figure on the ground. *Dulcima!* Clad in a soiled buckskin riding outfit, she lay on her side, one arm flung out and the other under her body.

I knelt, still keeping my pistol on Powers, and clutched the girl's shoulder, then shook her. "What the hell's the matter here?"

But I already knew.

"Indians!" Powers' lips trembled. "They got her dead-center with their second shot. God, we shouldn't have come up here! She didn't want to. I should have listened. But—"

"But you had to follow me after the gold!" I cocked the Colt and leveled it right at his head. "Well, damn you, you've lost the gold and you've lost me that girl!"

"*Never!* She never cared a plugged peso for you. Dulcy and I've been lovers ever since I picked her up on the streets of Frisco!" Powers stiffened, and made a move to reach for his rifle, then shrugged. "I guess Lady Luck was against us all from the start." He leaned against the tree, tears starting from his eyes again.

While we stared at each other and I debated putting a bullet into the pandering villain, there came three shots from the hill—closer now!

"Get to hell out of here, before I or those people up and cash you in for keeps!" I jammed the Colt into his ribs, and yanked the pistol from his holster. "She'll be taken care of. It's all I can do for her now. Get while you can, and if those Indians nail you, it's all you damned well deserve!"

Powers took one last look at Dulcima's crumpled form, then turned toward a beautiful black mare tied to a tree with a small brown horse some twenty yards off. "You should know that we were firing just to bluff you away from the gold. Never meant to hit you. Now, I wish to hell we had!" Then he was mounting the black, and gone beyond the trees.

I stood looking down at Dulcima, remembering how she'd told me of her fear of this country from the time the Comanches killed off her folks, and how much she wanted to get away from its wildness—and its Indians. And then she'd followed me to this hidden valley, with Powers, and found nothing but death! Well, it was one sure way to get away from everything.

I listened but heard no unusual sounds, then knelt at the girl's side and rolled her limp form over, thinking of the last time I'd held her. I crossed her pale hands on her blood-soaked breast, closed those wide blue eyes and then the tears came, for she seemed again like that wistful waif of the daguerreotype—the tragic daughter of the lost lady of the medicine hand.

Some slight movement jolted me out of myself, and I whirled, gun in hand, to find Rosita Almada, in a green leather riding outfit, standing at the edge of the grove, with Joaquín Murieta close behind her, a pair of rifles cradled in his arms.

Rosita brushed past me to kneel by Dulcima. She crossed herself, then rose to stare at me, without the least expression. "Where is Powers?"

"Gone! Those Indians shot her, and I let Powers go." I looked down at Dulcima, and back at the Almadas. "He loved her—"

"*Sí*, he loved her, as he loved money." Rosita's smile was cold. "That is why he fought with your brother . . . and finally shot him down in the night!"

"Powers killed Josh?" I was rocked, though I knew Rosita and her brother knew just about everything going on around San Francisco. "But —Powers was nearly a hundred miles away that night. Dulcima told me that weeks ago!"

"Dulcima! She'd lie to you as easily as she'd lie to me. That *pobre criatura* was wild about that scum!" She paused and glanced at her brother, then turned back to me. "You forget that Powers, for all his evil ways, is one of the *campeón* horsemen of California. Doubtless he rode that hundred miles in one night just to take his revenge!"

Francisco spoke in an undertone to Rosita, then slipped off into the underbrush, where I could now hear their horses moving about.

I stood numbly by, watching him go, my mind in a perfect jumble. So

Powers *had* killed Josh, and not Carlos Hechavarría! But why had Carlos tried to drygulch me?

As though she could read my every thought, Rosita spoke, "Someone of the little sheriff's posse learned that you were the source of the information, and talked. Word came to Carlos, and he watched for a chance to catch you in an ambush." Again she gave me that impersonal smile. "He was stalking you and became careless. But, obviously, you were the better man. So, now Francisco and I have disbanded the company. At some later time we shall be in a more favorable position to aid our poor country."

"You're leaving?" I took a step toward her, but she backed away. "Put up your pistol, Roy, and come to the rocks. We are taking enough of—our gold to establish ourselves *elsewhere.*"

I silently followed her from the grove, leaving Dulcima, lying like a shattered doll, in the dappled green and golden shadows of the trees.

"What about those Indians?"

"Francisco says this is a valley sacred to the Yuki tribes. That is why they attacked Powers. You were lucky his shots drew their fire. We hadn't seen you yet, having come into the valley from another pass—though we'd followed both you and—"

Whatever else she was about to add was never spoken, for we each stopped short at the sight of her brother, minus the weapons, hands held high by the central boulder.

"Be so good as to approach, señorita!" And Salvador Salazar and three heavily armed Mexicans stood by the giant boulders, pointing pistols and rifles at us. "*Sí*, it is *muy bueno*, scooping up so many birds in one net!" Salazar doffed his battered sombrero in a lop-sided salute. "Ah, my young Bean, we trailed this fine pair, while they followed that Powers." He looked closely at me. "Where is that hellhound, and the little señorita?"

"Gone," I croaked, my throat tightening as I watched Salazar's deputies hunkered down, piling the scattered coins back into the ripped sack, and tugging out the rest of the bags from under the boulder. "He's gone, and Dulcima's dead! She's over there in the timber. *Indians!*"

"We heard the shots and hastened to find you." Salazar pulled off his sombrero and ran his hand meditatively over his vanished scalp before replacing the dilapidated object. "Poor young lady. Old *Señor Destino* came for her, after all!" He squinted up at the hills. "*Sí*, this is the land of the Yuki, and by the arrows of San Sebastián, I don't want any of it!"

"What about the gold?" I looked at the motionless Almadas, as they watched the deputies staggering to their horses with the bags.

"Ah, the bloody loot of Joaquín Murieta, and the *renegado* Jefferson

Kirker!" Salazar glanced at the progress his men were making with the loading, then motioned for Rosita and her brother to lower their hands. "You behold, young señor, that I know a thing or two about this gold. I've watched and waited for years to get that money back. And you've been the bait, my *hombre joven!* As soon as those 1847 gold eagles began to appear around San Diego, I knew that, sooner or later, you would lead me straight to the stolen treasure!"

"Well, take the blamed stuff, and let's get the hell out of here," I snapped. "I don't feel like setting myself up as a target for any wild Indians—even if I've been nothing but a dumned Judas goat for the likes of you!"

"Softly, my young *amigo,* all in good time. First we must pay the proper attention to your friends here. This, I'll be bound, is none other than the charming Red Rosita. *Sí,* I remember you very well, señorita, from the many pleasant but profitless hours spent in your former establishment at San Francisco." Salazar thoughtfully tugged at his drooping mustachios. "And your handsome caballero—ah, reminds me of someone. But never mind, we shall discover just who at the proper time." He shouted an order to his busy deputies, then pulled a pair of wrist bracelets from his coat. "That *imbécil* of a Captain Love may have destroyed Murieta, but I think these people may be wanted somewhere. They knew the stolen gold was cached right here—and that's enough for me!"

He motioned Rosita and Francisco to hold out their hands, and as he reached for Rosita's wrist with the gyves, I pulled my Colt.

"Tell your day laborers there to drop everything and get their hands up —and you too!" I emphasized my orders with a good poke in Salazar's ribs.

Not a word was spoken as I waved Rosita and her brother on their way to their horses back at the grove. Rosita stopped once at the edge of the timber and looked back. "Dulcima?"

"She'll get a proper burial." I motioned them on again.

I already knew, from the look on Rosita's face, that she had no wish for me to join them—and that hurt as bad as anything!

"Now, young Bean?" Salazar scowled at me. "You've let those *bandidos* go; how about us?"

Keeping an eye on both Salazar and his people, I edged to where I could reach far enough to scoop out a handful of gold pieces from the torn sack. "I'm leaving—if it's all right with you!"

Salazar lowered his hands, motioning his deputies to finish loading the sacks on their horses. "*Sí,* I think you had better leave. And I think I better not find you in these parts again—and that means San Francisco. You cannot seem to keep away from dangerous people. It is a fault that will bring you *mucho* trouble!" He looked me in the eye, then stepped forward and gave me a bear hug. "We'll see the poor young lady has a decent burial. *Adiós,* my young friend. Ride!"

I walked away from the law—and the gold—without looking back, to where my horse and pack mule waited, stamping and whickering. Untying both, I mounted White Lightning and rode.